THE
HOLY GHOST
SPEAKEASY
AND REVIVAL

THE
HOLY GHOST
SPEAKEASY
AND REVIVAL

a novel of fire and water

TERRY ROBERTS

TURNER PUBLISHING COMPANY

Turner Publishing Company
Nashville, Tennessee
www.turnerpublishing.com

Holy Ghost Speakeasy and Revival

Cover design: Maddie Cothren
Book design: Tim Holtz

Library of Congress Cataloging-in-Publication Data
Names: Roberts, Terry, 1956- author.
Title: The holy ghost speakeasy and revival show : a novel of fire and water
/ Terry Roberts.
Description: Nashville, Tennessee : Turner Publishing Company, [2018] |
  Identifiers: LCCN 2018007090 (print) | LCCN 2018012539 (ebook) | ISBN
  9781684421657 (epub) | ISBN 9781684421633 (softcover) | ISBN 9781684421640
  (hardcover)
Classification: LCC PS3618.O3164 (ebook) | LCC PS3618.O3164 H65 2018 (print)
  | DDC 813/.6--dc23
LC record available at https://lccn.loc.gov/2018007090

9781684421633

Printed in the United States of America

18 19 20 21 10 9 8 7 6 5 4 3 2 1

The words of the Preacher,

The son of David,

King in Jerusalem.

Ecclesiastes 1:1

To Lynn
. . . whose essence is kindness

Acknowledgments

THERE ARE TWO HISTORICAL CHARACTERS—and I do mean characters—who make an appearance is this novel and must be acknowledged. Jedidiah Robbins's Courthouse Sermon is based on Billy Sunday's infamous "The Saloon in a Coward" diatribe and, I hope, reproduces much of Sunday's fantastical invention and full-throttle spit and spittle. Similarly, H. L. Mencken's determination to expose our Preacher as a fraud as well as his later backhanded endorsement is entirely typical of Mencken. It was no end of fun both to reshape Sunday's words and write in Mencken's voice for a few pages.

One other historical note worth mentioning here is that the high water mark of Ku Klux Klan activity in America occurred during the 1920s as a violent sideshow to Prohibition, and indeed, those two historical phenomena crawled out of the same puritanical and self-righteous hole in the American psyche.

When it comes to Jedidiah Robbins and his fellow travelers, I owe my agent Emma Sweeney my deep and abiding appreciation for believing in their story. In addition, the team at Turner Publishing—especially editor Jon O'Neal—has been nothing short of brilliant in presenting them in the best possible light.

A number of friends have read this book in its various stages, but most importantly, I have to thank Wendy Ikoku for repeatedly bringing her kind but sharp editorial eye to bear.

I want to also thank my children—Jesse, Margaret, and Henry. My sincere hope is that their characteristic humor and patience shine through these pages.

And finally, I have to mention my mother, Helen Roberts. Fifty years ago, when I was a boy, she would sit by my bed each night in that old farmhouse at Sanders Court while I recited the 23rd Psalm and repeated the Lord's Prayer. If not for her, neither Jedidiah nor I could even begin to convey the poetry of the King James Bible.

THE
HOLY GHOST
SPEAKEASY
AND REVIVAL

IN THE BEGINNING

August 1904

THE THING THAT HAS STAYED WITH ME for the rest of my life is the smell. It has haunted my sleeping and waking dreams for these many years since.

The farm pond where my wife died stank in that midsummer with a fecund richness—duckweed, rotting cattails, and a green cloud of pond scum. There are always dragonflies floating in the thick, radiant air of my memories, and the memories themselves are running with sweat.

So wretched is that day that it remains fully present in the depths of my mind. Even now.

My wife's screams, and those of her sister, silence the surrounding world. Birds and crickets and the very moles under the ground cease, for a moment, to be. Screams surrounded by dead silence as I turn away from the picnic strewn over the blanket in the field above the pond. Silence as my heart stops beating in my chest and my limbs chill for want of blood. Silence except for the shrieks of sister Isobel as I sprint down through the thick, sharp stubble of freshly mown hay. A yellow jacket's sting that I won't notice till later, much later.

Silence except for the hoarse voice of Isobel, tearing her throat out as she screeches for help.

I am ripping my shirt off as I scramble over the barbed-wire fence at pasture's edge and leap far out into the flat below. Stripping my pants down to my knees and abandoning them in the

1

sucking mud. Struggling against the whole desperate weight of the world to get to the water.

The water where my sister-in-law clings to a downed tree, pointing with an algae-stained arm to the center of the pond. I see beyond her flung hand the upturned rowboat that the two had gone exploring in. Neither girl a swimmer, neither with the sense to wait for me to come back with their jar of wine and a piece of cake.

Finally I am in water deep enough to wrench my feet from the mud, and I am swimming free from the gasping, clinging clutch of earth. Swimming high in the water, yelling now. I call out her name. I cry, from the pit of my lungs, as if to tear the air. Thinking that she can hear me, even deep in the water, even deep beneath the blue-green surface of pond scum and water beetle.

I see nothing when I reach the rotten boat. Not her arm or her hair. Not her hand flung high or the bubbles of her breath. And I dive straight down, my eyes open in the slant, green light beneath. I am twisting my head madly side to side, searching in the underworld till my lungs sear and burn. Up again, I scream her name.

Diving again and again until it is all I can do to cling to the upturned shell of the rowboat. Weeping now into the water beneath, my skin, my heart, my guts logged with filthy water. My arms and legs weak from lack of air, my brain stunned into silence so that I can only whisper her name. Rachel.

It takes them two days to drain the pond. They find her body at the upper end, tangled by her muddy dress in the limbs of what had been a submerged tree. Her fingers scraped raw from her struggle to escape and climb into the light. Her mouth gaped open in silent wailing.

My name? I would wonder later as I lay all night alone in our bed. Was she screaming my name or that of our daughter? Was she screaming for her baby? What was she calling out as the blind water seeped down her throat and into her bloody, pulsing lungs?

I refuse to have her embalmed. The law decrees that if she isn't embalmed, she must be buried immediately—within two days. I refuse because I know that she's pregnant. Not far gone but with child nonetheless. Full with—dear God—our second child, a copy perhaps of two-year-old Bridget, the sweetest and kindest to bird or beast. Perhaps it is a boy. I dream that it is a boy, but how to ever know?

Refuse because I cannot bear the thought of a stranger's cold hands cutting into her, draining her blood, filling her and the babe with a wash of icy chemicals.

On the day of the funeral, I fling myself into the open grave. I am distraught, crazed such that suddenly and irrationally I am convinced that she yet lives. Might rise up if I can only tear the lid off the coffin with my bare hands. With the strength of ten desperate men, I might retrieve her from the depths of the dirt-strewn world beneath the grass.

Later, they would say I fainted or even that I was drunk. They would say that I was lost to the rational world and torn by grief.

Two strong deacons dragged me from the grave. Deacons of her parents' church who find my uncontrollable weeping and savage fighting against them a sort of demonic possession.

But they don't know death. Don't know its naked, intimate touch, as close as a tongue-locked kiss or a whispered secret. They don't know death as I will come to know death. The rasp of bone on bone. The frigid embrace.

They drag me away before filling in the grave, convinced that I have lost my mind and might harm myself or attack them. And so in this long-ago season of weeping, I lose her body to the underworld.

It was she who thought I would become a preacher. She hoped I would become a devoted man of God, like her father. And, in so doing, make her proud in the years to come.

PART ONE

AUGUST 1926

CHAPTER ONE

He is preaching from Proverbs, as he so often does on the second night in a small town. He has started them off with John 3:16, the one verse even the dirt-farming dolts know by heart. But then he shifts them over seamlessly into Proverbs, a territory in which his mind ranges freely, happily.

Even in this dirty rag of a town, they fill the union hall on the second night, and he can tell that the Gospel is moving the red clay under their busted brogans and stained dress shoes. The Holy Spirit is hot in the room. Two women have fainted, and a third matron now flings her sweat-soaked arms into the air and begins to spin in place among the battered folding chairs. Men are growling with the Spirit, young girls starting to sweat and scream.

"God does not care…," he shouts over the growing din. This is apparently a speaking-in-tongues sort of backwater, and the tongues are shouting out tonight. "…what you wear. He cares not. God does not care what you have in the bank." I care, he thinks, but God doesn't. "No! He does not care. God does not care who knows your name or speaks to you on the street. He does not care. He cares only whether you call out to Him when you are in need. Whether you kneel to Him when life kicks you in the gut."

"Take me, Jesus! Oh, take me now!" The spinning woman shrieks and crashes to the floor, taking several lesser mortals and a chair or two down with her. There is a rising hum of muttered singing to go with the occasional scream, a Tower of Babel rising in the room. A tall man begins to shout and pummel the people around him with his fists, the Spirit running rampant.

He has to rise above it all to be heard, but he is a past master at making himself heard, come riot or storm. He has proven he can preach above thunder or gunfire. "Trust in the Lord!" he shouts, such that the rafters shake and dust sifts down on the sweating heads. "'Trust in the Lord with *all* thine heart: and lean not unto thine own understanding.'" He pauses for effect, waves the Bible above his head, open to the third chapter of Proverbs, and skewers the people below him with the long, forbidding forefinger of his right hand. "'In *all* thy ways acknowledge Him, and He shall direct thy paths.'"

He has them now. Women, mostly older but a few in the first blush of holy passion, are dropping as if struck down by lightning. Grown men with beards to their belts are throwing their arms in the air and whispering—or—shouting, "Amen," "Oh my Jesus," "Amen, God almighty!"

He nods to the young blond woman at the piano, and softly, ever so softly, she begins to play "Shall We Gather at the River." "Oh, my brothers," he intones. It sounds almost as if he's whispering, though he can be heard in the farthest back row. "Oh, my sisters. 'Be not wise in thine own eyes: *fear* the Lord and depart from evil.' The Word of the Lord. Come down to me now where you'll be safe. Come *down* to the front of this room. Find safety in the arms of your Savior." In the midst of his call, he notices a young man half walking, half staggering into the back of the hall with what looks like a whiskey bottle in his hand. An angel, he thinks, sent to sweeten the altar call. "Come," he shouts, "to the safety of the risen Lord! Come to your Father who art in Heaven!"

The dulcet tones of the piano chords grow louder, and there is a surge of human flesh toward the front of the room. Individual souls pushing over chairs, shoving past family members, drawn as if by gravity toward the stage at the front of the old, dusty auditorium.

Down below the stage, the floor is thickly strewn with straw to soften the hard oak boards under the collapsing bodies and bending knees. "Just as you are, He loves you," he shouts. "Come just as you are to the risen Jesus, who will wash away your fears, wash away your sins, rinse the dirt out of your very soul, the ache out of your human heart.... Oh, come down to me now, come to *Jesus!*"

The various members of the Gospel troupe are below the stage, ankle-deep in straw: Mother Mary, weeping as she goes from soul to soul; Brother Andrew, the mute who can only sing, but with the tongue of an angel; the Bundren twins, James and John, earnest young deacons and teachers who quote the Bible in their sleep. All working the crowd, pausing to pray with a gasping sinner, holding close a screaming teenage girl, helping a hugely fat matron onto her knees. "Heal me, Jesus," the matron mutters, "heal my sorrows now."

He can see a young drunk with what looks like a whiskey bottle stagger straight down the center aisle, forcing himself past singing, swaying figures. Below the pulpit, he stumbles to a stop and looks up at the preacher. The boy flings the whiskey bottle at him, but it shatters harmlessly against the pulpit. "Kneel down before you fall down," the Preacher says quietly to the boy, who, almost as if hearing him, tumbles over backward into the heaving mass of kneeling, falling, fainting humanity.

An hour later, they have prayed and blessed and consoled till they are all, except Andrew, hoarse as crows. The Preacher bends over the last remaining sinner, the young drunk who had tried to nail him with the whiskey bottle. The girl from the piano, Bridget, is kneeling beside the boy, trying to scrub the vomit off his face with a rag. "Won't do any good," the Preacher whispers to her. "Too drunk. Get a bucket of water." He says to one of the twins who is standing nervously by, no telling which.

When the bucket comes, he nods at the boy. Bridget edges back to a safe distance, and the twin douses the boy with the water.

He woofs and sits up suddenly as if he's being attacked, flinging his hands up to protect his head. "Jesus...cold," he mutters. And then looking up, the boy focuses on the Preacher. "Hell of a show you all got here," he says, and coughs to clear his throat. "I only caught the last act."

The young woman Bridget smiles at him. The Preacher nods slowly.

"But I tell you what."

"What?" the Preacher rasps.

"You need your own goddamn tent. You need a big top that you...can haul from...town to town. If you ever spect to make a livin at this."

The Preacher nods to the twin, who puts down his bucket and helps the boy to his feet.

"Odd you should mention it," the Preacher whispers.

Bridget finishes the thought. "Cause we just may have one."

The Preacher reaches out casually and pulls up the sleeves of the boy's shirt, first the left and then the right, revealing a hastily inked tattoo on the meat of the boy's right forearm. TAMPINI BROTHERS SHOW. "Greatest on Earth?" the Preacher asks gently.

The boy nods.

"Bring him," the Preacher says to the twin, who's holding the boy upright, barely. "The Good Lord works in mysterious ways."

The nighttime walk to the freight yard sobers the boy Gabriel. Enough so that he can begin to make sense of what he sees. The first train they come to, parked on a spur line, is the *Sword of the Lord*, explains the girl. Four cars, including the engine. Behind the engine: a baggage car, the passenger car, and what looks for all the world like a private railcar set up for business and sleeping. Starting with the engine, each is painted in bright red letters with part of a Bible verse that if you take in the whole rig reads as follows: TAKE THE HELMET OF SALVATION—AND THE SWORD OF THE SPIRIT—WHICH IS THE WORD OF GOD. EPHESIANS 6:17.

All but the Preacher and Bridget stop at the *Sword of the Lord* and say good night. The two walk farther up the track with Gabriel to a long, unlighted train that sits abandoned in the dark. Gabe knows it immediately as the main rig of the Tampini Brothers Circus. It stinks in the heavy air of manure and grain, wet canvas and something else, something metallic like wet iron and rust. Gabriel sees no sign of the animals anywhere, and he wonders if they are loose in the Carolina woods...or have been butchered for meat.

Bridget and the Preacher lead him to a flat railcar that is loaded with rolls of brightly painted canvas lashed down over long, tapering poles.

The Preacher tries to speak, but his tired throat cracks. Bridget takes over. "Is this what we think it is?" she asks Gabriel.

"It's the Tampini Brothers' main top," he says to the Preacher, assuming the young woman is translating. "It's the very goddamn thing. Covers half an acre." And then, after a pause, "It's what you want. If it was me, I'd hook this car up to your rig and drag it on off."

"Steal it," Bridget says helpfully.

"Hell, yes."

"Too late. Already bought it," the Preacher croaks, "along with the train."

"You don't need the train," Gabriel says impatiently. "You got your own engine and coal car. Damn, but you Christians are stupid. You should have bought the men who know how to throw it up if you was going to buy something. Them and the horses. The Perch-air-rons."

"Well, hell," the girl says to the Preacher, but gently, reflectively. "I *told* you we'd need the horses."

"Do you know how to put it up?" the Preacher asks Gabriel. "Can you take it up and down?"

"Does the goddamn sun rise in the east? But I can't do it by myself. I'd need a dozen men and half a dozen of them horses."

"The Percherons," says Bridget helpfully.

"Damn the horses," the Preacher says irritably. "The horses are at the livery stable. Five of them. They agreed to hold them till the day after tomorrow before putting them on the block."

"How much?" The girl.

"More than we've got, even with tonight's take and the fat woman's purse."

"What fat woman?" Gabriel asks.

"We've got to do at least one more night," Bridget says. "For the horses. And to hire the men he needs for the tent."

The Preacher looks up at the Carolina sky, beginning already to lighten over the hills to the east. Ripple of birdsong in the air, and the faintest breath of cool air. Even so, he shakes his head as if bone-tired.

"Go lay down," she advises, "and sip that hot lemon shrub you like for your throat. Tomorrow night, preach the Ecclesiastes that you love so much. That's worth a thousand dollars all by itself."

CHAPTER TWO

Midmorning the next day. Rays of dusty sun penetrate the open windows of the last car in the *Sword of the Lord,* the club car that makes an office and sleeping quarters. The Preacher, Jedidiah Robbins, and the young woman, Bridget, are having what is for them a late breakfast. Eggs scrambled up with scraps of beef, along with bread toasted over a wood fire in the small cookstove vented out the back of the car.

"What do you make of him?" he asks quietly. "The boy, I mean. Gabriel."

"Did you name him that? Angel Gabriel," she asks. Ignoring the question.

"I didn't say he was an angel. I said he was a boy."

"Well, *he* says he's a Portugee. From East Tennessee. And that he barely knows who his father is."

He glances at her. Under lazy, hooded eyes. "Had time to converse with him, did you?"

"I didn't tuck him in, if that's what you mean. You told me to show him to the saints' car. Tell him where to wash and where to sleep."

He nods. "Fair enough. So what do you think of him?"

"Dark skin. Almost green in lamplight. Not so much of a beard. Blue eyes, which don't match his face. Dark, curly hair, but nothing that screams Negro. Why?"

"Do you know the term *Melungeon*?"

After a moment's reflection, she shakes her head. "How would I know it if you hadn't taught it to me? Godforsaken country. Which reminds me—we need books. A box of books from the local library would be nice, before we move on."

"A Melungeon is a mystery man—or woman—of some mixed blood. A mountain-bred creature that might be Indian, might be English—of long-lost Roanoke blood—might be Spanish from the earliest Europeans, or might be plain old Negro blood mixed light in mountain skin. East Tennessee or North Georgia, West Carolina. Mustache but no beard. Blue eyes or green."

"Do they stand out? Do people hate them?"

He shrugs his shoulders. "Not so much unless their skin turns too dark." And then after a moment. "I'd say that our angel boy is a Melungeon."

"Should I send him on his way?"

"No. He needs us." He smiles at her. He can't help himself. "He needs us for rest and food. Show him what a family is."

"And we need him." It wasn't a question.

"Oh, yes. We need him to ride the advance train into town. Spread the Word like John the Baptist. Post our bills on every telegraph pole and porch post."

"What about the tent, the big top?"

"Erect the big top. We need him to do that."

"And sell the goods?"

"Let's don't bring him in to that just yet. Let Boss manage the goods. He knows just what to do. If they get to town two or three days ahead of us, Boss'll have most every man in the place in desperate need of redemption by the time we arrive. Women furious and men hungover. The Lord never saw such a perfect field of play. Spread the Gospel Word and spread the goods at the same time."

She smiles at the audacity of the Preacher's plan. "He'll need help. Some of the men who the Tampini Brothers threw away."

"Send him out today. Tell him to gather up who or what he needs and we'll find a way to pay them."

"Can I—"

"No, you cannot. These men will be in the bars and whorehouses on the worst side of town, and you have no business there. It's enough that you get him up and moving. Tell him he can have a dozen hands. No animals other than the horses, and no women. Send him out today before the men he needs are either dead or in jail."

She raises her eyebrows, as if to say, "No women?"

"No women. Not on the advance train. You and Mother Mary are enough for the *Sword of the Lord,* at least for now. Eventually we will want a choir. Of angels. And then, if you like, you can handpick the girls who will sing us all to sleep."

She grins at him. "Young and comely, no doubt. *Your* angels?"

He smiles back at her. "Comely at the very least, even if not young," he says. "Virginal. Let them all be virgins."

She laughs. She loves him as much as he her. Equally deep and untouchable. Equally mysterious in response to the world. For she is his beloved. His only child, his daughter.

The boy Gabe is standing outside the saints' car when she finds him. Bathing by dipping a rag he's discovered somewhere into a metal washtub full of cold creek water. Scrubbing his chest and arms vigorously. Bridget appraises him silently for a long moment, while his eyes are still closed in the chill ecstasy of washing. He would do, she thinks, even though there is what appears to be a name inked over his heart. Probably his mother, she thinks, gone on to Jesus.

When his eyes open finally, he grins at her—even as his face flinches at the suddenness of light. Definitely hungover. "You wouldn't happen to know if I have a job, would you?" he asks and coughs to clear his throat. "I went to Sunday School when I was a boy. Learned my books of the Bible in order."

"Order of importance or their chronological order?"

"Well, the order God put em in, accordin to that Bible your boyfriend keeps waving around."

She crosses her arms and shifts her weight to one leg to study him more closely. "You mean my father?"

He stares at her, confounded for the moment. "God, your father?"

She laughs. "No. No, the Preacher is my father. Jedidiah Robbins, though everybody out there in the world calls him Solomon. He doesn't allow any boyfriends."

"Well, then, you should know if I have a job, shouldn't you? I don't remember last night so well, especially after that mob at the union hall."

"You were drunk to puking. It's a wonder you remember your own name."

"Gabe Overbay."

"Well, Gabe Overbay, your job is John the Baptist. You are to go forth and prepare the way, arriving in town two or three days in advance so you can spread the good Gospel Word with posters, placards, and handbills. Your job is to set the stage for the mighty act to follow."

"What about the big top?"

"That too. You are in charge of the advance train, and you need to go forth this morning and hire the men you need to erect that big…tent. Spread the Word and set the table for the communion of souls."

"Did you grow up with your daddy?"

"Of course. Who else?"

"You talk like him."

"I think like him too. And today we want you to go forth and round up a dozen men who can help you spread the Word and put up the tent."

"Roustabouts?"

"Yes. God's holy roustabouts."

"They ain't pretty. These men you're talking about. Rough as a corncob froze solid."

"We'll teach them the Gospel. You teach them the rest."

"So I'm a foreman?"

"You're God's own foreman in the first rank," she says with a smile. "The Old Testament precedes the New. You," she points at him, "are Old. I am New."

"And your daddy?"

"He brings in the sheaves."

"I don't know what that means, but fair enough. What am I to be paid?"

"For now, ten dollars a week and your found."

"Do I sleep with the saints?" He nods toward the car where he'd spent the night.

"No. You'll have to sleep on the advance train most of the time. Now, go find yourself a dozen saved roustabouts. Get em here by tonight so they can hear the sermon."

That afternoon, after arrangements for the evening service are concluded, Bridget goes to visit the horses. Five hulking Percherons that are dozing on their feet in the shabby corral behind a barn on the edge of town. It is 1926, and yet the faded red paint on the front of the barn still decries it a LIVERY STABLE.

She has never seen anything as large as these horses. The huge animals stand comfortably shoulder to shoulder in the shade cast by the barn, for all the world like five monstrous cats asleep by the fire. She carries them bucket after bucket of cold water that she pumps by hand from a wellhead beside the barn. They slurp and blow in the water, and they nuzzle her with soaking-wet lips. She drags an empty barrel into the shade beside them and stands on it to curry their dusty hides.

She combs them until they gleam like silver in the damp shade of the barn. And as she combs, she talks quietly to them. "Tomorrow you'll be mine," is what she tells them. The brutes rub their great Roman heads together, stare at her out of impossibly deep, intelligent eyes, and are satisfied.

CHAPTER THREE

On this night, he begins with Ecclesiastes. But not the verses Bridget expects from the third chapter—a time to be born and a time to die, a time to plant and a time to pluck up. Not those verses, which after all contain some consolation. To her surprise, he starts out of the darkness in the first chapter, the vanity verses. She can tell that those in the crowded union hall who have come to be lifted up are confused at being reminded of their own misery first and foremost.

The Preacher prays silently for a long moment and then begins fast, as though swimming in a strong current of wind or water. "'What profit hath a man of all his labor which he taketh under the sun?'" He pauses and looks out over the crowd, pointing at them with his eyes. "'One generation passeth away, and another generation cometh: but the earth abideth forever. The sun also ariseth, and the sun goeth down, and hasteth to his place where he arose. The wind goeth toward the south, and turneth about unto the north: it whirleth about continually: and the wind returneth again according to his circuits. All the rivers run into the sea: yet the sea is not full: unto the place from whence the rivers come, thither they return again. All things are full of labor; man cannot utter it: the eye is not satisfied with seeing, nor the ear filled with hearing.'"

Again he pauses. Again his eyes roam over the restless crowd. "'Vanity of vanities, saith the preacher, vanity of vanities: all is vanity.'" He bows his head to pray, silently. His eyes shut, he cannot see the crowd of red-clay farmers and their wives. He has no idea if he's reaching them.

Bridget wonders if he's been drinking during the long, hot afternoon. He can dive deep when he drinks, too deep for these hillbillies to follow. He needs to keep them with him tonight for the collection plate to fill and overflow. He needs to remember who he's talking to.

Suddenly he looks up. "We cannot save ourselves," he says evenly, almost in an offhand way. And then he says it again, only slightly louder: "We cannot save ourselves." As if conversing privately with each person in the hall. He begins to bear down hard on certain words, almost growling deep in his chest. "As hard as we WORK and much as we STUDY, we cannot save ourselves. It is VANITY to believe that we can. Only God has the POWER to lift us up from the mire in which we live. And even then, God must take a great LEVER in His hands to pry us out of that slick, red sin that clings to us like blood-soaked clay."

Almost whispering. "And do you know what that lever is?" He clasps his hands above his head and suddenly those hands appear huge, almost menacing. "Sister, do you know?" His eyes sweep the crowd below him as his arms quiver. "Brother, you look like a workingman. Do you know God's lever? Have you felt it prying at you?" All anxious eyes strain toward him; anxious faces shake almost imperceptibly. No, no, we don't know.

The Preacher's hands crash down on the pulpit. "GOD'S GREAT TOOL IS HIS SON. And know Him you must if you expect to be saved!"

From where she sits demurely at the piano, Bridget can see her father's back, his hands clenched above his head and then smashing down on the pulpit. She smiles to herself. He just may bring this off, she thinks. She just may get her horses. Although God only knows what dark road he meant to travel when he started off in the vanity verses.

The Preacher sees eight or ten rough, shabby men standing with Gabe Overbay at the rear of the hall. The circus roustabouts the boy had been sent to collect. He focuses his words on those men, those ten scabbed, tattooed souls. Save them, he thinks, and you could save the world.

"Ecclesiastes teaches us that the world continues to turn, the rivers to run, the sun to rise and set; and every day that passes, we are worn to the quick. Our bodies lie down tired and rise up tired; all is vanity. Our stomachs revolt at the food we swallow; all is vanity. Our eyes lose their luster and our hearts their passion; all is vanity. Each day we return to the fields only to see another inch of metal worn from the hoe blade and another day of life worn out of our bodies. All is vanity." He could see the ten roustabouts shifting nervously from foot to foot. He knew that hangovers raged in their heads and that their guts clung to their backbones, but something was brewing there—something from their long servitude to the Tampini Brothers.

"And yet," the Preacher cries. "And yet. There is hope. God is at work in the fields, striving to bring home His children. Though they be starving, though they be alone, He brings them. God seeks to make a great harvest. He grasps the greatest tool of all, His son Jesus Christ, and He pries us up out of the miserable mire of our lives. And I ask you now, can you feel Him at work? Can you feel—"

He is interrupted by a scream from the rapt crowd. Mother Mary, precisely on cue, hurls herself to her feet and screams again. "O, lift me, Jesus. O, lift me up from this miserable, hateful body!" Two men beside her struggle to hold her upright as she sways from side to side.

The emotional dam has broken. Women scream and men dance, flinging their hands into the sultry air. "O, my great

God almighty!" calls out one of the roustabouts and begins to force himself forward through the crowd, pushing people aside with brawny arms. As if on signal, the other roustabouts start calling out, "Amen," "Praise Jesus," "Lift up my soul," as they move through the crowd, creating a tidal flow forward toward the altar.

He can feel more than hear the piano begin to play behind him. Bridget, with her deft sense of timing, has begun ever so slowly the opening chords of "Shall We Gather at the River." He can see the boy, Gabriel, circulate through the crowd with a metal bucket, collecting offerings of bills and coins from each man, woman, and child. The words LOVE OFERING are painted on the side of the bucket. The coins ring into the bottom of the pail.

He throws that seeming quiet voice of his forward over the crowd, a whisper that reaches the back wall fifty feet away. "He doesn't care if your crop has failed. He doesn't care about the baby you killed. He doesn't care if the banker owns your house. He doesn't care what you have done or what has been done to you. He can forgive you *anything*. Your sins are the vain things of this world. He only cares that you lift up your hands to Him. Lift up your hands now. Reach up to Him. Reach…."

That night, they raise $1,259 dollars in bills and change, plus a strand of pearls and a pocket watch thrown voluntarily into the bucket. Plus another three billfolds and a leather purse collected by one of the Tampini roustabouts whom even the Preacher hasn't noticed. A slight, leathery man wearing a clean striped shirt and a straw boater. A man named Spivey, nicknamed Fingers.

The Preacher asks Gabe how certain he is that Fingers has turned over *all* of his special brand of love offering. Gabe replies that he is "dead certain. He don't care for the money. He just likes the challenge of the crowd, though he says your crowd runs itself so crazy that it ain't much of a challenge."

"Can he help you with the horses and big top?" he asks.

"No. Too skinny and too particular. He don't like to get his hands tore up. But here's the thing: he can do anything else you dream up. Anything. He was the main accountant for the Tampini Show. He's a traveler."

"A communist?"

Gabe nods solemnly. "And a good one too. Irish. Despises money, like I said. But what he purely loves is trains. And I told him he could ride ours."

"Trains?"

"Yep. He can ride the advance train if you don't favor no commies."

"No, he can ride with me. You and your boys will corrupt him. And God knows, if we keep this up, we might need an accountant."

At dawn, Gabe and two of the roustabouts go with Bridget for the horses. The huge gray brutes recognize her from the day before and seem happy to see her again in their corral. One hundred dollars cash for each she pays the livery stable owner and another fifty for all the harness and tackle. The horses follow her docilely back to their own home, now the advance train for the crusade, while the men walk along behind, carrying the tack and staying well clear of the horses' hooves.

That afternoon, Jedidiah Robbins, the Preacher, sits with four other people in the club car on the *Sword of the Lord:* his daughter, Bridget; the new accountant, Fingers Spivey; the boy, Gabe; and a mystery man that neither Spivey nor Gabe has met before. The stranger has straight black hair with a full beard, and his skin is a dark olive brown from sun and blood. He is stocky with long, thick arms and powerful hands that are covered in scar tissue. Even Gabe notices that he does not sit easy in an upholstered chair.

Bridget starts the introductions. "Mr. Spivey and Mr. Overbay, this is Boss Strong. Boss, this is Fingers Spivey and Gabriel Overbay. They are joining the crusade from the Tampini Brothers Circus. Mr. Spivey is an accountant—"

"Call me Fingers," the thin man interrupts her. "Everybody does."

Strong nods and smiles, revealing one or perhaps two missing teeth. Bridget continues. "Mr. Overbay is in charge of the roustabouts and has brought along with him the engineer and fireman from the Tampini Brothers train."

"Gabe," the boy says by way of acknowledgment. "Just Gabe."

Again Strong nods.

"And just what does Mr. Strong do for the show?" Gabe asks Bridget. Who answers the question by nodding to her father.

The Preacher answers, "It's not a show. Always remember that. It's a crusade. Our purpose is not to thrill and entertain, but to save souls."

"By thrilling and entertaining the rubes?" Gabe is irrepressible.

The Preacher almost smiles. "Sometimes. Sometimes by scaring them. Making them smell the hellfire licking up through the ground and warming their toes. Sometimes by lifting them bodily off the ground with music. The Holy Spirit aflame on each man and woman's forehead."

Gabe nods at Strong. "Is he part of what scares them?"

Strong smiles back at the boy, which is itself frightening.

"No, Boss is part of the same chapter and verse as you. He rides the advance train just like you, and like you he prepares the way for the *Sword of the Lord*. You, Gabe, do it by setting up the Gospel tent and distributing flyers all over town. By visiting all the local preachers you can find, Bible in hand, and letting them know that Solomon's Crusade is on the rails, headed in their direction."

Bridget makes a mental note to buy Gabe a new shirt, maybe two. The one he's wearing looks as if it's been boiled in greasy water.

"So Boss is going to help with the tent and with the flyers?"

The Preacher shakes his head and glances at Spivey. "Can you help the boy to understand?"

Fingers nods. "He's a bootlegger, kid. Jesus, where you been?"

"But—"

Bridget cuts the boy off. "Where do you think the money comes from to pay for the crusade?"

"I thought—"

"Don't think so much, and don't talk so much. Listen more." It's the first time that Strong has spoken, and it sounds like the blade of a shovel being driven into gravel. Strong nods to the Preacher to continue.

"Here's how it works, Gabe. Tomorrow morning, the advance rig pulls out of the yard here headed for Marion, our next stop. By the time you leave in the morning, SAINT JOHN THE BAPTIST will be painted on every car. No more Tampini Brothers. You and your engineer are in charge of getting the rig there, finding a spot for the Gospel tent, and spreading the good Word. While you're searching out the various churches and preachers in town, Boss will be locating the speakeasies and pool halls. While you and your team are setting up the tent, Boss will be setting up the local boys by the pint and the gallon. Is that right, Boss?"

"Wholesale and retail," Strong replies, drawing out each syllable. Again the sound of gravel.

"There's only one problem with the big top," the boy whispers, afraid to speak now and afraid not to.

Both Bridget and the Preacher glance sharply at him. "What's wrong with it, Gabe?" Bridget asks. But the boy just shakes his head.

"What Gabe means," Fingers Spivey says, "is that it's a mite garish for a Gospel tent. What with the strong man painted all over the side of it, the elephant, the midget, the clowns, and so on. The bearded lady."

There is stunned silence, broken only by the harsh sound of Boss Strong chuckling to himself.

"Can you turn the damn thing inside out?" the Preacher finally asks.

Fingers Spivey shakes his head. "Then the bearded lady is on the inside, staring at you during the service. Better paint it. Put it up at dusk on the first night." He turns to Gabe. "Paint it in the dark and don't let any of the rubes get close to it till the paint dries. What color?" This last addressed to Bridget.

"Dark blue," she says. "White won't cover that multitude of sins."

Bridget and the boy are the first to leave the meeting, sent away so that the Preacher, Boss, and the accountant can talk money. How it may come and where it might go.

Once outside, she offers to help Gabe buy a new white shirt later that afternoon. Or perhaps two shirts, so one will always be clean. Then, just before they part, he asks her, "Why did he name the advance rig *John the Baptist*?"

"Because John the Baptist prepared the way for the Lord," she says, and then, in exasperation, "Do you even know how to read?"

He looks down at her feet and mutters something. She pokes him in the shoulder, and he repeats himself. "Not much," is what he says, and she is immediately sorry.

"I'll teach you how," she whispers. She stops herself from reaching out to touch his face or even caress his shoulder. She has so unexpectedly wounded him. "I can at least do that."

Inside the car, the Preacher has brought a bottle out of his desk and poured a generous portion into three clean glasses. "This is what Boss sells out in front of the Gospel," he explains to Spivey. "Being as you are the accountant, you'd better sample the goods."

After a sip, then another, Fingers pauses to consider before he whispers, hoarsely, "That, gentlemen, is what I call nasty good."

"Sin in a jar," Boss agrees.

CHAPTER FOUR

THE PREACHER STANDS WITH DAUGHTER BRIDGET to
watch the *John the Baptist* rig pull out of the Morganton, North
Carolina, yard early the next morning. Behind the engine and
coal car, there is a flatcar piled high with tent canvas and poles;
behind the flatcar is the passenger car, where the roustabouts
sleep; behind that is a boxcar that serves as a rolling stable for
the five Percherons; behind the horses is a boxcar stuffed with
hay and buckets and other accoutrements for the horses; and
behind that is a mystery boxcar that is painted red like a caboose.
The mystery car has sliding doors on both sides. Behind one,
the public door, are crates of Bibles for sale; the door is broadly
labeled God's holy word. Behind the door on the opposite side,
which remains mostly shut and locked, are crates of mason jars
brimful of corn whiskey or apple brandy. On each car of the train
is painted, in tall block letters, SOLOMON'S CRUSADE, and
beneath, in slightly smaller script but easily readable from a hundred feet away, THE SAINT JOHN THE BAPTIST TRAIN.

As they watch the rig gain speed at the far end of the yard,
the Preacher kneels in the gravel to pet a shabby stray dog that
has crept up to their feet. The dog is nervously wagging its tail,
ready to bolt at the first false move from the Preacher or Bridget.

"Last thing you need," Bridget says gently as she stares after
John the Baptist, "is a dog."

"I believe," he replies, "that you just came into possession
of five thousand pounds of horse on the hoof, give or take a ton.
They're not even out of sight, and you look lonely as lost time. I
might at least have a—"

"You do not need a dog. I will not take care of it for you." She continues to stare after the train, which is now disappearing around a bend in the track.

He gathers the thin, scruffy creature into his arms ever so slowly, continuing to kneel. The little fice quivers from fright, but then begins timidly to lick his hands. "We all need something," he says. "Need is the human condition."

"Not laughing or talking. You usually say talking and laughing make us human."

"Maybe laughter and words come from the need, from the loneliness." He's still fondling the dog, which is slowly relaxing in his arms. He looks up at Bridget and winks. "Ever think of that?"

"Well, then, that dog is not human; therefore, she doesn't need you."

"I wonder why," he says with a perfectly straight face, "I ever taught you to think for yourself."

She reaches down to take the dog from him. "Let me have her," she mutters. "She smells and she needs a bath."

Later that day, he sits at his desk in the *Sword of the Lord* and makes for himself a sort of chart. Once he is done, he means to share it with Bridget so that she will know what to do in case something happens to him along the Gospel trail. Two weeks previously, he'd fainted while preaching and has suffered from dizzy spells since. He smiles at the thought that the chart is a sort of will and testament. If so, then it's a *new* testament because the people around him are shifting, changing, and someone else needs to see the pattern he is weaving—someone with a mind and someone he can trust.

Which narrows down the list considerably...perhaps to just two—Boss and Bridget.

His first draft of the chart is a single sheet of soiled paper divided into four quadrants by vertical and horizontal penciled lines, each splitting the page. In the left margin, he scribbles "Saint John the Baptist" beside the upper-left section, signifying the people who ride the advance train; beside the lower left, he scribbles "Sword of the Lord" for those who follow on the Gospel rig.

After a pause, he writes at the top of the sheet over the left column the words "Knows the Business" and then over the right column "Knows the Lord." He then enters the names of his associates and his brethren into the four quadrants. Upper left— those in the advance train who know the business—he writes, "Boss Strong" and "Gabe Overbay." Of the two, he thinks, Boss knows far more than Gabe, but then perhaps Boss is Gabe's teacher, his pattern for what comes next.

Lower left—those in the Gospel train who know the business—he writes his own name, "Jedidiah Robbins," and then "Bridget Robbins" and "Fingers Spivey." Spivey is still a mystery, a man so self-contained that he seems to appear and disappear at will, especially in a crowded room. Can he be trusted at all? He pencils in a question mark beside Spivey's name.

Upper right—those in the advance rig who know the Lord. He catches himself about to write the names of the Tampini roustabouts but then realizes he doesn't know their names, and he doubts they know the Lord. Shakes his head at his own stupidity. How could he have let them out of sight with his property and couldn't call a single one of them by name? "Ask Spivey" he writes in the upper right, and then, after a moment, "Save their souls." As for the property—train, tent, horses—Boss would look after their investment as well as Gabe and the seven lost souls.

Lower right—those on the Gospel train who know the Lord. Here he is on safer ground, as the four souls whose names he writes here have been with him for some months and are now settled into their roles. "Mother Mary McManaway," "Brother Andrew" (no known last name), "James Bundren," and "John Bundren." Mother Mary weighs 250 packed-solid pounds and believes in the Lord so fervently that she begins to sweat at the mere mention of Jesus' name. A woman who can pray in a voice so loud and deep that it causes dogs and babies to howl. At the altar call, she will hug any repentant sinner and bury any weeping face between her massive, heaving breasts. Brother Andrew had been rescued from the insane asylum in Raleigh, where he had been imprisoned because he was both a mute and an albino. Eyes so pale, they turn pink in lamplight. Now he sings for his supper like an angel, and grown men weep to hear him.

James and John Bundren are identical twins, two country boys in their twenties, and both so thin that Bridget claims you can see through them in a strong light. They stink of tobacco from the furtive cigarettes they pass back and forth behind trees, churches, boxcars. Each with his well-worn Bible. The twins were delivered unto the Preacher after a night of heated negotiation with their mother, who desired him to train them up in the Gospel Word so that they would be a blessing to her in her old age. James and John can barely read but know long passages of the New Testament by heart. One stutters painfully, but he, the Preacher, can't remember which.

Staring at his chart, he wonders if all those who know the Lord are damaged somehow, lost and seeking.

That night, he draws the chart again for Bridget. To settle his supper he is drinking apple brandy, the best they have, made by a man named Freeman in Madison County and saved back for him by Boss. And for the first time, he pours his daughter a short glass full. She sips and grimaces while he shows her through the diagram of their traveling show.

"Who knows everything?" she asks finally. "Other than you, and now me, who sees it all clear?"

"Boss sees it all," he says without hesitation. "Knows how it all plays. But he can't ride the Gospel train."

"Does Boss even believe in God?"

"Hard question," he says after swishing a sip of apple brandy around in his mouth. "Boss is a drinker and a fighter. Loved any number of women. But I know no man more moral. No man closer to his code."

"Is it even remotely Christian—the code Boss follows?"

He smiles at her, his heart swelling. "Close enough," he whispers. "Such that if something happens to me, if I fall by the wayside, I want you to turn first to him. He's no preacher, nor would he choose that for himself. But preachers are a dime a dozen in these hard times. You'll need a man to hold the troupe together, a man to make the trains run."

"What the hell do you mean, if something happens to you?"

"Boss once shot a man in Erwin, Tennessee, for whipping a dog. Said the dog was considerably smarter than the man."

She can feel the brandy warm in her belly, rising into her head. "I will tell you right now, goddamn it, that you're not going anywhere. Not without me."

"And I freely admit that he's loved many women. Did I say that already?"

"You are a young man yet. Not sixty nor even close."

"More than I can count."

"More what than you can count? Years?"

"The women Boss has taken to bed."

"How many truthfully?"

"Oh, dozens, I expect. But it doesn't seem particularly sinful in his case, does it?"

"Boss and his women is a topic for another day. What in God's name makes you think you're going to…?" She can't bring herself to say the word.

"You know, it was your mother who wanted me to become a preacher. I never felt especially suited to it."

"I think she would be proud of you," she whispers. "And she would want you to live."

The dusk is slipping in through the open windows of the car and gathering around them, pooling almost like dark water. He gets up to light a lamp and, after fussing with the wick, pours a dollop more brandy into her glass. His as well, although he gives himself less than her.

After he sits back down, he says, simply, "I hear voices."

"What in the world?" She sips from her glass. "Voices?"

"Used to be only late at night, but this summer I hear voices talking with me even by the light of day. Bright noon."

Protected by the growing dark, the little dog—by now the "official" office dog—creeps out from under his desk and rests her chin on his thigh. He pats her head, and she licks his fingers. "I cannot predict," he admits, "what it means. But the voice I hear most often is that of your mother. And she talks with me as if she's in the room. As if we share a here-and-now. A place that has nothing to do with this earth, even though I do try to interest her in what we're doing here."

"You are precisely fifty-nine years old. A young man, and everyone on that chart there," she points with her glass and slops brandy onto the paper. "Everyone on that chart of yours needs you, and I need you most of all. None of this will go on without you to speak the Word."

"I have no desire to leave you," he says quietly. "Make no mistake. I am overly fond of this world, if you must know the truth. And I would live many years with you just to see what you make out of this life. But sometimes…"

She stares at him with tears in her eyes, mingled frustration and love. "Sometimes what?" she whispers.

"Sometimes I feel the breeze itself blow right through me as if I'm not here. As if I'm made of mist."

CHAPTER FIVE

IT IS THREE NIGHTS LATER in the small foothills town of Marion, North Carolina. A warm August night, the heat of the sunny day drenched in a late-afternoon thunderstorm.

Solomon's Crusade is about to embark on a new chapter in its history, performing for the first time as a bona fide tent meeting—the former Tampini Brothers big top standing proud in the ball field behind the elementary school. The canvas is stiff with a new coat of blue, and the lacquer smell of oil paint masks the ghostly odors of manure and straw that once followed the circus. The roustabouts have knocked together a rough stage at one end of the tent, covered the ground with busted-up hay bales borrowed at night from a nearby barn, and nailed together splintered benches for the crowd out of boards donated over the back fence of a local lumberyard.

The members of the crusade—Bridget, Mother Mary, Brother Andrew, and the Bundren boys—have been welcoming the local people as they drift into the tent before the service. A minister named Agape Bailey, brought forward by Gabe, is standing with the Preacher in the open door of the tent, introducing him to local personages, including the members of Bailey's own First Baptist congregation.

The people are mostly tired and careworn, farmers and shopkeepers, the men's eyes guarded if curious. They stare openly at the Preacher, wondering about the celebrity evangelist, this Solomon they've read about in the newspaper. The women have dressed in their Sunday best to celebrate the coming of something fine and ethereal into their midst, a spectacle they can enjoy as much as, or more than, the men because it is a pageant pure and spiritual, not tainted by the flesh. The matrons are openly happy to have naked, unadorned religion in their midst, knowing it's the only nakedness inside this tent. They have brought pound cakes and peach pies for the Gospel troupe and left them on the back bench by the entrance.

One woman has brought a chocolate cake that draws hungry glances from the two roustabouts standing just outside the tent. She comes forward demurely to be introduced to the Preacher. "This is Cassandra," Agape Bailey explains, "my wife and my helpmeet in the service of church and Lord." The Preacher does something unusual then, at least for him: he reaches out and shakes the woman's hand and holds it firmly until she looks up to meet his eyes. He realizes with a shock that Cassandra Bailey must be twenty years younger than her husband and has skin like Old Testament alabaster.

"So you are the great Solomon come to us from afar," the woman whispers.

The Preacher grins. "I am. Come to aid your husband and good men like him."

She glances at her husband, who has turned away to meet the mayor of the town, glad-handing and gushing. "Well, he needs all the help he can get," she says to the Preacher, blushing slightly. Barely aware of what she's saying.

The Preacher bends to look into her eyes. They are chocolate brown, like the cake, but not so innocent. "Will you pray with me after the service?" he asks her. "Pray for relief."

She smiles, but she doesn't answer as, at that moment, her husband presents the mayor, who is wearing a tie so garish it defies description.

◇◇◇

He had meant to ease the crowd into the New Testament with the usual pleas and platitudes. John 3:16 and similar pabulum. Jesus standing in the doorway with hand outstretched—a kindly, bearded young man full of soft understanding. But for some reason, Cassandra Bailey has thrown him off the standard track, and he veers away from calm reassurance into the flames of Pentecost. Acts, the second chapter:

"'And suddenly there came a sound from Heaven as of a rushing mighty wind, and it filled all the house where they were sitting.'" He pauses to stare out over the crowd. "'And there appeared unto them cloven tongues like as of fire, and it sat upon each of them. And they were all filled with the Holy Ghost, and began to speak with other tongues, as the Spirit gave them utterance. And now hear we every man in our own tongue, wherein we were born? And they were all amazed, and were in doubt, saying one to another, What meaneth this?'" Again he paused, this time for effect. "This is the very word of God, like an iron hand squeezing your heart," he shouts. "God whispering in your own ear, like the mighty wind rustling through this room."

He continues. "The lesser preachers teach that speaking in tongues means that you growl and grunt and fling yourself on the hard ground. But the book of Acts doesn't say that, sister. The book of Acts says just the opposite, brother. It says that we shall understand each other—each to each—regardless of where we're born or what language we speak. The Acts of the Apostles say we will speak through our tongues to each other in the broad light of day, and *that* is the gift of the Holy Spirit. That we shall understand and love one another, no matter our origin, no matter the lies we tell ourselves. The Spirit is poured out upon the flesh, and the anointed flesh shall know God."

That night he preaches with the madness and fire he'd known when he was a young man, when Bridget's mother had just died and he was furious with the world. He preaches with the passion of youth flaming out of his vitals, smoking from his nostrils. It was as if he'd set himself on fire in the pulpit in a self-immolation of words. And the crowd melts before him almost as if *his* apostles—the Tampini Brothers roustabouts—had doused the people in smoking kerosene. They scream and collapse and dance in place as if possessed by some winged angel composed of smoke and ashes.

Is the Holy Ghost in the room? Yes, he thinks. Yes! Dropped from the sky as if from the mists above. Floating on fluttering dark wings into this sweating canvas pyramid.

Fainting women are trodden on by worshipers who dance the hectic jig of spiritual fervor. Children are shoved roughly out of the way as the people begin to push forward toward the altar. People who would tear him limb from limb to touch the bold fire within his body.

He sees Bridget slip from the piano stool and motions her behind him where she'll be safe. She is crying. She shakes her head no, and jumps down from the platform into the crowd, where she pulls the frightened children to one side, out of the way of their own parents.

Led by Gabe Overbay, the roustabouts advance quickly, forming a rough line before the altar to keep the crowd from crushing onto the stage and tearing the clothes off his body, the flesh from his bones. He is still shouting about the fervor of the Holy Ghost even after he realizes that he's called down something he may not be able to exorcise. He lowers his voice several registers and begins to whisper, humming and singing almost in a deep tone, trying to calm the stampede.

He recites the twenty-third Psalm, slowly and soothingly—"'The Lord is my shepherd; I shall not want'"—even as one roustabout knocks down a shrieking woman with his fist. Mother Mary wades into the crowd, parting the waves with the broad prow of her bosom. She lifts the stricken woman and carries her under one fat arm—"'He maketh me to lie down in green pastures'"—as she moves slowly through the waves of sweating, shouting people, caressing crying faces and stroking heaving backs with her free hand.

The Bundren boys are circulating as well, their open Bibles held at arm's length above their heads as they testify—"'He leadeth me beside the still waters'"—and receive professions of faith from frightened, leaden souls now shedding their burdens. One woman begins to tear at her own clothes, ripping her dress down over her arms and shoulders, bare to her waist. Her husband ceases spinning beside her to cover her with his suit coat.

The crowd begins to quieten as his voice pacifies them—"'He restoreth my soul'"—and they listen to the well-worn, familiar strains of the only Psalm that most of them can recite from childhood. "'He leadeth me in the paths of righteousness for His name's sake.'" They whisper the words along with the Preacher, as if falling under a quiet shepherd's spell rather than that of the violent Pentecostal Ghost.

He can see Fingers Spivey flitting through the crowd—"'Yea, though I walk through the valley of the shadow of death'"— comforting the afflicted as he gathers their unwitting offerings.

"If you come unto the Lord," he intones quietly, "you need fear no evil—'Thy rod and Thy staff they comfort me'—and if you join the ranks of the saved tonight, you may 'dwell in the house of the Lord forever.' You will live forever at the foot of the throne of God."

On this night, the crowd is restless before the altar, even with the soothing oil of the twenty-third Psalm poured over their sweating bodies. They surge backward and forward almost as if a single unconscious being, made of water now rather than fire. As if waves washing back and forth, crashing against a rocky shore.

Gabe Overbay returns through a side door from where he's been helping Bridget manage her small herd of frightened children. He nods to the Preacher to say that they're safe and begins to circulate through the crowd with his bucket: LOVE OFFERING. The other roustabouts break their line as well, now that the Preacher is safe from inundation. The pails begin to ring with conviction, as spare change follows the soft flutter of dollar bills into the collection.

The Preacher steps down from the stage and joins Mother Mary and the Bundren boys—praying, blessing, absolving—saving the distracted, filthy souls of Marion, North Carolina, by the dozen. The blood of the Lamb washing away sins real and imaginary. Girls and women reach out to touch the hem of the Preacher's jacket, one woman pulling the string tie from around his neck to give to her bedridden mother.

They have the best night of collections that they have ever experienced: $2,459 plus four wallets, two pocketbooks, and three gold rings. The Preacher raises his eyebrows at Fingers Spivey. "Rings?"

"Rings are hard," Spivey admits. "But you had them rubes so bemused, I coulda borrowed their underwear, and when they got undressed, they'da thought Jesus took it."

Once the crowd begins to dissipate, Bridget knows better than to follow her father directly to their car on the Gospel train. There will be women seeking his guidance—indeed, his very touch—to ease their troubles. She stands with Gabe Overbay outside the tent as the crowd finally begins to ebb, watching him eat pound cake with all the avidity of a starving dog. It is then that she sees Cassandra Bailey for the first time, when Cassandra stops to ask where the Preacher is. "He asked me to pray with him," she says by way of explanation, "for the sins of our community."

Bridget points to the club car at the end of the *Sword of the Lord*, where yellow lamplight glimmers behind drawn shades. "He'll be in there washing up," she tells Cassandra. "Knock on that last door if you're sure you need to see him."

"Wha th hell tha about?" Gabe mumbles around a mouthful of cake after Cassandra has walked away in the direction Bridget has indicated.

"Dad preached from Acts tonight. Pentecost and fire. It always brings out the dewy virgins."

Gabe swallows. "You mean…?"

"Acts, chapter 8, verse 17," she smiles grimly at the boy. "Which I don't expect you to cipher. It says that there will be a laying on of hands and she will receive the Holy Ghost."

"Shitfire. No offense, but he's…"

"Too old? You'd be surprised." She studies him for a moment and then reaches out to brush the cake crumbs off his once-new white shirt. She knows the streaks of blue paint on the sleeves will never come out, even with borax. "Come on, Angel Gabriel. I don't have anything to do for a couple of hours, and it's time you had your first reading lesson."

It is late, midnight or after, when she walks from the *John the Baptist* back down the tracks to the club car on the Gospel rig. She has taken Gabe through the alphabet and a number of short words that are easy to recognize, using a hymnal she found in the saints' car. He is a quick study, so ravenous for language that she finds herself moved by his simplicity, his willingness to struggle with words like *life* and *blood* and *lamb*. All the more reason, she thinks, to liberate a box of books from the local library before they move on. Spivey could deliver such a box, she thinks, but what books in particular does she need?

When she reaches the club car, she sees Spivey himself sitting on the iron steps, nervously smoking a cigarette. He gestures her over to him. "I need to see the Preacher," he says, "and…"

"Let me guess. There's a woman in there?"

Fingers shakes his head. "No, that other preacher's wife left out that door a half hour ago."

"Then he's likely asleep by now. Can't it wait till morning?"

"This can't wait," Fingers mutters. "Boss Strong is in jail."

CHAPTER SIX

THE FIRST THING THE PREACHER SAYS to Bridget is *coffee*. "Fire the stove and make the whole pot, please." And then, to Fingers, "How in the...?"

"Boys say they took him up an hour ago. Sheriff's deputy caught him delivering the goods to a little Negro speakeasy. Other side of this burg."

"Damnation!" he says.

"No need for you to say that." Fingers grins. "I already said it enough for both of us."

"What time is it?"

Fingers pulls a watch from a vest pocket and shakes it, a watch that Bridget is fairly certain he didn't have that morning. "Midnight. Just after."

"Does the sheriff know that Boss is with the crusade?"

Fingers shrugs. "If he don't, it shouldn't take him long to figure it out. New man in town, never seen before. Showed up same time as the advance rig."

"Then we've got to get the booze off the train. Hide it somewhere." This from Bridget as she pours grounds into the basket of the big tin coffeepot.

Fingers glances at the Preacher. "Where do we put it? I inventoried over forty cases in that boxcar."

The brindled fice is asleep and dreaming on an old towel beside the stove. Her legs twitch and she half growls in a nightmare chase. The Preacher has been watching the dog absently as he listens to Bridget and Fingers. He looks up suddenly and grins. "Better to move the whole car. Has

Boss been selling the goods off the train, or carrying jars into town?"

"Mostly into town," Fingers says. "I know, cause he had some of the boys making deliveries." And then he adds, "One or two of the smart ones who know to keep their mouths shut."

"Then we'll hide the whole car. There's an empty railroad repair shed a quarter mile on down the siding. All the way back in the trees. We'll uncouple the Bible car and hide it there till we're ready to pull out."

"Unhooking the car ain't no problem, Preacher, but how in the...how in heck do you mean to move the car without firing up one of the engines and attracting all kinds of attention?"

"Bridget can do it," the Preacher says simply.

His daughter glances up sharply from the scarred table, where she's just poured three cups of strong, black coffee. "Me?"

"Her?" Fingers says.

"Well, her and those horses of hers. It's time they earned their keep."

Bridget glances at Fingers as she hands him his coffee. "Do you think they can do it? Pull an entire railroad car?"

"For me, no. For the Preacher, no. For you, they'd pull the whole damn train and think you're taking them to a picnic."

She blushes. Something he, the Preacher, hasn't seen so much these last years.

The pungent smell of coffee is strong in the club car. The little dog settles back into quiet sleep, her nightmare over. After a moment, the Preacher, who is fully awake now with his mind ranging over the coming hours, tells Bridget and Fingers, "The two of you are in charge of moving the car. As quietly as possible, with as few of the roustabouts as you can manage. The fewer who know where the car is, the better, in case the sheriff of this little Eden decides to play rough. It all needs to be done before first light."

"What about Boss?" Bridget asks. "Are we going to leave him where he is?"

"As soon as I finish my coffee and consult the Scriptures," the Preacher says, "I'm going down to the jail to visit with the prisoners. They may not let me in till first light, but I need to have prayer with Mr. Strong before the sheriff has a chance to get at him."

"Should we use Gabe for the horses and the Bible car?" Bridget asks.

The Preacher pauses to consider. "No, I'll take him with me. He's been all over town hawking the crusade. Let the locals see him with me. Besides, it's time the boy learns the daylight ways of the world."

The jail is in the basement of an old storefront building a block behind the McDowell County Courthouse. The sheriff's office is on the first floor, at the front of the building, which consists of a lobby, off of which there is a locked storeroom and a closed door that must lead to the private office of the High Sheriff himself, of whom there is no evidence this early in the day.

The Preacher and Gabe Overbay sit side by side in a couple of chairs facing one of three battered desks in the lobby. Behind the desk is the deputy who arrested Boss Strong the night before. He is a tall, ungainly man with a sadly confused look on his face, for he has been listening to the Preacher read aloud from the Gospel of Matthew, starting with chapter 1, since well before daylight. He has heard about the generation of Jesus, the son of David, the son of Abraham. He has been privy to the virgin birth of Jesus in Bethlehem, in the days of Herod the king. He has learned about John the Baptist, preaching in the wilderness of Judea (which was of particular interest to Gabe, if not to the deputy).

The first light of day filters into the office through the grimy windows, and the deputy—Jimbo Banks is his name—is hearing of Jesus in the wilderness, being tempted over and again by the devil. He has been up all night, and he can't understand why the devil wants Jesus to turn stones into bread.

"Stop," he says finally. "They's only so much Bible a man can take in one sittin. I reckon it's close enough to eight o'clock so that you can see the prisoner now anyway." Jimbo rises to his feet much like a stork or crane takes flight from a river bank, all sharp angles flung together. Gabe's eyes follow him as he bends stiffly to pull a set of keys from a bottom desk drawer. "I can only let one of you in there at a time," Jimbo tells the Preacher. "We got rules. Rules and regulations."

"My associate can remain here with you in the outer room," the Preacher says gently. "I assume you'll need to lock me in with the prisoner."

"I'm sorry," says Jimbo. "It's them rules. He looks to me like a mean son-of-a-bitch, Preacher. Are you sure you don't want to just read to him through the bars?"

"I'm not afraid," the Preacher says gently. "God is with me, even in the midst of the wilderness. Besides," he adds helpfully, "I need to kneel with this sinner in prayer. A good, long prayer if he is as bad a man as you say."

While Jimbo with his keys starts down the steep stairs to the basement cells, the Preacher leans close to Gabe long enough to whisper, "If the sheriff shows up, stall him. I need long enough with Boss to work out a plan."

Gabe nods, though just the thought of a sheriff makes him sweat.

Jimbo and Gabe sit together halfway up the stairs where Jimbo can see the Preacher and Boss Strong kneeling together in Boss' cell. The Preacher's Bible is open on the bunk in front of them, while they lean on the bunk to take the pressure off their knees. "How long you reckon they'll stay like that?" Jimbo asks Gabe.

"Oh, I've known the Preacher to pray for hours at a stretch," Gabe explains. "And that man you got down there is sure a bad un. Why don't you and me go back upstairs where it's a little more comfortable?"

"We're both too old for this," Boss whispers mildly, too quietly to be heard more than a few feet away, though even his whisper is rough in the throat. "Kneeling in the cold dirt like a couple of monks."

"If you don't care for it, why did you get yourself arrested? You in the damn calaboose was never any part of the plan."

"That boy up the steps caught me red-handed, walking into the back of a nigger juice joint carrying a tow sack full of liquor jars. The whole place no bigger than this cell. Pine planks laid across a couple of barrels to make a bar."

"You're telling me you let that string bean upstairs bring you in? *You* must be getting old."

"He had a little pistol he seemed anxious to try out. I would've had to break his arm to take it away from him, and I figured you didn't want no deputy laid up in the hospital and me on the run."

The Preacher grins down at the soiled wool blanket on the bunk. "No, you're right. This is better."

"Well, if it's better, Jedidiah, how you plannin on getting me out of here? I don't like livin underground. Smells like the bottom of a privy down here."

"It's not been twelve hours. 'Be not hasty in thy spirit to be angry: for anger resteth in the bosom of fools.'"

"Sounds like some of your Proverbs. I'm not angry—yet, but I do like my sunshine, and I do need a drink. In a few days, I'll rip the bars out of that window and climb on out of here."

"You won't have to. You're going to have a conversion experience."

"How you mean? You gonna save my soul?"

"Yes, I am, me and Christ. You're going to see Jesus and talk to Him. And He's going to tell you to forego your sinful ways. Give up that demon in a bottle."

"I can do that. At least till we get out of this sorry excuse for a town. Where am I supposed to do my testifying?"

"I'm going to ask the locals to try you straightaway for violation of the Volstead Act."

"Sons a bitches can't even spell *Volstead*."

"Probably not, but they can get you into a courtroom, and before the locals find out you're wanted in Virginia."

"Don't forget that mess in Tennessee."

"And Tennessee. You're going to find Jesus in the most public place possible, and I'm going to rise up and bless you and ask the judge to deliver you into my custody as a bright and shiny man of God."

"Like a new penny?"

"Exactly."

"And if that don't work, can I bust out of here and meet you at the next town?"

"You can tear down the whole damn building like Samson if you want, but this will work. And it will sell, and there won't be a warrant waiting on you when we get to the next stop on down the line."

"If you say so. Just make it soon. I don't favor a cage. And Jedidiah?"

"Yeah?"

"What the hell did you do with the hooch? If they find it in the Bible car, you and that child Gabe'll be in here with me."

When the Preacher and Gabe arrive back at the depot siding, it is obvious why the sheriff hasn't appeared at the jail. He is waiting for them along with a deputy, standing beside the *John the Baptist* rig and arguing with Bridget. The Preacher is relieved, as the Bible car is nowhere to be seen.

It strikes the Preacher that the High Sheriff of McDowell County is an almost invisible man. He is of average height with eyes of no particular color. Sandy hair that might be turning gray. Pale skin, but not so pale as to stand out. A perfectly round face with rimless spectacles that hide his eyes. The most colorful thing about him is his uniform, which is as clean as the day it was made, the crease in the trousers as straight and sharp as an arrow pointing down at his polished shoes, and the shirt starched to minute perfection. The deputy looks tall, fat, and shabby standing beside him.

"I'm the Preacher," he says as he shakes the sheriff's hand.

"Have a name, Preacher, or is it just Solomon?"

"Jedidiah Robbins, and this is my daughter Bridget, and my associate Gabriel Overbay."

"I'm Sheriff James."

"As in Jesse James?" Gabe's nervous joke.

"No." The sheriff doesn't pretend to smile. "William."

Not Will? the Preacher thinks. Bill or Billy? William!

"Sheriff James wants to search the *John the Baptist* train," Bridget explains, "but I told him that I believe a search warrant is necessary in the United States of America." There is an edge to her voice.

"Actually I want to search both trains," the sheriff says evenly, his voice as gray as his appearance.

"Including our personal quarters?" the Preacher asks. Offhand, helpful. He nods down the track. "The club car on the *Sword of the Lord* is where Bridget and I live."

After a moment's consideration, the sheriff says, "Yes, the law requires it."

"What are you looking for, Sheriff, if I may ask? We bring the Word of God to the masses, and you can have all of that you need without a warrant. Free of charge."

"I'm looking for contraband liquor, Mr. Robbins. Your employee, this Boss Strong, was arrested late last night, carrying six gallons of distilled spirits with the intent of selling them to my constituents. He had to transport the contraband into my county somehow, and so it stands to reason that the liquor came in on one of your trains." And after a moment, almost as an afterthought, "I'm not saying that you or your daughter knew about it."

"What are you—" Gabe starts to speak, but the Preacher lays a hand on his arm.

"Between such men as ourselves, Sheriff, there is no need for a warrant. We are both servants of God and his chosen ones. I invite you and your deputy to search every nook and cranny of our two machines. I'm shocked—shocked and appalled—by Mr. Strong's actions, and I will—"

"If you're so shocked, why did you go to visit him before dawn?" There is a marked pause, and the tension mounts. Bridget has never seen anyone interrupt her father before.

The Preacher smiles sadly. "Outrage knows no hour, Sheriff. When I heard what Mr. Strong had done, I was compelled to confront him with his sin. How would you feel if one of your deputies was caught ensnaring innocent people in the fiery net of liquor?"

The sheriff glances at the rumpled deputy standing beside him and almost smiles. "They ain't the brightest boys in the world," he admits, "but I don't pay them to think." He looks straight into the Preacher's eyes. "Like you, I pay them to do what they're told."

The Preacher knows he's been threatened. Personally. And he realizes that the sheriff is so bland precisely because he chooses to be. A form of hiding in plain sight. He smiles back into those colorless eyes. "I admire your style, Sheriff," he says. "Bridget, Mr. Overbay, and I will be in the club car. Search to your heart's content. But I should warn you."

"Warn me?"

"Be careful of your good shoes. There's horseshit everywhere."

That afternoon, a Saturday, the Preacher is summoned to the McDowell County Courthouse—a block from the jail—for a meeting with the local judge, a man named Mabry. The message is delivered by Jimbo the deputy, and when the Preacher asks him what Mabry is like, Jimbo only shakes his head sadly.

"He hates liquor and he likes his rules. Likes his Bible too," he mutters. "He's a First Baptist, and if he starts to quote the Ten Commandments at you, look out. Somebody's going to prison." Jimbo's thin face brightens a bit. "But you might come out all right with him, since you got most as much Bible as he does."

The Preacher doesn't trust Gabe to keep his mouth shut in front of the judge, so he takes Bridget with him. She at least has enough sense to trade in her denims and work boots for a Sunday dress, and just before they leave, she combs her long hair back and twists it into a demure bun, as so many of the country women wear it.

As they walk together to the courthouse, he asks about the Bible car, and her face lights up. "The horses were so good," she says, almost purring. "They stepped into their harnesses as if they knew exactly what I wanted, and pulled like heroes."

"But what about the car? I'm not worried about the horses."

"It's as if it disappeared off the face of the earth. It's down in that abandoned railroad shed with the doors pulled. Fingers and two of the boys are sitting peaceful, playing cards with an old Negro man who lives in the shed. When I took their lunch down there, Fingers said to tell you to take your time. They like the easy life."

"I expect they do. But my guess is we'll need to leave soon, and we may need to leave fast. You might let Fingers know that when you take them their supper."

She nods. "What about today? What about this meeting?"

"Depends on who the boss in the room is," he says. "If it's the sheriff, we may be in trouble. He's way too clever for a town like this. If it's this Judge Mabry or some other local, then we may be all right."

"*All right* meaning…?"

"That we'll take Boss with us when we leave this hole in the wall. He won't be either in jail or a fugitive in yet one more state. That would be all right."

"Why do you care for Boss so much?" They were standing now in the worn, patchy grass outside the courthouse, ten minutes before their time. "It's like he's your blood brother or something."

He stares at his daughter speculatively for a moment before answering. "Think of it this way," he says finally. "Boss is who I would have become if I hadn't met your mother. And if we hadn't had you."

"The civilizing influence of women saved you from a life of crime?"

The Preacher grins. "Either that or it saved me from a hell of a lot of fun."

CHAPTER SEVEN

THE JUDGE'S CHAMBERS consist of a barren room tucked away behind the courtroom on the second floor of the courthouse. It holds a large oak desk with a matching chair permanently tilted at a dangerous angle, a rusty set of file cabinets, two plain wooden chairs afflicted with rickets, and a well-used spittoon. The room smells of rancid tobacco juice and the old, blistered shellac that is turning black on the floors.

The judge wears, of all things, a white linen suit with a string tie. He is well fed to the point of portliness, and his face is flushed and heavily veined. At first glance he is a happy stereotype of the privileged Southerner. Drinks like a whale, the Preacher thinks as he shakes the judge's hand.

Judge Mabry is gallant with Bridget before ushering them into the courtroom. "My quarters are too poor to host our meeting," he explains. "I expect the sheriff, who is always punctual, and several of the spiritual leaders of our community to consult with us over this unusual situation."

The Preacher raises his eyebrows. "The local ministry?"

"Precisely. They are fully engaged with us in the fight against that liquor sickness." He folds his fat fingers together to illustrate. "If the sheriff is my right hand, the local ministers are my left. Together we present one unbroken wall to protect the people of McDowell County."

Bridget smiles, thinking of the children's rhyme. Here's the church and here's the steeple. Open the doors and see all the people.

Together they sit down around the prosecuting attorney's table, borrowing chairs from here and there in the front of the courtroom. The sheriff is suddenly present, as if materializing out of the dust motes in the air. His attire differs from this morning in that he's now wearing a tie: black, the only color on his gray frame. His shoes are spotless. Despite the horses, the Preacher thinks.

The sheriff nods curtly at the Preacher and almost smiles at Bridget.

"Did you find any contraband on our two trains?" the Preacher asks, conversationally. And then to the judge by way of explanation, "The sheriff and one of his fine deputies searched *Saint John the Baptist* and the *Sword of the Lord* this morning. I believe they were looking for illegal spirits."

"Oh, I know about the search," the judge says, tapping his chest. "The sheriff keeps me apprised of all his actions."

I doubt that, the Preacher thinks, smiling back at the judge. "And what did you discover?" again to the sheriff.

"A shotgun, two pistols, six knives, and a shovel handle sawed off to make a club—all on the flying squadron." The sheriff turns to the judge. "That's the advance train he styles *John the Baptist*. None of it particularly illegal, but strange equipage for a Christian crusade. Your boys must be expecting the devil to attack them in their sleep."

This is almost a joke from the gray man, and the Preacher smiles in appreciation.

From a bag at his feet, the sheriff takes two matching switchblade knives and a half-empty jar of apple brandy. "This was in the second train, what he calls the Gospel train. Switchblades are illegal in this county, Judge, as you know, and the brandy as well." He turns suddenly to the Preacher, and the tone of his voice actually rises a bit, as in accusation. "The switchblades belong to those twins of yours, name of Burden. And the illegal liquor was in your own car. I found it before you got back from visiting the prisoner, and it must be yours." He nods solemnly at Bridget. "I doubt if your daughter drinks it."

Again the Preacher smiles. "The twins are named Bundren, and they aren't smart enough to carry knives. I suggest you give those to your deputies."

The sheriff doesn't smile. "And the booze?"

The Preacher nods at the jar. "That thing of darkness I acknowledge as mine. As my daughter will attest, I suffer from severe headaches, and from time to time I have to take a teaspoon of medicine to ease the pain."

"A teaspoon will do it?" the judge says wonderingly.

"Bullshit," the sheriff says.

"Maybe," the Preacher to the sheriff. "Maybe bullshit. But then again, according to the Volstead Act, it's not illegal to have a small amount of spirits in your private possession. It's only illegal to make, transport, or sell the devil's stew."

The judge glances back toward his chambers, and suddenly the Preacher knows where the old goat keeps his own bottle. Has to be the file cabinet, he thinks.

Someone pushes open the large double doors at the back of the courtroom. Everyone but the sheriff turns to see who is entering. Bridget recognizes Agape Bailey, the Baptist minister, from the crusade the night before and, with a shock, his wife Cassandra, whom he is pulling along beside him with a painful grip on her elbow.

Bailey is wearing a wide, garish tie—like some sort of pitch-man for God—but Cassandra is dressed as if in mourning. She has on a long, black, shapeless dress fit for a grandmother, and matronly black shoes. And though she has let down her hair to hide it, her pale white skin shows up one eye swollen shut and her cheek bruised black. Bridget doesn't normally care for the women her father takes to bed, but her heart goes out to Cassandra. She knows the woman couldn't have chosen that dress and those shoes for herself, nor did she deserve her husband's fist, and Bridget cringes in sympathy.

Behind the couple come several more lean and hungry-looking men in plain white shirts and dark pants, one with a worn suit coat but no tie. The lesser preachers from this small, foolish foothills town. Literate perhaps but with no training other than deep immersion in the King James Bible.

Everyone but Judge Mabry and the sheriff leaps to his feet and begins adding and rearranging chairs to make room for the newcomers—almost as if around some grim dinner table. Bridget lets herself be separated from her father so that she can casually but deliberately sit next to Cassandra Bailey, meaning to offer her another woman's support if and when it is needed. The result is that Mabry, continuously beaming a toothy smile, sits at one end of the table and the sheriff at the other. Along one side, to the sheriff's right, sit Agape Bailey, then Cassandra, who has yet to look up, and then Bridget, just at Mabry's left hand. On the other side, the Preacher sits between Marion's Methodist and Presbyterian ministers—the Presbyterian of course wearing the suit coat.

Judge Mabry nods, and the sheriff says, "Now, about this liquor being sold by the crusade, we—"

The Preacher interrupts him smoothly, evenly, to say, "Aren't you forgetting something, Sheriff? Shouldn't we open a gathering of this significance with prayer?"

It's as if a subtle electric shock goes around the table. Bailey's mouth drops open; his wife looks up for the first time, to glance at the Preacher. Bridget nods and whispers, "Amen." And the two spare ministers also nod, suddenly aligned on their side of the table with the one suggestion that none can refuse.

Mabry is still smiling and nodding, in part perhaps because Bridget is patting his arm encouragingly, following her father's lead impeccably.

"Prayer?" the sheriff mutters stiffly. "I suppose so. Brother Andrews, why don't you do the honors." It's as if he's asking him to say grace at Thanksgiving.

Andrews, the Methodist, nods to his right. "I been wanting to hear Brother Solomon light it up. And he is our guest." The formal courtesy of one preacher to another, natural enough, but something the sheriff hadn't counted on. The sheriff swallows the urge to shout that the man's name isn't Solomon.

The Preacher wastes no words on thanking the Methodist but rather reaches out to grasp the hands of the two men on either side of him. Both men have calloused, work-worn hands, and he files this away for further reference. Unlike Bailey, they are weekday farmers and Sunday preachers, called straight from the field to the pulpit.

"Great God in Heaven," he intones quietly. "Who made us out of dirt and spit. Who shaped us to walk on two feet above the animals around us. Who endowed us with hearts to feel and minds to think. Who gave us the freedom to choose and so the freedom to return to Thine embrace.

"Almighty God, to whom we all bow in ready obedience. Look down upon us now and bless this august gathering with your own wisdom: the wisdom to know what is best for the people of this fine town, the wisdom to work together to protect and inspire your people, the wisdom to join together arm in arm for the good of that poor, lost soul who is—like your servants the early Christians—languishing down in the local jail. Let us not forget his soul as we deliberate for the good of this, your community.

"Bless this fine judge and these wonderful ministers of your church, bless this sheriff charged with bringing your law to the people. Bless Sister Bridget and Sister Bailey, who are here to remind us to be gentle and to be kind. And most of all, bless the humblest of these. Myself. Who seeks ever to obey your will.

"Guide us to work together, not at odds with one another. Guide our thoughts and guide our words such that we may work together to defeat the demon liquor. For together we follow you, while alone we may stray. Amen."

The preachers on either side of him mutter "Amen," their grips on his two hands plow-handle tight. "Amen," Bridget almost sings. "Hallelujah," intones Mabry, and when the Preacher looks up he is satisfied to see the sheriff glaring the length of the table at the judge.

Judge Mabry nods to the sheriff, ignoring the angry stare. "Sheriff, where should we start?"

"We should start with the tow sack full of white lightning that came into our dry town from these supposed Christians. We should start with this man named Boss Strong, who works as an advance agent for him," nodding at the Preacher, "one Jedidiah Robbins, the evangelist who brought this poison into our midst."

The ministers on either side of the Preacher shake their heads and mutter at this naked accusation, but Agape Bailey nods furiously in support of the sheriff.

Judge Mabry shifts his gaze from the sheriff to the Preacher and raises his eyebrows to invite a reply.

"Boss Strong is guilty as sin," the Preacher begins and lets the idea settle. Bridget stares, wondering. "Guilty of attempting to sell six jars of contraband corn liquor to citizens of your fine town. But there is no proof, Your Honor, that the liquor came in on one of our trains, and as wise a man as he is, the sheriff is in no position to claim that any of our people are guilty other than Mr. Strong. I know Boss," this as an aside to the ministers, "and he is a poor, sad soul who has lost his way."

The sheriff guffaws. "Lost his way? Lost his way! Judge, Boss Strong is as hard as a pine knot and mean as a rabid dog."

Bridget shakes her head in denial of the sheriff's description.

"Nonsense." The Preacher again. "He has had a hard life, but I would trust Boss Strong with the care of my own daughter. And Sheriff, if you had a daughter, you'd feel the same way— once you got to know him."

The sheriff's eyes haven't left the Preacher's face. "It will surprise you to know that I do have a daughter," he says slowly. "She's seated at this table. And the last group I would entrust her with is you people."

Cassandra Bailey looks up to meet the Preacher's eyes. There is pleading in her face, as well as defiance, and beneath both there is infinite sorrow. Bridget reaches over at this point to take her hand, and beneath the tabletop Cassandra clings to her.

There is a long silence as the various people around the table take stock. In that moment, the Preacher knows that the trap is sprung. His enemy in the room is Agape Bailey—in addition to the sheriff, obviously. The Preacher doesn't know how much they know, but the fact that Cassandra is here doesn't bode well. He glances at Bridget, who has leaned over to whisper something to Cassandra. Cassandra replies to Bridget, who looks up at her father and nods ever so slightly.

He stalls while his mind searches for the next step. It looks at this moment as if Boss might end up paying the price for the Preacher's prayer meeting with Cassandra Bailey rather than for six jars of homemade corn. "Does it say in the Bible, gentlemen," this addressed to Bailey and the other two ministers, "that liquor is to be foresworn? I have read the Ten Commandments many times and I don't find it there. Judge, what do you think?"

The judge nods in appreciation of this point and smiles benignly.

"Jesus did turn the water into wine," notes the good Presbyterian, with an ironic smile. "Which my Baptist friends seem to forget."

"What about the sixth damn commandment?" Agape Bailey growls.

There is a pause while those that know count down the list. "'Thou shalt not kill' ?" the Methodist asks.

"I believe he means the seventh rather than the sixth," the Preacher says evenly. And to the judge in explanation: "'Thou shalt not commit adultery.'"

Judge Mabry turns his eyes to Cassandra Bailey, studying her face for the first time. He scowls and then looks back to the sheriff. "We're not here about your damn family problems," he says. "Or yours either, Mr. Bailey. We're here about the goddamn liquor." Bailey starts to speak, but without even bothering to look at him the judge raises his hand for silence.

"Sheriff, do you have enough evidence to fine this Boss Strong character?"

"Six gallons worth of evidence." The sheriff has regained the control that he'd almost lost.

"What's the fine?"

"Fifty dollars."

"Seems high. Make it forty. And if he can't pay, you can have him for thirty days. Mr. Solomon."

"Yes, Your Honor?"

"Has Mr. Strong repented of his sins? Is he right with God?"

"Yes, sir, he has. In the strongest possible terms. And he would say so, right here in this very courtroom if necessary."

"Good. Because on Sunday morning at eleven o'clock, he's going to offer his personal testimony. And you, sir, are going to preach the strongest antiliquor sermon that's ever been heard in these mountains. You are going to raise up enough hellfire to sweat the booze out of every drinker in this town." He glances at the ministers on either side of the Preacher. "Satisfied?" he asks.

They nod. "Amen," the Methodist adds.

"Where do you want Solomon here to preach? Which church?"

It's the Presbyterian who again reveals a glimpse of humor. "Why don't we do it right here in the courtroom, Judge? Your sanctuary holds more than any of ours."

As the Preacher and Bridget walk back to the rail yard, he asks her what Cassandra said.

After a moment, she takes his hand, their shoulders warmed by the late-afternoon sunshine. "They made her wear her dead mother's clothes to shame her," she says. "And, Papa?"

"Hmmm?"

"It wasn't her husband who hit her."

"Her father?"

Bridget nods, and begins to cry, her composure finally breaking.

He pats her hand. "I know," he says. "He gives no warning, that sheriff. But he's the very snake in the garden."

CHAPTER EIGHT

THE SATURDAY-NIGHT TENT MEETING draws an even larger crowd than the one the night before, because word has circulated through the small, foothills town that there is something mysterious, even disreputable, about Solomon's Crusade. One member of the crusade, perhaps even the great Preacher himself, is in jail, probably for murder or some worse debauchery.

The Preacher steers clear of Pentecost since the crowd has outgrown even the big top, and too much Holy Spirit might cause an inferno. Rather, he falls back to the Sermon on the Mount as inspiration for the poor, the meek, and the hungry. Though the crowd is larger and more restless, the financial take is less than that of the night before by several hundred dollars—perhaps because some are saving up their nickels and dimes for the main event the following morning. At the end of the night, Bridget carefully counts out forty dollars and sets it aside in an envelope for Boss Strong's fine.

After the service, the entire company meets inside the saints' car on the *Sword of the Lord,* with Fingers and several of the roustabouts standing guard outside to keep the curious, especially any curious deputies, out of earshot. The plan is revealed. The roustabouts will tear down the crusade tent and pack it—along with every other piece of equipment—onto *Saint John the Baptist.* Early the next morning, they'll load the horses, and then, while nearly the entire town along with the sheriff are crowded into and around the courthouse, Gabe and his roustabouts will back *Saint John the Baptist* a hundred yards down the spur to the abandoned shed and couple up the Bible car. From there, they will pull out up the mountain grade to the next stop: Asheville, North Carolina.

Once the liquor sermon is over and Boss is freed, the rest of the company will take their sweet, sanctified time in boarding the *Sword of the Lord* and departing for the hills. The Preacher sends the Bundren boys and Mother Mary with Gabe on the advance train but keeps Bridget and Fingers Spivey with him. He wants only calm heads around once the courthouse sermon is over. Bridget's job is to get Boss out of the courthouse and onto the train with as little noise as possible. Privately, he tells Fingers to stay out of people's pockets the next morning and to shadow the sheriff. "No matter what he does, you stick to him till you hear the train whistle blow, and then you run hell for leather so we don't leave you."

"What are you afraid he'll do?" Fingers asks. "He don't carry a gun."

"He'll try something to keep one or more of us in that jail of his. What, I don't know. But I know I don't trust him."

"Can I stop him if he gets to interfering?"

"You do what you need to. But be careful. He doesn't look like much, but he has a nasty mean streak."

Fingers smiles. "Shit on him," he says.

The courtroom is packed wall-to-wall with spectators, sitting, standing—children on the shoulders of their fathers, wives prim in the laps of their husbands, Sheriff James and his deputies struggling vainly to keep more of the crowd from pushing their way into the back of the room.

After the judge calls the proceedings to order and several of the local preachers lead the masses in a hymn, Boss Strong gives testimony to his fallen and now redeemed state—it sounds not unlike rock being broken into gravel with a sledgehammer— and then kneels before the entire congregation, Bridget kneeling beside him. From where he sits in the witness box, the Preacher stares, sure that Bridget is the only person on earth who could get Boss to kneel to anyone or anything.

When Judge Mabry nods to him, the Preacher stands and climbs the three steps to the judge's bench, where he opens his crusade Bible and begins. He nods down to Bridget, who leads Boss quietly out through the door behind the bench as the Preacher starts to shout.

"Brothers and sisters, members of the family of God: my dear friend Sheriff James tells me that before the wise counselors of this nation passed the Eighteenth Amendment, this small community, this McDowell County, North Carolina, had at least fifteen saloons in it. Fifteen! And I am come here today to tell you that the saloon is a coward and a liar. And it makes cowards and liars out of us all!"

He knows he is here to play a role onstage more than to deliver any sort of real sermon. And so he lets out all the stops, yelling and stomping and flapping his arms like a rooster. It is a parody more than a sermon, and it's exactly what he's been ordered to deliver.

"I tell you, the saloon strikes in the night. It fights under cover of darkness and assassinates the characters that it cannot damn, and it lies to you and about you. It attacks defenseless womanhood and childhood. The saloon is a coward. It is a thief; it is not an ordinary court offender that steals your money, but it robs you of manhood and leaves you in rags and takes away your friends, and it robs your family. It impoverishes your children and it brings insanity and suicide. It will take the shirt off your back, and it will steal the coffin from a dead woman and yank the last crust of bread out of the hand of the starving child; it will take the last bucket of coal out of your cellar, and the last cent out of your pocket, and will send you home bleary-eyed and staggering to your wife and children. It will steal the milk from the breast of the mother and leave her with nothing but booze with which to feed her infant. It will take the virtue from your daughter. It is the dirtiest, most low-down, damnable business that ever crawled out of the pit of Hell. It is a sneak and a thief and a coward.

"The saloon is an infidel. It has no faith in God; has no religion. It would board up and burn down every church in the land. It would hang its beer signs on the abandoned benches of this very courtroom. It would close every public school. It respects the thief and it esteems the blasphemer; it fills the prisons and the penitentiaries. It despises Heaven, hates love, scorns virtue. It tempts the passions. Its music is the song of a siren. Its sermons are a collection of lewd, vile stories. It wraps a mantle about the hope of this world and that to come. Its tables are full of the vilest literature. It is the moral clearinghouse for rot, and damnation, and poverty, and insanity, and it wrecks homes and blights lives today—or it would if our wise legislators hadn't given the good sheriff and his men the power to close down the saloons of McDowell County.

"I say to you the saloon is a liar. It promises good cheer and sends sorrow. It promises health and causes disease. It promises prosperity and sends adversity. It promises happiness and sends misery. Yes, it sends the husband home with a lie on his lips to his wife, and the boy home with a lie on his lips to his mother, and it causes the employee to lie to his employer. It degrades. It is God's worst enemy and the devil's best friend. It spares neither youth nor old age. It is waiting with a dirty blanket for the baby to crawl into a wicked world. It lies in wait for the unborn. "It cocks the highwayman's pistol. It puts the rope in the hands of the mob. It is the anarchist of the world, and its dirty red flag is dyed with the blood of women and children. It sent the bullet through the body of Lincoln; it nerved the arm that sent the bullets through Garfield and William McKinley. Yes, it is a murderer. Every plot that was ever hatched against the government and law was born in, bred in, and crawled out of the grogshop to damn this country.

"Like Hamilcar of old, who swore young Hannibal to eternal enmity against Rome, so I propose to perpetuate this feud against the liquor traffic until the dove of temperance builds her nest on the dome of the capitol of our great state and spreads her white wings of peace, sobriety, and joy over these mountains that I love with all my heart."

The Preacher pauses to take a sip of water from the glass provided for him. He mops his face with a handkerchief—both motions the stylized stock of his trade. He wishes the water were something much, much stronger, for it is dry and dusty and hot in the crowded courtroom, and he is sweating the stinking sweat of the self-righteous. He has always wanted to dance this dance just for the pure, ridiculous hell of it, and now he has a packed house to cheer him on! He can't help but smile but hides the grim humor on his face with the damp handkerchief. He lowers his voice several octaves and begins again.

"If our Savior and Lord Jesus Christ descended to McDowell County today, he might walk down the street and say to the first mill he came to, 'Hello, there, what kind of a mill are you?'

"'A sawmill.'

"'And what do you make?'

71

"'We make boards out of trees.'

"'Is the finished product worth more than the raw material?'

"'Yes.'

"'Then godly men will make laws for you. We must have lumber for houses.'

"Jesus goes up to another mill and says, 'Hey, there, what kind of a mill are you?'

"'A grist mill.'

"'What do you make?'

"'Flour and meal out of wheat and corn.'

"'Is the finished product worth more than the raw material?'

"'Yes.'

"'Then come on. We will make laws for you. We must have bread for families to eat, and we will protect you.'

"Our Lord goes up to another mill and says, 'What kind of a mill are you?'

"'A paper mill.'

"'What do you make paper out of?'

"'Straw and rags.'

"'Well, godly men will make laws for you. We must have paper on which to write notes and mortgages. We Christians must have paper to print our money.'

"Our Savior goes up to another mill and says, 'Hey, what kind of a mill are you?'

"'A gin mill.'

"'I don't like the looks nor the smell of you, gin mill. What do you make?'

"'Liquor.'

"'What is your raw material?'

"'*The boys of America.*'"

He is spraying spit and flinging sweat all over the front row.

"I've got the figures right here." The Preacher waves a blank piece of paper from his coat pocket. "According to these here statistics, if we make liquor legal, the gin mills of this country must have two million boys or shut up shop for lack of raw material. Say, walk down the streets of Marion, count the houses and homes. Every fifth home has to furnish a boy for a drunkard. Have you furnished yours? No. Then that man there will have to furnish two of his sons, two of his flesh to make up the difference.

"'Say, then, saloon gin mill, what is your finished product?' Christ asks.

"'Bleary-eyed, low-down, staggering men and the scum of God's dirt. Women who will sell their sacred bodies for a drink of liquor. Abandoned mothers and starving children. Full prisons and penitentiaries. Full madhouses and jails. Broken families and crying children.'

"I tell you that the curse of God Almighty is on the saloon. That is why legislatures are legislating against it, and spiritual leaders like your own good ministers are preaching against it. That's why your good Judge Mabry invited me here today into his own courtroom to rail against it. The fraternal brotherhoods are knocking it out. The Masons and Odd Fellows and Knights of Columbus are closing their doors to the whiskey sellers. They don't want you wriggling your sodden bellies across the floors of their lodges.

"Yes, sir, I tell you, the curse of God is on the saloon. The saloon is on the downgrade. It is headed for Hell, and, by the grace of God, I am going to give it a push—right here in Marion, North Carolina, today—with a whoop and a holler, for all I know how. With your help, sister, and your help, brother, we are going to send the saloon down to Hell today where it belongs, and, in the process, we are going to save you, and you, and you from going to Hell instead!"

The crowd is stamping and yelling. Several women are crying and punching their husbands or brothers or sons, pounding them on the backs as if to beat the whiskey out of them. A hymn breaks out in the back of the room but is drowned out by the general cheering and hollering.

As the Preacher slips through the backdoor of the courtroom, toward the judge's chambers, he is joined for a moment by the Presbyterian minister who'd suggested the courtroom in the first place. The Presbyterian is laughing and shaking his head.

"Why do I think that's the first time you've ever done that?" he says to the Preacher. "'What kind of mill are you?'" He laughs again.

The Preacher can't help but smile back at the man. "You should try it," he whispers. "In fact, I read that last part in a Billy Sunday pamphlet, and I hereby bequeath it to you."

"I notice you didn't touch your Bible."

The Preacher winks at the Presbyterian. "Truth to tell, I couldn't find a suitable text. Liquor preaching isn't exactly biblical, brother, if you know what I mean."

In the balcony at the back of the courtroom, a young reporter from the *Charlotte Observer* furiously finishes writing his notes while the crowd stomps and cheers below. Clutching his notebook, he leaps down the steps and out the courthouse door, pushing his way through the milling, singing people. He knows that there is a public telephone in the drugstore on the corner, and he sprints there to phone in his story. His editor will absolutely love this one—a hick town so nuts against liquor that they hold church in the courthouse to fight the demon rum.

As the *Sword of the Lord* bucks slowly up the Old Fort Mountain grade late that afternoon, Bridget sits with Fingers Spivey and her father in the club car. They are entering the high mountains now, and from time to time the engine slips and grabs like a goat on the rails, straining at the climb.

"At first he refused to kneel," Bridget admits. "Said he could testify all right, for swearing a false oath comes natural enough when you are forced, but he would kneel for no man."

"Then, how did you…?" Her father lets the question hang in the air.

"I told him that he wasn't doing it for them—or for you. I told him he was doing it for me, and that in case he hadn't noticed, I wasn't a man."

The subject of this exchange, Boss Strong, comes in at that moment, through the door at the end of the car that connects it to the rest of the train. He has heard the end of Bridget's recounting and grins at her. He sets a quart jar full of a warm, brown liquid on the Preacher's desk.

"Where in the hell did you get that?" the Preacher asks him.

Boss shrugs as if to say that his ways, like those of the good Lord, are mysterious. He nods to Bridget, who unscrews the lid from the jar and brings four glasses to the desk.

"I got something for each of you," Fingers says suddenly. "Since we seem to be having our own little communion service."

From the floor beside his chair, he produces a surprisingly thick book and hands it across the desk to Bridget.

"A dictionary?" she says, her voice full of wonder.

"Since you's kind enough to teach that boy," he says, "I figured I'd stop by the library for you."

Then without seeming to even reach in a pocket, he tosses the Preacher a thin metallic object, larger than a coin.

After a moment, the Preacher grins. "It's the sheriff's own badge, isn't it? How in the hell…?"

"I borrowed it off him while he was busy arresting me," Fingers says. "Shoulda cuffed me, but he let my hands go free while he was hustling me down those stairs to the cells."

"How come you ain't still in the cells?" Boss' gravelly voice.

"Cause I offered him to stay instead of me," Fingers says. "That sheriff handled me a little too rough for my liking, sneaked in a rabbit punch or two once we got to the bottom of the steps." He tosses the keys of the McDowell County jail cells onto the desk. "I got these for you as I was leaving out," he says to Boss. "Souvenir of your happy times in that burg. Plus it'll make it some harder for them deputies to get their sheriff out of jail."

Bridget has been busy pouring, and now Boss raises his glass. "I like him," he says of Fingers Spivey to the Preacher. And then to Fingers himself: "You just the kind of disciple we been needing to help us spread that Gospel Word."

Interlude

TWO DAYS AFTER what has become the infamous "Courthouse Saloon Sermon" in Marion, North Carolina, a writer
in Baltimore, Maryland, reads a colorful account of the event
that has spread from the initial report in the *Charlotte Observer*
through various channels into the offices of the *Baltimore Evening Sun*. He starts out laughing, but by the end of the article is
cursing and kicking his scarred old desk. He balls the newsprint
up and throws it forcefully into the trash bin and kicks the bin
across the room. "Ignorant, inbred, misbegotten hicks," he yells
loudly enough to bring several men from other offices to his door.
"Goddamn them all, these ignorant preachers and Anti-Saloon
League do-gooders—rabid, inbred vermin dragging the whole
nation to its cultural knees!"

He lays his cigar on the corner of his desk and tracks the trash
bin down to the corner of the office and retrieves the article to
reread it, knowing full well it will only feed his itching, buzzing,
restless fury. He reads aloud from the sermon as it was recorded
on the fly by the young reporter, stopping every few sentences to
pound on his desk and offer profane commentary. At one point,
he growls, "A sermon in a courtroom. Do they even know what
separation of church and state is down in North goddamn Carolina? Do they even care?" And after a moment's further reading,
"I swear to God I will go down there and find this Solomon's
Crusade—can you even believe that: *Solomon's Crusade!*—and I
will reveal Solomon and the rest of his crusaders for the imbecilic
hypocrites that they are!"

The other journalists turn away, realizing that their colleague is starting to wind down and they won't witness a full-bore explosion this day. "The old goat's on a tear, though, ain't he?" one says to the other. "Think he'll do it, go down there and feed the Christians to the lions?"

"Might do it," the other replies. "If he don't have so much to drink tonight that he can't remember who he's mad at tomorrow."

The old goat is Henry Louis Mencken.

PART TWO

APRIL 1927

CHAPTER NINE

I̵T IS LATE APRIL 1927, almost eight months since the Courthouse Saloon Sermon and the notoriety that came with it. Having
worked longer and harder than in any previous year, the crusade is taking time off in preparation for the summer run. *Saint
John the Baptist* and the *Sword of the Lord* are parked together
on a long siding in the little mountain village of Hot Springs,
North Carolina. The big top is erected in the stubble of a hay
field beyond the two rigs. It stands empty there in the spring sunshine as two coats of royal purple paint slowly dry, much of the
previous year's blue veneer having peeled away from hard use.

During these long, languorous spring nights, the Preacher
dreams of those he has known. He is often troubled by these
dreams, the urgency of desperate men and women, the demands
of other lives reaching out to him. It's almost as though, when
he finally lies down to rest, the dim and smoky lineaments of the
past seep through into the landscape of his mind.

He dreams of his mother, whom he barely knew except as a
shadow in the house and in his heart. A woman so obsessively
silent that she made the singing of the birds in the trees seem
strident by comparison.

During the daylight hours of this springtime respite, he
is also reminded of his father, the man who, for all intents,
raised him. His father and his father's mother, Grandma Robbins, nurse to half a county and the world's best friend to one
small boy.

But his father doesn't follow him into sleep; he is a daytime
ghost, spun out of dust motes in sunlight. Rather, his silent

mother comes to him in his dark dreams. And after her, the many men and women he has met over the years who needed him, who needed the Jesus in him. His kindness, compassion.

One man in particular has become his constant companion in the long-fallow fields of midnight life. He does not know the man's name; he never knew it.

It was when he was still young. After Rachel, but before his time on the rails and the crusade. When he was a dirt-poor apprentice minister in a local Baptist church. Widower, Bible-mad scholar, secret drinker.

A burg not unlike the worn-out boot heel of a place such as Valdese or Marion or Hickory. A small-town Baptist church—meaning that no secret was safe from shifting eyes and pointing fingers. Meaning that he kept his jar of pure moonlight liquor all but buried behind his landlord's barn.

He recalls walking home late one night after sitting up with a grieving family that had lost a pregnant daughter to consumption of the lungs. Witnessing the helpless weeping and the stifled curses muttered, shouted at God. He had no explanation to give the family, he discovered, no reply to the curses and the cries.

He treads the midnight streets back to his rented rooms, then in his memory and now in his dreams. He finds a man slumped to his knees, leaning against the side of a run-down shanty of a grocery store. Haggard and rough, stinking of piss and sweat, a week's worth of gray beard against a sagging sunburned face. He knew the man obscurely, as we all know someone we've seen before but cannot name.

"Brother," he says, as he kneels by the man in the mud beside the store. "Brother, can you stand? Can you walk?"

The man looks up then—then in memory, *now* in the dark and liquid world of his dreams—and there are his eyes, rheumy and tired beyond all description and beyond the reach of our understanding. "They ain't no help for me, Preacher," he whispers hoarsely. His throat clogged with the bloody spit that drools from this lips. "No help a'tall except maybe a sip of something hard. Something hard to ease this awful pain." The man gestures first to his groin and then raises his gnarled hand to his shoulder, his left shoulder.

"Do you mean medicine? A sip of medicine?" The question embarrasses him, even in the swim of his dreams, for it is a foolish question, and he knows it, then and now.

"Naw." The man starts to laugh but is immediately racked with a gut-deep and retching cough. Bloody phlegm on his lips and into his beard. "Naw. Naw, I mean that bad old liquor, Preacher. Just a sip, for I am dying. My heart is...blowed up." The man starts to slip forward, into a muddy puddle, and the Preacher struggles to hold him up, out of the dirty water. "It hurts so," the old hobo mutters. "Hurts so, this life."

"Stay with me," he whispers fiercely to the dying man. "Stay here with me."

"I can't," the old man mutters, suddenly racked with tears. "I see...."

"See *what?*" He would never know. The old man's breathing was slowing, slowing. "'In my father's house there are many mansions,'" he says into the man's filthy ear. Then louder, repeats himself. "'Many mansions.' They are warm and dry. You and I will be all together there. We will meet on the golden streets and live together there."

Though his body is failing, the old bum lifts his head one last time. One eye is already shuddering closed, as if in the hideous parody of a wink. Even so, the other eye flares with light, the last sparking match tip of a thought. "I will know you," the hobo says, "I will know your face. And maybe then I will have a home." And again, as if the thought surprises the old man, "A home."

"I'll meet you there," the Preacher says aloud, to the darkness all around him—in memory, and now, in the fluid depths of his dream. Flickering starlight obscured in flying cloud. "I will meet you there, no matter."

And so it is this man—and this promise—that visit him at night when his dreams dive deep beneath the surface of the waves. Into spectral places where no living person would choose to follow.

CHAPTER TEN

THE CRUSADE IS TAKING ITS APRIL VACATION in Hot Springs because the surrounding mountains are home to a surprising number of craftsmen, artisans who make fine, pure corn whiskey and strong, dark apple brandy. The government cannot taint this alcohol, as it flows directly from the stills, and so it is free of the poisons federal agents pour into mass-produced lubricants and medicines. While the preacher soaks in the medicinal hot springs and Bridget continues Gabe's reading lessons, Boss Strong circulates through the surrounding hills, sampling the wares and negotiating with cash money for hundreds of fruit jars carefully sealed and delivered.

The crusade's winter trek through Georgia and north Florida has drawn record crowds, even though the Preacher has refused time and again to reprise his infamous gin-mill performance. Cassandra Bailey joined the crusade in January while they were encamped for a week in Jacksonville, Florida. She came nursing a broken arm and seeking sanctuary with Bridget, who persuaded her father to add Cassandra to the troupe. She has proven to have a profoundly sweet contralto voice and now sings at the beginnings of services.

In the months since Marion, Gabriel Overbay has progressed from the simplest beginners' readers into Horatio Alger pluck and luck—*Ragged Dick, Paul the Peddler, Joe the Hotel Boy, The Young Outlaw*—where he would have stayed for all eternity had not Bridget nagged and pushed him on into stronger fare.

She had thought that *Little Men* might be next, but the Preacher mercifully intervened at that point and armed her instead with Jack London. Gabe is now halfway through *The Call of the Wild*, with *White Fang* and *The Sea-Wolf* waiting on the shelf.

While on winter tour, the Bundren boys found their natural place in the Gospel scheme—baptism. One or the other or both would wade into any standing body of water—no matter how frigid or muddy—and immerse long lines of penitent sinners, shouting or stammering the words "In the name of the Father and the Son and the Holy Ghost" as they did so. In the salt waves off Jacksonville Beach, in the slow, malarial meanderings of lowland rivers, in the icy run of mountain creeks, they would baptize. Sometimes by the hour, their soaked pants and shirts clinging to their stick-like frames, until they grew too weak to lift up the newly bathed souls.

Though he loved the water and had been a powerful swimmer since his youth, baptism was the one ministerial sacrament Bridget had never seen her father perform. She knew it was because her mother had drowned while boating with her sister Isobel in a farm pond. Drowned because she couldn't swim after their rowboat overturned. Drowned as her father strove in vain to swim down to her and raise her reborn from the water. He would not, could not baptize.

For the 1927 tour, they add ginseng to their stock, in part because the Preacher wants a private supply for himself, and in part so that Cassandra and Bridget can brew up and bottle a ginseng tonic that is good for what ails you. And especially good for one specific ailment: the limp male member of the congregation. Fingers Spivey is in charge of finding mountain farmers who will harvest ginseng in the woods for ready cash, just as Boss is in charge of the liquor resupply.

The Preacher goes with Boss Strong on one of Boss' expeditions to a place on the Tennessee line called Paint Rock. Bridget is jealous of their jaunt, for it is too far to walk to Paint Rock, and they are to ride a horse and a mule that Boss has leased for the season. Boss has been on horseback for most of the spring, picking his way along dim trails into mountain coves that suddenly open up into sun-washed vales, where isolated families produce whiskey and brandy all but undisturbed by the local law enforcement, and where federal revenue agents fear bushwhack.

On this day, Boss rides the big paint gelding he's had all season, and the Preacher is set ignominiously on a mule so lazy that it requires a switching from time to time just to stay awake. His mule's name is Sadie—short, or so he tells Boss, for Sadistic.

"Careful what you say," Boss warns. "She bites and she can hear you." Boss leads a second mule with a length of plow line. The second mule, black and leggy, is to haul back the product that Boss has already placed a down payment on—forty jars of pure white liquor from a man who lives just off Paint Rock Road and who keeps his still on an island in the middle of the French Broad River.

Fresh spring water is piped from a quarter mile up the mountainside underneath the road and through twenty yards of rushing current out to the island operation. The man who cooks the liquor—who must remain nameless—tells them tales of sheriffs come and gone, federal agents nearly drowned in pursuit, and angry wives come to shut him down.

They sample the goods while standing by the river's edge— the liquor is hot and hard—and then work together to load the jars, padded and wrapped in tow sacks.

When they start back, it is near dusk and Boss is relaxed and happy. "Wouldn't it be fine?" he says as they ride slowly along River Road, "Wouldn't it be fine if ever day was like this day here? Sun and river. A sip of liquor and a good story to follow it along? No goddamn sheriffs to shut up the day, no preachers to throw handfuls of guilt on a man."

"That would be fine," the Preacher admits. "Maybe add in a woman or two."

"So long as they don't talk too much," Boss agrees. "Cause you know, women will talk into your ear even when there's nothing to say."

The sun slants across the river, throwing cool shadows into the hot afternoon glare. Even the paint is willing to plod along at the pace of the mules, and the air is thick and sweet with late spring.

Out of the unguarded moment, the Preacher speaks before thinking. "Boss, if something happens to me, you have to take over the crusade. You know that, don't you?"

"What do you mean if something happens to you?" Boss' voice is still dreamy with whiskey and the buzzing dusk. He's all but napping in the saddle.

"Well, if I should die or something."

"Hell, no."

"Could happen, you know. And somebody would have—"

"Hell, no, you ain't dyin. And by the by, I ain't no preacher." Boss is sitting up straight now and reins back till the paint is shoulder to shoulder with the Preacher's mule.

"Somebody else can preach, Boss. Nobody but you can sell the product and run the show." They are suddenly in the deep water of this parley, and he's not quite sure how to explain.

"Yeah, but your theory bout that event got one big problem." Boss' voice is thickly serious.

"What's that?"

"You can't die. You got too much to do in this sorry-ass world. Raise your daughter, for one thing. And keep me company. I won't allow it."

"How you going to stop it? Death, I mean."

Boss reaches down to grasp his shoulder. "If you even look like you're considering to die, I'll…I'll slap you so damn hard the brains'll run out your ears," he growls. "You understand me?"

"That should help," the Preacher says. And he laughs, though Boss still stares at him strangely.

CHAPTER ELEVEN

THE NEXT AFTERNOON PLUS ONE OR TWO, the Preacher is walking alone toward the old bathhouse where for fifty cents you can soak for an hour in the hot, hot mineral water that is piped straight from the river bottom.

He proceeds slowly, relaxed inside his skin, enjoying the breeze that ruffles the leaves in the oaks and maples along the path. It is the crispness of the air moving over his face, he decides, that makes the long walk of his life worth living. The beauty of the wren's fussing as she follows him along, upset with him for looking into her nest. The loveliness of budding leaves as they unfold wetly to the world. This is the true world, he thinks, not the world of men and women, not the world of books and words, but the world of the river, sluicing and whispering beside the path. The world before men came and after they are gone. The larger, God-haunted world that reduces all human despair to an afterthought, a footnote. Peace be unto you, he thinks in response to the laughing call of a blue jay and the soft cooing of a dove.

Bridget has gone off with Gabe on a picnic—ostensibly for a reading lesson, but the Preacher suspects something more. It is the softest, freshest time in the mountains, and the air is rich with new warmth and liquid bird song. He's seen his daughter stare speculatively, perhaps even longingly, at the Portugee boy since they've been encamped at Hot Springs. Now that she's actually begun to civilize him, maybe she has other plans as well.

Does he care if she seduces the boy? Has him for a season? As he walks along the dirt road that leads down to the bathhouse, he thinks no, he doesn't care. She's old enough to have something of her own, to at least see what bare skin warmed by the sun is all about. He wishes that he had talked to her about preventing babies, his job to do since her mother isn't here to explain. But she's, what, twenty-two? Twenty-three, perhaps. Surely she knows enough to…

At the bathhouse door, he pays his two quarters to the sleepy attendant, who gestures toward a stack of laundered towels on a wooden bench. Inside, painted arrows on the facing wall point men to the left and women to the right. He takes the left-hand hallway and walks all the way to the end before turning into a cubicle. Each closed section of the tubs has its own small dressing room. He latches the hallway door carefully behind him, because he doesn't have a bathing costume and prefers to enter the water as naked as sunlight.

The tub itself is perhaps five feet square with tile steps leading down into steaming water, waist deep. He piles his clothes carelessly on the chair in the cubicle and is just about to ease down into the bath when he hears an almost timid tapping on the door.

"What the hell?" he mutters to himself, assuming it's the attendant. He wraps the towel loosely around his waist and unlatches the door so he can open it a few inches. Peering through the crack, he's shocked to see that it's not the drowsy attendant on the other side, but Cassandra Bailey clutching a towel to her chest. "Let me in," she whispers. "Before that boob up front wonders where I went."

He doesn't know what else to do, so he opens the door another few inches, and she pushes her way inside. He latches the door behind her.

"What are you doing here?" he whispers, even though he knows full well how stupid the question sounds. In the months since Florida, her arm has healed, along with the other bruises and scars she brought with her from her marriage to Agape Bailey. Under Bridget and Mother Mary's care, she's even gained a little weight, so that she looks almost plump standing there in the faint bars of sunlight that filter in from the gable end of the bathhouse.

All these weeks and he hasn't been alone with her, even though more than once he's caught her staring at him when no one else was paying attention. She would blush and look away, but not before holding his gaze for a moment.

"Bridget told me you came to bathe every afternoon," she finally whispers. "And I followed you. I wanted to see you."

"You see me every day."

She shakes her head almost fiercely. "Not like that. Not in a crowd." She steps closer to him, and he can small a faint scent from her hair. Citrus—oranges, perhaps. "I wanted to pray with you like that night on the train in Marion."

For a moment, he isn't sure whether she's said *pray* or *lay*.

He starts to speak, but she reaches out to place her hand over his lips.

"If you want me to go," she says quietly, "I will. And no one will ever know. I'll say I wandered down the wrong hall and opened a door by mistake."

He can't reach out to touch her without dropping his towel. He's afraid to speak, for he doesn't know what he would say. So he does the only thing he can think to do: he nibbles her fingers. Which taste faintly earthy, like a spice he can't name.

After a moment, she drops her own towel and reaches out her other hand to caress his cheek, both hands now on his face, palms warm and dry against his careworn skin. He closes his eyes, perhaps because to both see her and feel her touch is too much. He senses the gentle pressure of her fingers against his lips all the more intensely, massaging his cheek in simple grace, while his tears seep out to dampen her hands.

With his eyes shut, his own nakedness no longer seems to matter so much, and without thought he lets go of his towel and reaches out to her waist, his hands finding the slight swell of her hips and resting there on the soft linen of her skirt. She is real, he decides, not a dream after all. She is real and so utterly unexpected.

"What is your name?" she says aloud after what seems only a moment, though the moment has stretched out like a cat before the fire. "Not Solomon, surely, or Preacher—your real, given name?" She removes her fingers from his mouth so he can answer.

"Jedidiah Robbins," he says slowly, syllable by syllable, his voice hoarse. "Though only Boss calls me that."

"Well, from now on, it will be Boss and me," she says. "Jedidiah."

It is only later, when they have come together in the hot, silky water and floated gently afterwards, that she tells him the rest of the story. "It was Bridget," she says, "that sent me. I have been wanting to come to you, God knows. Waiting and wanting, yearning for you, and yesterday she said it was time."

"Why now?" He is so relaxed in the mineral bath that he barely hears himself speak.

"Because now you will need someone."

He stands upright in the pool and opens his eyes to look down into her porcelain face. "Why will I need someone?"

"Since she's taken up with Gabe, you'll need someone to look after you. Someone to care for you. And…"

"And?"

"She wants me to help persuade you…persuade you to let her marry him."

He closes his eyes and slips back down into the water. "Don't count on that last bit," he says after a moment. "Not marriage."

CHAPTER TWELVE

THAT NIGHT, after they have eaten their supper, Bridget makes her own case. This time, it is she who pours them each a glass of brandy.

"She can be everything to you that I am. And more. Surely you realize that."

"She's young enough be your sister. Meaning young enough to be my…"

"And she loves you. Not like I do, of course, because she's only known you for a short time. But she loves you nonetheless."

"She's another man's wife. Another preacher's wife, even."

Bridget guffaws. "Don't play righteous with me. When has either of those slim facts ever stood between you and a willing woman?"

"More often than you might think. More often than not, actually."

"This other man you're throwing up—Cassandra's goddamn husband—he beat her like a drum, just like her daddy did. He broke her arm, for God's sake."

"And that means I'm free to love her? And who, by the way, gave you permission to curse like that?"

"You gave me permission by a thousand examples. And yes, that means you are free to love her. Lord, at the very least, that means she is free to love you."

"What about your mother?"

"I don't remember my mother, except as a vague scent and some scraps of cloth. The quilt you gave me that she made. My mother's gone, and I don't even know where she's buried."

"To me, she's not gone. She lives inside my mind."

"Papa, her memory can't keep you warm at night."

"And so I'm free?"

"We're both free, Papa. Look at me. Look straight at me. I'm twenty-five years old and lonesome for things that other girls have known since they were fifteen. I will never leave you this side of Hell. But I want a man of my own. A man who I can raise up and a man who will give me babies."

"Whom."

"What the hell, *whom?*"

"You want a man *whom* you can raise up."

After a long pause Bridget shakes her head. "She loves you. You know that."

"She doesn't even know me. I'm as difficult as a black dark night and cold as winter rain."

Bridget stands up, tempted to throw the brandy jar at him. But, instead, she pours them each another tot. "You are kind. You are caring. You give of yourself when others have thrown over giving. You crave a warm woman in your bed and you cannot deny it. And she needs you just as much as you need her. Don't try to pretend otherwise."

"Goddamn it, Bridget. Just because I might enjoy her companionship now and again doesn't mean you have to run off with that Portugee boy. That…"

"Who gave *you* permission to curse like that? And besides which, Gabriel is a fine young man, or at least he will be when I'm through with him. And I am not—*notice I said 'not'*—running off with him. I'm staying *here* with him. At least as much of a here as we've got to offer. I'm going to stay with him on *John the Baptist,* and Cassandra is going to move back here to the club car to stay with you. If you'll have her, that is. It's settled."

"It is not goddamned settled. Nothing about this is settled.
The natural next step is for the boy himself to approach me on
his hands and knees and beg permission for your hand in marriage. And there are no guarantees—*note I said 'no guarantees'*—
that I will accept him as a...what? A son-in-law."

"Then why in the hell did you take him on in the first place?
If you didn't know that you'd accept him, why did you throw
him in my way? Knowing what you know and seeing what you
see, why did you give him to me all wrapped up with a bow if
you weren't willing to take him on as a son? Answer me that!"

He comes to a full stop. Stymied. After a pause, he says the
only thing he can think of. "He needs to ask me himself. And he
will be a son by law, not a son by blood."

"Fair enough. He'll come to you tomorrow on bended knee.
And if you're not kind to him, you'll have to answer to Cassie
and me both."

The boy Gabriel surprises him early the next morning, before
he even has a chance to escape the train. He is sitting with his
second cup of coffee when there is a pounding on the door of the
club car. Startled, he almost splashes the coffee over the letter
he is writing.

When he rises to open the door, he sees first the boy, standing embarrassed on the rear platform of the train, his fist still
upraised as if to knock again. When he stands aside to let Gabe
in, he glimpses a strange sight beyond: his daughter Bridget and
her friend Cassandra Bailey are sitting at a rough table that the
roustabouts have knocked together under the trees. They built
them for the troupe's evening meals, often eaten together when
there is no rain.

The two women are not talking over coffee, as you might expect, but are pointedly facing the club car and staring back at him before he shuts the door.

Gabriel Overbay's white shirt is not only clean; it is ironed. It is not only buttoned at the neck; the boy is also sporting a thin, dark necktie, carefully knotted. For a moment the Preacher is nonplussed by the sight, but then he realizes that the tie is one of his own, borrowed no doubt by Bridget for the occasion. He glances down at Gabe's faded jeans, almost expecting the boy to be wearing a pair of his own pants too.

"Yes, Gabriel, what can I do for you?" He has no intention of making this easy for Gabe. It is a real test for the boy, even if the women have already made up their minds on the matter.

"I, well…I need to speak with you," Gabe mutters. "Sir." The boy bends to glance out the window, toward where the women sit waiting.

"They can't help you, Gabe," he says. "No matter how formidable they are."

"Formable, sir?"

"*Formidable.* It means impressive, decisive, dangerous."

"They sure are, all of that dangerous part, sir."

Gabe has never once in the past eight months called him "sir" until today, and suddenly the Preacher feels sorry for the boy. "Sit down there by the desk, Gabe, and let's talk. Would you like some coffee?"

"I'm afraid I'd spill it on your…on my tie, sir. And my stomach, it don't…." The boy collapses into a chair, almost toppling over.

"Did they scrub you all over with a brush before they sent you in here?" the Preacher asks him, almost kindly.

The boy blushes. "No, sir. But they made me comb my hair till my scalp bled."

He stifles the urge to laugh. Not yet, he thinks. Let him stew for a bit. "What do you want to talk to me about, Gabe?"

"I am in love with your daughter, Bridget, sir, and I have come here today to ask for your request—your permission for her hand in marriage." The boy says it fast, all in a gulp, without breathing. And then begins to cough, as if he'd just spit something out.

He can't help himself now. He laughs. "Oh, Lord, boy, did she write that out for you?"

Gabe nods miserably. "Her and that Cassandra. They made me memoralize it."

"Fair enough. Can you say it over again, more slowly?"

"No, sir. I don't think I can."

"But you do want to marry her."

"God, yes. I'd do anything for her."

"Well, that's a start. Have you ever been married?"

"Oh. No, sir."

"So you're not married now—to someone else." He realizes even as he says it that he wouldn't be the least surprised if the boy had picked up a wife somewhere along the way. Circus life, circus wife.

"No, sir. Thought about it once, but nothing come of it."

"You mean to say that *nothing came of it*. Do you have any children that you know of?"

All the color drains suddenly out of the boy's face, and he looks wretchedly down at the floor.

"Boy or girl?"

Gabe mutters something.

"What did you say?"

"I heard rumor it was a boy."

101

"Was? Still is a boy, I expect." The Preacher is flooded with anger and sadness all at once. Perhaps more sadness than anger. "What is his name?"

Gabe shakes his head, still staring at the floor.

"You don't know, do you?"

More head shaking, fitful now, as if confused.

"Where does he live, your boy?"

"Morganton, sir."

"And you've never seen him?"

"No, sir."

"Well, damn, Gabe."

The boy looks up at him, his face a horrible blotch of hot pink and starched white skin stretched across his high cheekbones. "Yes, sir. It is…sir."

"Does Bridget know?"

The boy stares helplessly at him, the thought that he might have told Bridget apparently just entering his mind. "I guess you don't want me to marry her, then. Bridget, I mean."

He thinks for a moment. What should he say and how should he say it? He glances at the letter he'd been writing when Gabe first knocked on his doorjamb. It's a letter to his dead wife, telling her about Cassandra and asking her what he should do. He delivers such letters by putting each carefully in an envelope with her name on it, sealing the envelope, and burning it in the stove. He wonders what she would think about this mess now. He already has a sense of her intentions concerning Cassandra, just from writing, but what about this poor boy and Bridget? He smiles suddenly, unexpectedly.

"I guess I should go," Gabe interrupts his thoughts. "I'm sorry to have busted—"

"Sit still for a moment," the Preacher says gently. And then, after a pause, "I'm not disturbed by your son. It's not me you have to worry about when it comes to that. But I will tell you what you'd better do. First, you had better write today and find out what his name is and any other news you can get from the mother. That sort of thing matters to women more than you or I can imagine. Do you need me to help you write?"

Gabe nods that yes, he needs help.

"You and I can do that together. We'll do it before you walk out that door. The next part I can't help you with. Once we hear back about his name and perhaps how he's progressing in life, then you have to tell Bridget."

"I don't think that's such—"

"Trust me, Gabe. I won't tell her for you, but you have to, or it will go badly when she does find out."

"What if she doesn't want to…?"

"Marry you after you tell her?"

The boy nods.

"I've known Bridget for over twenty years, Gabe, and I doubt very seriously if it will slow her down for long. Oh, she'll have something to say about it, make no mistake, but she's older in the ways of the world than you might imagine. And I will tell you this—mind what I say. She won't rest till she's laid eyes on the boy. And she's as stubborn as a goddamn mule."

The boy's eyes are huge, his mind almost overwhelmed by the twisty turns of his own life. He swallows audibly, painfully. "What do I tell her about…about our talk? Here today, I mean?"

"Oh, hell, Gabe. Tell her that I give my permission. I'd lead her on for a bit if I were you, just to make her wonder, but tell her that I said I can't imagine why you'd want her, skinny as she is."

CHAPTER THIRTEEN

AFTER THEY WRITE THE LETTER, he follows Gabe out the door of the club car and down the iron steps of the rear platform. Bridget stands up when she sees them and, after a searching glance at her father, follows Gabe along the path beside the gravel siding, toward *Saint John the Baptist*.

The Preacher sits at the picnic table across from Cassandra. Her chocolate eyes also probe his face, but he gives nothing away. She looks past him, and he can see the concern growing in her features. He can't resist, so he turns just enough to see Gabe and Bridget thirty feet away, whispering furiously, her standing with her hands firmly on her hips, bent forward from the waist in frustration.

"What did you tell that poor boy?" Cassandra whispers. "Jedidiah?"

He shakes his head ever so slightly. "Just watch," he whispers back.

Suddenly, Gabe grins, and it is as if the sun is breaking through blue-black clouds, like healing through a bruise. Bridget straightens and, after a moment, reaches out to touch the boy's face. Then she bends over and picks up a rock from the siding, turns and throws it at her father. The rock skips off the table top, narrowly missing both him and Cassandra.

"You told him to lead me on a string, didn't you?" she yells.

He grins before he turns back to Cassandra.

"We're getting married, Daddy," she yells even louder this time. "Whether you like it or not!"

He stands to face them, even as he feels Cassandra's hand on his arm. "So I hear," he says evenly, smiling at the two of them—Bridget and her Gabriel. "In the fall," he says after a moment longer. "Let the wedding be in the fall, when sane people get married. Or, better yet, next spring."

He turns back to Cassandra, letting the young couple have their time and place, afraid there will be tears if he stares at them any longer. Tears in his own eyes if no one else's.

"You know they're sleeping together?" Cassandra asks quietly.

"So I imagine."

"Just saying you may not want them to wait that long."

"I want them to wait that long or longer," he says as he meets her eyes fully now. "In case the boy decides to run off or she changes her mind. Women have been known to do that, change their minds, on a moment-by-moment basis."

"All women? Everywhere?"

"Since Eve in the garden," he says with a perfectly straight face. "Eve and her pet serpent."

CHAPTER FOURTEEN

T HAT EVENING, HE SITS IN THE CLUB CAR with Fingers Spivey and goes over the roster for the upcoming summer season. Cassandra has asked if she can read in the car, where there is lamplight and a soft chair, so when Fingers shows up with his sheaf of papers, the Preacher is faced with asking her to leave or letting her listen. Listening, it seems to him, is the best. Perhaps hers is another mind that might see further into who and what they are.

He and Fingers begin with the crew of the advance train, *Saint John the Baptist.*

"Boss Strong," Fingers says quietly, pen poised.

"Foreman," he replies. "Fifty dollars per week."

Fingers nods as he makes a note. "Gabriel Overbay?"

"Crew boss. Forty dollars per week."

"Bridget Robbins?"

He is momentarily nonplussed and glances at Cassandra where she sits reading. "Publicity," she suggests without looking up from her book.

"Publicity," he repeats. "Thirty dollars per week."

Fingers shakes his head. "Better pay her same as the boy. Or more. Or she'll have it out of him."

He glances at Cassandra, who nods in agreement.

"Just who is in charge here, anyway?" he asks the room, but neither one of them answers. "Make it forty, then. We'll probably go broke."

"Spect we will," Fingers says dryly. And then: "Noah Cederberg, engineer and roustabout."

"Cederberg?" he asks. "Odd name."

"He's a Swede," Cassandra says, "and a Lutheran."

"Well, then thirty dollars per week for the engineer."

"Fowler Sheedy, fireman and roustabout."

"Is *he* a Lutheran?"

"No," Cassandra says, and finally shuts her book and looks up at the two men. "No, *he* is an out-and-out atheist. Irish but not Catholic. Shebeen and shanty, but no pope. Curses like a sailor."

"Twenty-five dollars per week, then. For our atheist."

Fingers nods and continues through his list:

Ezekiel "Zeke" Scully, roustabout / $15

Jeremiah "Jerry" Blaesius, roustabout / $15

Levi "Doc" Klein, roustabout / $15

James "Lost John" Stoddard, roustabout / $15

Hackney "Hack" Ramsey, roustabout / $15

Micah Ramsey, stable boy / $5

As he writes, Cassandra provides a running commentary on each man and boy: Scully, Catholic with a tattoo of the Virgin on his thigh; Blaesius, German, speaks almost no English; Klein, the best at doctoring man or beast and oh, by the way, Jewish; Stoddard, lost for a week in the woods as a boy; Ramsey, local man who has just joined up in Hot Springs; and his son Micah, who loves the horses and is loved in return.

"My God almighty, where do they all sleep?" the Preacher asks.

"Boss has a private bunk in the Bible car," Cassandra replies. "I imagine Micah makes a pallet in the stable car, in an empty stall so he won't be trampled. The rest in the passenger car."

"Bridget and Gabriel?"

"The men are walling off part of the passenger car just for them, building a bed out of several benches. They all treat Bridget like the Queen of the May, just so you know."

After a moment's pause, he turns to Fingers. "How much total for the advance train?"

"Two hundred sixty-five per week plus their found. Just over a thousand per month in wages. You ready to discuss this rig? The Gospel train?"

The Preacher nods. His little dog is awake now. He pets her gently behind the ears, and after a moment the fice leaves him and jumps into the chair with Cassandra. "Whore," he says to the dog, but gently, gently.

"Jedidiah Robbins, boss man," Fingers says.

"You forgot 'Minister of the Lord.'"

"That too. How much you want to pay yourself?"

"Whatever's left after you heathens get through with giving it all away."

Fingers smiles. "I'll see if I can't pick you up a little something on the side. Mother Mary McManaway? Whatever you call what she does."

He glances at Cassandra, who shrugs. "Put her down for saint. I've never known her to sin except with a knife and fork. She'll dig her own grave with a spoon."

"How much?"

"Twenty dollars."

Fingers shakes his head. "You have to pay the performers more than the crew."

"Why?"

"Because it's what they're used to. My boys love what they're used to. And if you upset the natural order of things, there will be hell to pay."

"Thirty, then. Like our engineer."

"Bundren—the one that's left—assistant preacher."

"James," Cassandra adds. John just left us for that grass widow he discovered in South Carolina."

"James Bundren, then," the Preacher says. "Thirty dollars."

"Cassandra Bailey, musician," Fingers says with no inflection in his voice, as if she weren't in the room.

"Thirty dollars?" the Preacher says.

"You asking me or telling me?"

"Hell if I know."

"Thirty's fair. For talent."

Cassandra clears her throat, and they both look at her. "I'm still here," she says. "And yes, that's fair."

"Fingers Spivey," says the Preacher, "Engineer and accountant. Forty dollars. Is that fair?"

"It's fair, but I won't take it," Fingers says. "Against my principles as a Party man."

"What party?" Cassandra asks.

"Communist," the Preacher answers. "We'll put it by for you, Fingers, in an envelope with your name on it. Against a rainy day. Against you find yourself a grass widow of your own along the way and need a stake."

Fingers shrugs and then says, "I was married oncet. I don't care for the state. One more. Jesus the-Son-of-God Smith."

"Who in the hell is—?"

Cassandra laughs. "That sweet Negro man who joined last summer in Marion. The one who was living in the railroad shed."

"I thought his name was Son," the Preacher says, "or Sonny." He looks at Fingers. "You're having me on, right?"

Fingers takes off the straw boater to rub his head. "Nope, I ain't. That's the man's name, though you can tell it's a weight to him."

"Why is he moving over to this rig?"

"Cause I need a fireman," Fingers says, "to stoke the boiler when we get underway."

"Should we pay him the same as the roustabouts?"

"Hell, no. He's a fireman, a railroad man. Who do you think makes this whole outfit run down the track but the railroad men?"

"Well, then, put the-Son-of-God down for twenty-five a week. Does that suit you?"

Fingers nods, as does Cassandra.

"Is that the sum total of our associates and brethren?" the Preacher asks.

Fingers nods. "Costs us $380 per week in payroll. Or $1,520 per month. I ain't including myself. Take some good whiskey and strong preaching to cover that sum, but I figure we got both." He stands and gathers his papers. "You want to do the rest of the ledger tomorrow?"

The Preacher nods.

After Fingers is gone, the Preacher glances at Cassandra, who has resumed her book.

"How is it you know so much about all these people?" he asks. "From Zeke Scully to Mother Mary?"

She meets his gaze. After considering for a moment, she says, "You spend most of your time talking to God. Or your dead wife, whose name, by the way, I do not know. I spend most of my time asking after living people."

"Her name was Rachel."

"Well, at least you said, 'her name *was*' and not '*is*.'" She smiles at him. "She's not on the payroll, is she?"

CHAPTER FIFTEEN

THE TROUPE HAS SETTLED into a comfortable pattern during its weeks at the Springs. There is ample rest and hot food, even for the roustabouts. Gabe and his crew repaint the words and images on the sides of the two trains and replace several cracked tent poles under the big top with trees hewn from the woods. Boss and Fingers refresh their supplies of whiskey and brandy and lay in baskets of ginseng roots. Bridget accepts delivery on a shipment of new Bibles, which join the liquor in the Bible car. Cassandra Bailey moves into the Saints' car on the *Sword of the Lord*. From her new home in the Saints' car, she studies how to slip easily and quietly in and out of the domestic life of Jedidiah Robbins. She brews him a cup of ginseng tea each evening, liberally laced with sugar and a teaspoon of whiskey, which she insists he drink before bed.

The Preacher goes each afternoon to the bathhouse, sometimes with Cassandra and sometimes alone. "He leadeth me beside the still waters. He restoreth my soul." One afternoon, as he returns from the bathhouse, loose and relaxed, a little boy comes running up to him all in a dither. After a moment, he recognizes the gasping child as Micah Ramsey, the stable boy from *Saint John the Baptist*.

"Bend over and put your hands on your knees," he tells the boy. "Breathe deep. Breathe slow. Slower. Easy now, and tell me what it is."

When Micah straightens back up, the Preacher can see that his swollen, red face is awash with tears. He is crying so hard that his nose is running and he can't speak. He only shakes his head roughly and grabs the Preacher's hand. He pulls him toward the river. After a moment of hard tugging, the boy has the Preacher jogging toward the rushing water.

They trace a path through the trees studded with roots and rough gravel. Suddenly, near the edge of the woods, the boy slides to a stop and pushes the Preacher forward onto a beach. There is a disturbing rotten smell, and for a moment he thinks the boy must have found a dead creature of some kind, some huge fish. But then he sees. Among the rocks and driftwood and half-buried in the wet sand by the water's edge is a small body. He throws himself to his knees and bends over the form, first to be sure that it is human and then to be sure it isn't alive.

It is human, but it isn't alive. Hasn't been for at least a day, according to the smell.

The body is that of a little girl wearing the torn remnants of a flour-sack dress. One leg is buried in the sand, the other free. An arm is raised up, half the forearm stretching toward the sky, the small fingers curled loosely in the air, almost into a fist. Though part of her head and neck are buried, the girl's face is free and her brown hair washes back and forth in a rivulet that reaches out from the deeper run of the river. The skin of her face is a mottled gray, and when the Preacher touches her cheek, the flesh is hard, almost rubbery, and inhumanly cold. Her eyes are partially closed, with only a crescent slit of white orb showing beneath the lids. A trickle of brown water runs from her nose into the corner of her mouth, where the tip of her tongue shows gray between her stained teeth.

The sight of her crushes him with memory. Of Rachel's ashen face and dead eyes.

With a gasp, he forces the thoughts of his dead wife out of his mind and instinctively begins to pray for the little girl's soul, homeless now and adrift—perhaps even close by, in the trees. To pray for her mother, who must be terrified and searching, upstream. To pray for her father, whose prize darling she must be. And back to her soul, the soul of a girl who should be playing this bright morning, running and shouting, but whose body is made all of water now, brown water and harsh sand.

He feels a small hand on his shoulder as he prays, and for a moment is startled by the thought that the spirit of the girl is reaching out to him. But when he opens his eyes and turns, he finds Micah standing beside him, refusing to look down at the dead face, but standing beside him nonetheless, supporting him as he prays.

"Do you know the Lord's Prayer, Micah?" he asks.

After a moment, the boy shakes his head roughly.

"Then close your eyes and bow your head, and I'll line it out for both of us." Which he does, squeezing the boy's hand while he recites the words.

A moment's silence afterward, and then, "Run into town, Micah, and locate the policeman or a sheriff's deputy. Tell him what you found and bring him back here. I'll stay till you get back."

"You won't run off?" Micah asks.

"No, I'll stay right here beside her till you bring the police."

"Shouldn't we get her out of the water? She must be awful cold mired up in there."

"We'd best not move her till the policeman comes. You go on now. You can walk if you don't feel like running."

When Micah runs off the way they have come, the Preacher stands up and finds a large rock to sit on, perhaps ten feet away from the body. Where he had been warm and relaxed before, walking from the baths, he is cold now, and stiff. His arms and legs feel like rough lumber, lashed with frayed cords to the trunk of his body. The river is all before him, fifty yards wide at this point, gray-brown and rushing away to the north, torn into rapids now and again by boulders and stinking vaguely of mud and fish.

What he couldn't tell the boy, could tell no one, except perhaps Boss or maybe now Cassandra, is that the girl speaks to him. Whispers to him with the drowned dead voice of his wife, Rachel. Asking to be saved. Asking to be torn from the heavy drapery of water that is pulling, dragging her down.

As he sits, he apologizes yet again to Rachel, pleads for the hundred-thousandth time for her to forgive him for letting her die alone that July day. Letting the water take her when she had a long life stretched out before her. And as she always does, Rachel whispers her forgiveness, tells him that she is happy. She is beyond death now. She is not the little girl trapped in the sand.

After a moment, his breathing slows and he can see more clearly what is before him. The sand is wet and carved by current halfway up the beach. The river, then, has been at least a foot higher during the night and must have brought the body there while in flood. And left it there in the early hours of the morning.

He studies the sand while he waits and, after a moment, realizes that in addition to his own tracks and those from Micah's smaller, bare feet, another set of tracks leads to the body from upstream. To the body and back again the way they have come, which means that someone else has been there that day and seen the drowned girl.

He rises and follows the tracks upstream into the tangled underbrush—blackberry vines and dog hobble. There is the barest trace of a path along the riverbank, worn no doubt by fishermen. Fifty feet farther upstream, he comes to a man sitting on a log. He is wearing clean, carefully pressed overalls that sport patches on both knees. An equally clean white shirt, which, though it is worn almost ragged at cuff and collar, is carefully buttoned. An old gray fedora is pushed back on his head, with a cardinal's red feather set jauntily in the band.

He is the thinnest man the Preacher has ever seen, worn by some sickness or other down to bone. His hands below his shirt sleeves look almost skeletal. His cane fishing pole is propped at an angle over the log he sits on, with the line trailing out to a cork bobbing in the water. The man is reading a newspaper while his line and pole do their work.

The Preacher clears his throat, and the man looks up and carefully lays down his paper. Ironically, he's reading the local obituaries. He turns to the Preacher politely, and his thin, ravaged face breaks open into a smile. "Hidy," he says, and bobs his head. "You out fishin?"

"No. No, I'm not. I'm Preacher Robbins, from the crusade train. One of our employees found… Well, he found the body of a drowned girl just down the riverbank, and while I was waiting on the police to come, I saw some tracks leading up this way. I wondered if…"

"Oh, that was me," the man says happily. "I wandered down there a while ago and seen that girl you're speakin of. She's dead," he adds helpfully and bobs his head again.

"Did you send for help?"

"Naw. Naw, I don't fool with the authorities. If she'd been alive, there might've been something for me to do. But they ain't nothing can save her now."

"What's your name, if you don't mind my asking?"

"Why, I don't mind at all. My name is Festus. You might've heard of me. I'm famous round these mountains."

The Preacher waits. For something more in the way of a name or the reason for the fame. But nothing comes. Suddenly, for no particular reason, he asks, "Did you know that girl?"

"Oh, I know most ever-body around here."

"Did you touch her?"

"Why, Preacher, I put my hand over her mouth to be sure she wasn't breathin. Her mouth was full of that river water, and she was cold as the grave." Festus stands up, carefully folds his newsprint, sticks it inside the bib of his overalls for safekeeping, and bends to pick up his fishing pole. "Pleasure to meet you," he says, touching the brim of his hat with one long, bony finger, and then adds, "See you on down the road, I hope." He then disappears upstream into the deeper woods.

When he gets back to the girl's body, the Preacher discovers that Micah has returned, accompanied by the town's policeman and a doctor who's staying at the local hotel.

CHAPTER SIXTEEN

THERE IS PERHAPS A WEEK LEFT now in the crusade's encampment at Hot Springs. The mystery of the little drowned girl has been solved. Her name was Lillie Mae Goforth, and she wandered away from her brothers while they were fishing at night. The Preacher and Cassandra took Micah Ramsey to her funeral so he could see her in her coffin, laid out so prim and pure, and perhaps replace the frightening image of her buried in running, weeping sand, a picture to trouble his dreams.

The Preacher prays for Lillie Goforth at her funeral, a long impassioned prayer for all souls who drown, that they might rise again from the water, as though reborn in spirit pure and clean.

Because of this prayer—his prayer for the drowned—the minister who preached the funeral comes to the Gospel train and asks Jedidiah Robbins to baptize all his flock. At first the Preacher recoils at the idea, his old fear of the water rising up in him like gorge from his stomach. But the man before him is so simple and sincere that he finds himself agreeing even as his mind twists away from the idea.

The minister's name is Lester Caldwell, from the Highlands section of the county, and the good old man is certain that the Preacher has been sent to bless the members of his congregation. He has prayed about it with the little girl's family, and they are sure of it too. And so he wants the Preacher to take all of his little flock into the water.

Sitting with Lester Caldwell in the noonday sun beside the *Sword of the Lord*, the Preacher discovers that he has no answer to the old man's conviction. He agrees that on the following

Sunday morning, their last in Hot Springs, he will meet Reverend Caldwell and his flock at the pool below the Spring Creek Falls. Anyone in the village can show him where the falls are.

He reaches across the table to shake Lester's hand and seal this bargain, and when he does, the old man clasps both the Preacher's hands in his own, bows his head, and begins to pray. He prays in a high, singsong voice, stained with countless years of tobacco juice and field work. He prays a great thanksgiving to God for having sent the Preacher to him and his people, a man of the Spirit come to them in the springtime of the year.

Here is the odd thing. As Lester Caldwell prays, it's as if a surge of electricity courses through the old farmer's bones and sinews, through his wiry, calloused hands and into the Preacher. The Preacher's own palms begin to tingle and then his arms to itch. Rather than an old farmer's hands, it's as if he's grasping two cables shot with electric current. Sweat beads on his forehead as his chest and face grow warm and heavy. Something is traveling out of Lester Caldwell and into his body as the old man sings at God. Something powerful. Am I having a heart attack? he wonders to himself. Or is this mountain farmer some kind of saint?

As suddenly as it had come, the feeling begins to dissipate. Lester Caldwell is done and, after a tight squeeze, he releases Jedidiah Robbins' hands.

"What are you afraid of?" Cassandra asks him that evening, as they sit together after supper.

Before he answers, he tosses back his ginseng tonic and then rises to trim the wick of a glass lamp and light it against the gathering dusk.

Finally, he says, "I'm afraid that I won't be able to make myself go down into the water, into this Spring Creek."

She is at home enough now in the club car to bring out the brandy jar and two clean glasses from the cupboard. She pours for each of them.

"You've spent the last three weeks soaking in the hot tubs at the bathhouse, Jedidiah. Most every day in water up to your chin. Why is this different?"

"I don't know," he finally admits. "The water in the bathhouse is just that: a bath. It's been tamed somehow." He takes a sip. "The water in a river or a lake or a creek is living water, moving water."

"Wild water?"

He nods. "Wild water. It can trip you, pull you down. Drown you."

"It makes you think of her, doesn't it? Rachel?"

He nods.

"And when you think of her, you feel guilty, as if you should have saved her?"

"Why would you say that?"

She shrugs. "Bridget is my best friend. Women talk to each other, Jedidiah. She says that you were a champion swimmer in college."

He nods. "I was. At Berea, in Kentucky."

"And yet you're afraid of the water."

He nods again. Seems like all he does is nod. To what? Her looking inside of him?

"Jedidiah?" The brandy is softening her voice, taking the edge off the day and lending honey to her already sweet throat.

"Hmmm?" His voice, too...more relaxed.

"I can't swim a lick, but I'm not afraid of the water."

"You should be."

"No, because starting tomorrow you're going to teach me to swim."

He coughs up half a sip of brandy.

"There's an old swimming pool near the bathhouse. Relic from the Mountain Park Hotel that burned. The water's freezing cold, but it will do for swimming lessons."

"I'm not sure I can do what you're asking."

"I have faith in you, Jedidiah. Unproven. Untested. But faith nonetheless. If you're ever going to let me into your life—as something more than a once-in-a-while woman for a hot bed—you're going to have to teach me to swim so that you won't constantly fear for me. And God knows I need to learn. Starting tonight."

"You said tomorrow. I heard you say tomorrow."

"I think tonight, after a second glass of brandy, we should go wading at the edge of the river. Just wading. Get our feet wet, that's all."

"See what the moon is up to?"

"And see what the moon is up to."

He hesitates for what seems to him a long time. Thinking of Rachel and the fact that in a dream, she has told him to trust this woman. This Cassandra. To follow her. While he ruminates, she gets up and pours them both a second dollop of the apple brandy.

"Have you ever been baptized?" he asks her after a sip.

She shakes her head so hard that her hair dislodges from its combs and hangs fetchingly around her ears. "Hell, no. Of course I was dunked in a pool by that husband of mine. That Agape. But I don't count that. There was no love in it. And I'm not sure there was any God in it. He was grabbing at my breasts while I was under the water."

"I've never been baptized," he admits. "Not even my breasts."

She giggles, the heat of the brandy rising to her head. "Then we'll start with your toes. Tonight. In the River Jordan."

They only have three days to make peace with the icy water in the old hotel pool. But by the third day, Saturday, Bridget and Gabe come out to the pool to marvel at Cassandra, who can now swim slowly, laboriously from one end to the other and back.

Jedidiah walks beside her in the shallow end, stopping only when the water is lapping at his face. And then, when Cassandra is blushingly proud of what she's done, with Bridget screaming and applauding, he too suddenly begins to swim. Slowly at first, but then faster and faster: great comic looping strokes propelling him from one end of the pool to the other, effortlessly, happily through the water as if it is his native element. Once, twice, three times the length of the old pool and back, until he stands laughing and gasping in the shallow end.

Bridget, his child, is crying. She jumps fully clothed into the pool to throw her arms around her father's neck, laughing through her tears as though some thick mist has been burned away by the sun of their little family.

CHAPTER SEVENTEEN

SPRING CREEK FLOWS DOWN from between Bluff Mountain and Dogged Mountain to the west of Hot Springs, tumbling and falling and flinging itself between steep, rocky banks till it curls finally into town and joins the deeper, broader run of the French Broad River. A half mile above the village, where the creek has carved its way through the granite walls of a small gorge, there is a steep set of boulder-strewn rapids with a chest-deep pool below. The Spring Creek Falls.

When the Preacher finishes his second cup of coffee on Sunday morning and leaves the club car with his Bible—not his crusade Bible, but his own worn King James—he finds both Bridget and Cassandra waiting for him. They are wearing their crusade dresses—plain and unadorned but still appropriate for church. Cassandra clutches several towels in her arms.

"Where are you two going?"

"We thought we'd take a stroll along Spring Creek. Maybe see those falls we keep hearing about," Bridget says.

"I don't need you to go with me," he says testily. "I believe I can manage just fine by myself."

"It's a beautiful day," Bridget says, "isn't it, Cassie?"

"Fine day for a family outing," Cassandra replies, bearing down on *family*.

"We're going with you, Papa," Bridget offers, "whether you like it or not. Gabe will be along in a bit, after he finishes changing."

He grunts. "Well, are you bringing anybody else? How about the dog?"

Several of the roustabouts from *Saint John the Baptist* stand up from the picnic tables, and one—the German, Blaesius speaks up. "We might to come along too, Preach. Just to see what this like. Me and John here, Lost John, we never have baptize."

The Swede, Noah Cederberg, washes his mouth out with the last of his coffee and spits into the weeds. "I just might follow along too," he says. "My old mother always wanted me to be baptized. Thought it would do me good, come hallelujah time."

By the time they start down the dirt road to town, the entire company is trailing along in loose groups of two and three, seemingly everyone except Sheedy, the sworn atheist, who offers to stay with the trains, and Son-of-God Smith, who is nowhere to be seen.

A rough gravel road runs from the village up along Spring Creek. As they walk through the fresh sunlight, a few of the townspeople join them, slipping easily into conversation with the crusade grunts. Several of the older girls seem especially happy to walk with these men whom they've had no chance to meet before, new men who don't happen to be their cousins.

When they reach the spot on the road above the falls, the Preacher sees that they'll have to clamber down a steep path to a small patch of grass and a beach beside the creek. He descends first and offers a hand to Cassandra and Bridget. At the bottom, he finds Lester Caldwell kneeling in the dry sand before one of the creek-side boulders. He helps Lester to his feet, and the good old man feels almost light as a bird's wing. Tough as whitleather, no doubt, but thin as a knife blade.

Lester looks up and sees his own people as well as the strange men from the crusade picking their way down the path. "Well, I swan, Brother Solomon, it looks like you brought your own congregation right along with you."

The Preacher nods and smiles. "Some of those men are heathen through and through," he warns. "Don't smell of them when they get close."

Lester grins. "We're gonna wash all that stink of sin away, brother. Right here. I say we have a prayer and get to it. I'll baptize yours and you baptize mine, and between us we'll lay out every soul here as clean as lamb's wool."

Lester recites a verse or two out of Matthew, chapter 3, from memory; they each say a short prayer drowned out by the crash of the falls just beside them. Then, before Jedidiah has time to think, Lester takes his arm and they wade together into the frigid water. The pool is so cold that it blasts any lingering fear of the water out of his mind. When it reaches his waist, he feels his privates shrink in agony, and he says a brief prayer of his own that they don't disappear entirely.

Lester holds out his hand. Cassandra Bailey throws her towels on a rock and wades straight into the swirling water, her wet dress ballooning around her.

The Preacher looks up, and standing before him is a boy, perhaps fifteen years old, who looks vaguely terrified. He takes the boy's clenched fist and pulls him into the pool. "Do you accept Christ as your personal Savior, in this world and the next?"

The youth nods, his teeth chattering.

Suddenly, in a fit of common feeling, the Preacher hugs the boy to his chest, turns him slightly, and then covering the boy's nose and mouth with one hand, lowers him into the water. "In the name of the Father, and the Son, and the Holy Ghost," he intones and raises him back up. Cold water streams from the boy's head and shoulders, running in rivulets over his hands and arms. It seems the boy is crying, although it is hard to tell.

"Amen," whispers a woman, presumably his mother, who has waded into the water to meet him.

And so it goes. First one and then another. At one point, he glances up; through the radiant mist of the falls, he can see both Cassandra and Bridget sitting on a rock in the sun, with the towels they have brought wrapped around their shoulders.

One elderly lady, in her seventies at least, wades toward the Preacher. "Grandma, you been baptized a dozen times already," says Lester. "Once last fall. I done it myself."

The old lady smiles and keeps coming, straight for the Preacher, even as she almost falls on the slippery rocks that line the bottom of the pool. "Lester boy," she says, "I done some things here lately that I'd like washed away. Sides, I like the looks of this Solomon feller. I might a done some sinnin with him in another life."

He takes the old woman into the crook of his arm and carefully removes the fragile wire-rimmed spectacles from her eyes, placing them in his shirt pocket. "Do you take the Lord—"

"Son, I been takin him my whole life," she says. "Never said no to man nor God neither one."

She can't weigh more than eighty or ninety pounds, and he is ever so careful in lowering her into the flowing stream and bringing her back. When she comes up, her long hair washed totally out of its combs, she is laughing in delight. "I might just go sin again and come back to the end of the line," she cries out.

He has long since lost all feeling below his waist. His toes are only a distant memory, and he has forgotten his private parts entirely. He thinks they are through, he and Lester Caldwell, as all who were called have come to them. But now he sees that there is a double line of Negroes, dressed all in white and solemn black, waiting to be baptized. At the front of the line is none other than

Jesus the Son-of-God Smith, already immersed to his knees. "I brang you some of my own people just in case," he says to the Preacher. "I didn't want you and this other fellow to run short."

He turns to look at Lester, to be certain that he will accept this mixing of the races. That he is willing to touch each of these people in turn, hold them, bless them. But he needn't have worried; Lester already has his strong, electric right hand extended to Sonny Smith, welcoming him down into the spilling water.

CHAPTER EIGHTEEN

THE NEXT MORNING, the *Saint John the Baptist* train pulls out of the Hot Springs station for the short run upstream along the French Broad River to Asheville, North Carolina, the only town of any size in all the western end of the state. The Bible car is stacked to the roof with boxes of holy books of all sizes and colors, plus crates of pure, clean corn liquor and smoky, strong apple brandy. In the stable car, the five great Percherons are fat and happy, bored from lack of exercise. The train pauses at the Barnard Station just long enough to pick up Boss Strong, who is bringing in some jars of the best brandy from the Freemans on Anderson Branch, inventory strictly reserved for himself and Jedidiah.

The 1927 version of Solomon's Crusade will begin its holy work with three straight nights—Friday, Saturday, Sunday—at the Masonic Temple in downtown Asheville. Given what is expected to be a slightly more sophisticated audience—Mencken's booboisie—rather than the country rubes and hicks he normally preaches to, the Preacher has settled on the Sermon on the Mount for these three nights. From Asheville, they will head back down the mountain into familiar terrain: Old Fort, Morganton, Hickory, and then on into the Piedmont. Not Marion, though, as the troupe has no desire to see Cassandra's sheriff father or her First Baptist husband again.

The Masonic Temple is only nine years old, part and parcel of the manic building spree that is convulsing Asheville. Fronting on Broadway, one of the main thoroughfares through this tourist town, the striking pile of bricks is dominated by a tall portico of paired Ionic columns in front and a three-story, blind arched window on the side. The first floor includes offices, fireproof vaults for cabinets of mysterious Masonic records, lodge rooms, and a large banquet hall complete with fireplaces and second-floor balconies supported by columns of iron. Fingers Spivey has engaged the banquet hall for three straight nights of thunderous preaching and singing, having convinced the Preacher that the collective take will more than justify the expense. Boss and Gabe can decide if it's worth it to erect the big top near near the train station—just to draw a crowd and show off the horses.

The congregation that assembles on Friday night is like nothing Solomon's Crusade has ever seen. These are bankers and real estate investors, escorting plump wives and excited children. Doctors and lawyers, reeking of inherited money, high-dollar perfume, and bathtub gin. Expensive suits and even more expensive dresses, occasionally a fur piece or two against the chilly evening air.

Looking out at the crowd from a curtained alcove, the Preacher mutters to Boss, "You recognize any of these people? Think a single solitary one of them stooped so low as to buy our booze?"

"These ain't our people," Boss rumbles. "But their butlers and maids and chauffeurs are. That's who we sold to—for crisp, clean cash, which means those folks out there paid for it and drank it, but they ain't getting arrested for it. Let Boss and the chauffeur get arrested."

Fingers Spivey, who has joined them from the mysterious depths of the building, is whistling under his breath. "They may not be your people, Boss, but they sure as hell are mine. Look at the string of pearls that woman down front is wearing. You could dock an ocean liner with that rope."

"Tell you something else," Boss mutters. "The liquor we sold in this burg is probably already gone down the gullet, and I'm guessing the women out there drank their fair share. Rich women like them some booze."

"All the better," Fingers whispers. "For me."

"You saying there's not a lot of guilt to work with in this crowd? Guilt being the countrywoman's prerogative." The Preacher to Boss.

"Those people out there may be firsthand familiar with sin, but they ain't studying no guilt—man, woman, nor child," Boss says in what passes for a whisper. "And you ain't gonna teach em no guilt if you preach all night." Boss is absently patting Micah Ramsey on the head as he speaks. The boy had been shoved to the floor when the crowd pushed in and is sniffling.

"How about fear?" the Preacher asks. "You think they know what that is?"

Boss grins. "Maybe. Fear is good, but you best be careful. Remember the collection plate."

At the appointed hour, Cassandra walks onstage and, when the crowd slowly quietens, sings a long, slow version of "Amazing Grace." Normally, a country crowd would have joined in after the first line, but here only a few scattered voices echo her honey contralto.

The Preacher walks out on the low stage to where his large, ornate Crusade Bible rests on an improvised pulpit. It is open to Matthew, chapter 5, ready for the Sermon on the Mount piece he has prepared. But suddenly, on an instinct born somewhere in the depths of Spring Creek, he ruffles the pages forward to chapter 19 and begins reading at verse 16, knowing full well where he is going, that to these people he is preaching damnation.

"'And behold, one came, and said unto him, Good Master, what good thing shall I do that I may have eternal life?

"'And he said unto him, Why callest thou me good? There is none good but one, that is God: but if thou wilt enter into life, keep the commandments....

"'The young man saith unto him, All these things have I kept from my youth up: what lack I yet?'"

From where they sit at the piano to the side and behind the pulpit, Bridget reaches out and takes Cassie's hand. She knows what Cassie does not, that her father is off-script, and she senses an anger in him that she hasn't heard in years. She studies the crowd, not the least sure of how they will react.

"'Jesus said unto him, If thou wilt be perfect, go and sell that thou hast, and give to the poor, and thou shalt have treasure in Heaven: and come and follow me.

"'But when the young man heard that saying, he went away sorrowful: for he had great possessions.'"

Bridget's heart sinks as she listens. This might possibly be the worst passage in the entire Bible to throw up to these people. Cassie squeezes her hand; she must realize it too. "What in God's name is he doing?" Bridget whispers to Cassie. The other woman shrugs ever so slightly. "Something's made him mad," she whispers back. "Look at how stiff his back is."

"'Then said Jesus unto his disciples, Verily I say unto you, That a rich man shall hardly enter into the kingdom of Heaven.

"'And again I say unto you, It is easier for a camel to go through the eye of a needle, than for a rich man to enter into the kingdom of God.

"'When his disciples heard it, they were exceedingly amazed, saying, Who then can be saved?'"

He pauses then, to let the words settle. "Matthew, book 19, verses 16 to 25," he intones. "The word of the Lord." He can sense the unease in the high, ornate room. There is an ominous buzzing sound, as if he has whacked a hornets' nest with a stick.

From the middle of the beautiful room, someone shouts, "We don't have any camels here in Asheville, Preacher. Try again!"

He grins back at them, many already drunk for the evening, some on liquor Boss has sold them. "Do let me try again, brother," he calls out to the heckler. "Let me give you something you can identify with." He strikes a dramatic pose, with one hand raised, index finger pointing to the sky, almost but not quite in self-satire. "I say unto you, It is easier for you to drive a Packard Roadster through a barrel hoop than it is for a rich man to enter into the kingdom of God."

Bridget almost gasps. Careful, careful, she thinks. Don't insult them. She sees Boss standing in the wings, grinning, and she feels slightly better.

Because there is a ripple of laughter in the crowd. Not a tide by any means, but laughter nonetheless.

"Are we all going to Hell then, Preacher?" A different voice this time, a woman's voice. "Or is it just these bad men in the room, these bankers and such we're married to?"

He raises his arm again, almost as if he's playing a game with the crowd: tennis, perhaps. "'If thou wilt be perfect, go and sell that thou hast, and give to the poor, and thou shalt have treasure in Heaven: and come and follow me.'"

A different voice yet again from the crowd, this time down front, older, masculine—seasoned with cigar smoke and bonded scotch. "What guarantee can you give, Preacher, that there *is* a Heaven?" It seems almost a business proposition, and there are audible gasps in the room, as if this is a step too far, to challenge the existence of Heaven. "And if no Heaven," the voice continues, considering, "then perhaps I prefer my treasure here, where it is of use to me."

He can see the man who is challenging him, seated in the third row, between an older woman—his wife?—and a younger. The older woman pulls away from him slightly as he speaks, not wanting to be associated with the public sacrilege.

The Preacher pauses to consider. It has been years since he debated anyone but Bridget, and he feels a certain thrill at being challenged. He reaches out and lays his hand on the pulpit Bible. "If it is gold you seek, then," he says, "the next-to-last chapter in this good book speaks to your hunger. The book of Revelation, chapter 21, describes the city that is Heaven. And in this city, real estate values never waver. He recites from memory: 'And the twelve gates were twelve pearls: every several gate was of one pearl: and the street of the city was pure gold, as it were transparent glass.'"

"I'd like to know the price per foot for frontage on that street," calls out the wag from the middle of the room. "And what terms the owner offers." Again there is laughter, even more this time, as this is language they understand and can even hear ridiculed.

He shrugs. "We are gathered here this evening in a grand temple. An edifice to the power—even the generosity—of men. Is there a similar temple on the golden street, I wonder?" He makes a great show of turning to the back of the pulpit Bible, indeed, to the very last page. "Verse 22: 'And I saw no temple therein: for the Lord God Almighty and the Lamb are the temple of it.'" He gestures broadly to the center of the great hall, meaning to include both the wit who asked the question and all those around him who are still chuckling. "There's your answer as to the terms the owner is offering," he says.

"The owner of that property will make you a bargain today. He does not require a loan at interest, nor do you need to bring your attorney to the negotiating table. He will sell you a prime lot on that golden street for a single payment. The finest building lot in that city, and all you need do is cash in your current investments." He pauses for a moment, and his voice sinks to a deeper register. "'Go and sell what thou hast, and give it all to the poor, and thou shalt have treasure in Heaven.' It's a simple transaction, just like the ones that many of you in the audience make every day. Trading up, I believe it's called. And I expect that it's the very kind of transaction that paid for those pearls and those diamonds, the very sort of bargain that put silk next to your skin and a Packard automobile in your driveway, the very sort of real estate deal that made both your banker and your wife so happy to see you.

"But here's the thing that makes this transaction different. It is a dangerous mistake to call your estate here on this street, here in this city, *real,* because it is made of paper and it cannot last. You trade up and up, building your house on sand, always hiding your last debt in your next acquisition. But deep inside, beneath that embroidered vest and underneath that silk and satin, you know what's coming. You fear the day that the sands shift and the grand edifice you've built with your banker's help comes crashing down." He slams his fist into the podium so hard that every woman and most of the men in the hall visibly flinch.

"This city," he cries, flinging his arms out to the side to include all the great houses and halls around them. "This city will fall." His voice drops to a whisper. "And what's more, you know it. Deep inside, you know it and you fear it.

"But that city!" His arm shoots straight up, his hand a loose fist waving in the air. He can't point, Cassandra thinks, because he just broke his hand. "That city will not fail. It is built on stone, not sand. The streets are gold, not cracked and broken cement and asphalt. Not the weary brick! Those gates are pearl, and they do not open into the First National Bank. Those gates are made of the same simple words that hurt that rich man's feelings so many centuries ago: 'Go and sell that thou hast, and give to the poor, and thou shalt have treasure in Heaven.'" He pauses to catch his breath. The sweat is pouring from his scalp down over his face.

"Are there poor people in this town?" He is shouting now. No one answers. "Well, are there? You there in the second row, wearing the finest suit I've ever seen, ARE THERE POOR PEOPLE IN THIS TOWN?!"

The man at whom he is pointing nods nervously. The woman seated beside him, wearing a fox around her neck, answers. "Yes, Preacher, there are hundreds of poor, dirty people in this town. Some of them starving to death tonight."

"Thank you, sister. Your honesty becomes you. Many of you came here expecting to see a show. To laugh at the traveling crusade and to be entertained by the ranting and raving of the man whose picture you saw on that bill plastered to the phone pole. And I had every intention of doing just that, of giving you what you wanted. Of preaching platitudes and praising your generosity. But on the way into the hall tonight one of you—you probably don't even remember doing it—shoved a little boy out of your way.

"His name is Micah Ramsey, and he takes care of our horses. He was picking up a cigarette butt that one of your daughters dropped in the aisle and he was slow to get out of your way. And you shoved him hard against the wall just there, beside that column. Well, your problem is that I saw you knock the boy down, and I take it personal." With his broken hand, he slaps at his chest over his heart.

"Here is the truth you don't want to hear, and it's based on holy writ." He's pointing at them now with his left hand, his right arm hanging loosely, painfully by his side. "That boy will go to Heaven, and you will not. That boy will walk barefoot on translucent streets and you will go a-begging on street corners paved with fire. Unless you go out tonight and tomorrow and help the poor. Unless you trade up in spirit and build your house where time cannot touch it, you will go begging in the final hour of your life, and God almighty will have no mercy on your miserable soul."

He turns and walks off the small stage into the wings, catching Bridget and Cassandra so by surprise that there is a moment's long pause before the silent crowd hears the piano notes of "Just as I Am," followed by Cassandra's voice, husky with emotion.

CHAPTER NINETEEN

Boss HAS WORKED THIS TOWN BEFORE. He knows where to find a doctor at nine thirty on a Friday evening—in the all-night diner on the town square. The doctor, a portly, venous man named McGuire, agrees to meet them at his office in a crumbling brick building a block away, on the other side of the Vance Monument. After a quick conference at the front of the building, Fingers heads back to the temple to be sure that the night's take gets locked safely away while Boss waits in the downstairs hallway. When the Preacher asks why he wants to guard the door, Boss shrugs and offers, "You pissed on a lot of rich folks tonight, Jedidiah. Wouldn't be surprised if the chief of police won't be by to...check on us." And, after a pause, "Fingers says the same."

So it is only Cassandra who goes upstairs with him into McGuire's dusty, dimly lit waiting room. They can hear the doctor in the examination room beyond, cursing as he apparently tries to relight a cigar.

"You are a fool, you know that, don't you?" she whispers suddenly, not wanting the doctor to hear.

"For pissing on the rich folks?"

"No, fuck the rich folks. Well, yes, maybe, but I don't care about that. You're a fool for pounding on the podium like some star-struck kid who's just been called out of the potato patch to preach. Bridget says she hasn't seen you like that in twenty years. What the hell?"

He laughs at her. "I don't know," he admits. "I really did see some fat, old banker with a cigar stub clenched in his jaws push Micah down, and then Micah trying not to cry. And something snapped when I looked out at that sea of silk and satin. Top hats, for God's sake. Some of the men were wearing top hats."

"Come on in here where there's light enough to see." McGuire's voice sounds like it's been marinating in thirty years of cheap cigar smoke. He helps the Preacher up onto a wooden examination table and motions toward his own chair for Cassandra. "Sit down, girlie," he says, "and let's see what the old man did to himself."

"He slammed his hand into a pulpit," Cassandra mutters, "like an idiot."

"You a minister of the church?" McGuire asks with a curious, bird-like wink. "Cause if you are, my fee is double."

He has the Preacher take off his coat and helps him roll his sleeve up past the elbow. When McGuire bends over the wrist, hot ash from his cigar drifts down onto the Preacher's hand, and he flinches. "Sorry," McGuire mutters, and puts the cigar down on the edge of the exam table.

He manipulates, pokes, and prods at the Preacher's arm from elbow to wrist, and then, with strong, blunt fingers, begins to maneuver the hand slowly, carefully. The Preacher grunts out loud, and he can see Cassandra turn even paler in the strong electric light of the examination room.

"Can you make a fist?" McGuire asks. "Now stick your thumb and fingers straight out, spread wide." He taps the end of each finger experimentally; only the little finger elicits a slight flinch.

McGuire picks the cigar up off the edge of the table, and the Preacher can see a long row of burns where he's placed his stogies for years. "What do you think?" he asks the doctor.

McGuire turns to Cassandra before answering. "I think there's no fool like an old fool. You his daughter?"

Cassandra shakes her head, emphatically, no. But a smile creeps onto her face nonetheless.

"See," the Preacher says to her, "I warned you this would happen."

McGuire grins and turns back to the Preacher. "If not your daughter, I won't ask what, you old goat. I think maybe I should have gone into preaching."

The Preacher can't help but smile. "Know your Bible, do you?"

"No, but there doesn't seem to be much to it, and I'm a quick study." McGuire winks again.

"How about some doctoring first?" Cassandra says impatiently. "Is it broken?"

"Hell, no," McGuire says. "Should be, but it's not. Badly bruised, and you won't be able to do anything with it for a week or so." He pauses to wink at the Preacher again. "But you're in luck, because I don't need to cast it." He turns back to Cassandra. "I'm going to pad the heel of his hand and his wrist. And then strap the whole thing as tight as he'll let me. Your job is to make sure he doesn't take the wrap off for a few days. Can you do that?"

The Preacher is shaking his head, while Cassandra says, "Oh, yes. I can do that."

"Distract him. Get him drunk if you have to," McGuire says and winks again—this time at her. "But don't let him take that bandage off for a few days. There's a grand total of seventeen bones in the human wrist, and it's possible he managed to crush one of them. Let's see his range of movement on Monday."

"You sound almost like a doctor," the Preacher mutters.

"You sound almost like a Preacher," McGuire replies as he bends to his work.

While McGuire is padding and wrapping, they hear heavy footsteps on the stairs, and, remembering Boss' warning, Cassandra and the Preacher turn toward the door. It's only Boss and Fingers, not the police, and, though breathless from the stairs, they're both grinning.

"Tell him, Fingers," Boss says. "You're the messenger from the front lines."

"Listen to this," Fingers says, gesturing at Cassandra while looking the Preacher full in the face. "Five thousand, eight hundred and thirty-two dollars. Plus one fur stole, three gold rings, and a diamond necklace."

"What are you saying?"

"That's the take for tonight. That's what I'm saying."

"How much of it did you…?"

"I had no part in it. There were cops in the lobby and all over the street outside. My hands are as clean as…a surgeon's."

They all glance at McGuire, who is grinning around the stub of his cigar.

"That's more than we've ever made in one night." Boss starts to laugh.

"We have to give part of it to the poor," the Preacher says.

Boss looks at Fingers. "See? I told you he'd say that."

Fingers rolls his eyes. "We are the poor, in case you ain't been paying no attention. Three nights here could bankroll us for the rest of the spring. Make up for all those days and nights spent in them little tiny burgs where the one bank don't even hold five thousand dollars all at once."

"I thought you didn't care about money," he replies.

"I don't for myself. But I do care about keeping this show we got going alive. Remember the Tampini Brothers."

"Yeah," Boss adds. "Remember them brothers!"

Cassandra steps around the examination table, where she can stand beside the Preacher. She slips her hand behind the elbow of his good arm. "Are you sure?" she leans in to whisper to him.

"I'm sure," he says aloud. "They'll be watching. If we don't give to the poor—and make a big show of giving to the poor—we'll never get out of this town in one piece."

The doctor is nodding.

"How you aiming to help the poor you're suddenly so interested in?" Boss asks. "And just how much help we talking about?"

"We need to give a tithe," he says. "At least."

"What's that?" Fingers is looking at Cassandra. "I ain't never heard of no tithe."

"Ten goddamn percent," Boss says.

And Cassandra nods. "It's biblical."

Fingers whistles. "I make that five hundred and eighty-three dollars…and change."

"Give or take," the Preacher says. "Call it six hundred, counting the fur and the jewelry."

"How in the…?" Boss asks.

"Set up the big top down near the train station," the Preacher says. "And at noon tomorrow, start feeding people. Colored or not, I don't care. If they're hungry, feed em. And let the children ride the horses."

"Bridget will like that," Cassandra admits.

"Are you sure? It's a lot of money." Fingers the accountant.

"He's sure," Cassandra says, louder now, wonder mixed with resignation in her voice.

Boss is smiling again, having realized what may be at stake. "That means you can scare hell out of em again tomorrow night, don't it? If we feed the poor, I mean."

He nods. "That's exactly what it means. Doc, how much do we owe you?"

CHAPTER TWENTY

FROM HIGH NOON ON, the tent is the scene of tumultuous action. In less than twenty-four hours, the word has spread through Boss Strong's newfound network of speakeasies and blind pigs, so that dozens upon dozens of people have flooded down to the big empty field between the Southern Railroad roundhouse and the river.

One of the men, Scully, had been a cook on the Tampini Show, and, together with the others, he has managed with their one old, battered cookstove and several open fire pits to serve up gallons of a thick, brown stew and pones of cornbread cooked in bread pans that one of the grunts has scrounged or stolen from somewhere. There is even a stack of week-old pies that Fingers has bought from a local baker, along with buckets of fresh milk and tins of coffee.

When the Preacher asks Fingers where the milk came from, the latter jerks his head toward the *Saint John the Baptist* rig and says, "We now own us a couple of cows."

"How many is a couple?"

"Five or so. I ain't painted numbers on the side of them."

"What are we going to do with them when we pull out?"

"We're going to give them to some of these poor people you've suddenly took a shine to." Fingers grins, obviously enjoying himself.

"Who the hell milked them?"

Fingers looks down at the ground, embarrassed. He holds out his hands, artist's hands, and stares at them as if he has somehow betrayed those valuable digits. "I guess I did," he mutters. "I grew up on a farm in Pennsylvania."

He is haunted by the townspeople who are lining up for food, having come down the steep streets from town. Their faces are drawn and pale, the men as thin as fence rails and the women even thinner. He walks through the big top, where the boys have knocked together rows of rough lumber benches as if for a preaching. Once they've taken their plates and cups from the tables set up outside, they come in out of the air to eat. Their clothes, often dirty and patched, hang on them as if they are so many scarecrows walking. Even their voices are faded to a gray monotony.

Because the tent is set up near the rail yards, there are several dozen hobos from camps along the river's edge. These men—for they are all men—are jauntier than the townspeople, louder and more brazen with each other. They joke and laugh with the roustabouts. They are as bone-skinny as the townspeople, and many are missing fingers and teeth. They stink of sweat and urine and wood smoke. But somehow the freedom of the road has left them a tiny scrap of humanity, that and the ability to laugh.

It's the children who have the most spark left in them. Once they've wolfed down their plates of hot food, they race to the rough corral by the river's edge. Bridget, with Micah Ramsey's help, has them stand in line and wait for a turn with the huge Percherons, who have obviously done this before. The horses are as patient as Job with each child. After nuzzling and even lipping at an urchin's face and hands, one of the great horses lifts its head and allows the child to climb up the fence and onto its back for three—exactly three—circles around the ring. After which most of the children run back to the tent for more food before returning to the corral.

The Preacher smiles to see Micah's authority with these raw street children, many older than he is. His status with the horses is clear: he has with the brutes some magic of association, as if he were the bond servant to monsters. The boy's voice grows deeper while he herds the town children into line.

As he leans against the fence and watches the children, the Preacher realizes that Son Smith has been close by all day, often at his side. "What are you following me around for?" he asks the old man pleasantly. "Go get something to eat."

"Done ate," Son replies. "Sides, it's my turn."

"Turn for what?"

"Watch your backside. Me and Boss and Fingers plan to take turns."

"For what? My backside isn't much to look at."

"It ain't. But since you started flingin it in the face of all these rich folks, somebody'd better keep an eye on it or you'll end up in the river."

"I don't believe that," he says affably, watching Bridget comfort a little girl who is afraid the giant horses will step on her.

"Better start believing. And better start looking over your shoulder, as long as we're in this here town. Out in the country-side, where every living body is poor as the next, it don't matter. But here, you sawing against the grain."

"Still don't believe it. But even if it's true, who am I supposed to be looking over my shoulder for, some damn banker or lawyer with a ledger book?"

Son laughs. "To be so smart, Preach, you ain't got a grain of grown-up sense. You watch for the police, whether they in uniform or no. You watch out for the police first, last, and always. Who nailed my Jesus to the cross?"

For the first time, the Preacher turns to study Son's dark and ancient face. "I believe it was Roman soldiers," he says.

"Per-cisely," Son replies. "And the police ain't nothing but the Roman soldiers of the modern day." The creased old face breaks into a gap-toothed smile. "Do you need me to translate for you?"

CHAPTER TWENTY-ONE

THE SECOND NIGHT, the audience in the Masonic Temple is even more affluent than the one from the night before. The men don't bother to put out their cigars before striding boldly into the auditorium, flashing gold-headed canes and tipping their hats to one well-heeled acquaintance after another. The women look even more purebred and high-strung. It's as if the gossip has spread about the previous night's sermon, and rather than entering the arena cowed and afraid, Asheville's richest families are responding with a breathtaking arrogance. A number of the men have come from dinner wearing formal evening attire, their women equally exotic in dress.

From the same alcove they'd occupied on Friday night, Boss and Fingers watch the chief of police make his way down a side aisle, greeting a number of the luminaries by name. He is a beefy red-headed man who looks as Irish as a leprechaun—but in this case a very fat and dangerous leprechaun. He has two lieutenants with him, men with scarred faces and broken noses—beat cops who've come up through the ranks.

"What do you think?" Fingers whispers to Boss.

"I think I'm going to ease down front where I can see the crowd and stay between Jedidiah and the mob. I think you better go round up the boys and bring them backstage just in case. If trouble starts, they ain't doing us any good standing in the back of the room with their dicks in their hands."

The Preacher has known all day what he was going to start this night off with. It was the children, their arms and legs as thin as sticks, who set him thinking. They and their starving parents.

So he goes straight to the heart of the matter. Luke, chapter 16: "'There was a certain rich man, which was clothed in purple and fine linen, and fared sumptuously every day.'"

He pauses and looks out over the room. It is crowded tonight, more so than last night. He can sense privilege like a mist in the large, ornate space. It smells like cigar smoke and rich perfume. If silk and satin and lace had a scent, this would be it, he decides. "'And there was a certain beggar named Lazarus, which was laid at his gate, full of sores, and desiring to be fed with the crumbs which fell from the rich man's table: moreover the dogs came and licked his sores.'"

He pauses again, giving the audience time to think about that image. He remembers his own little dog, waiting in the club car on the *Sword of the Lord,* and he almost smiles. Cassie and he have named the dog Jezebel. "'And it came to pass, that the beggar died, and was carried by the angels into Abraham's bosom: the rich man also died, and was buried; And in Hell he lift up his eyes, being in torments, and seeth Abraham afar off, and Lazarus in his bosom.'"

He is reading slowly and carefully, emphasizing each separate word in its turn. He knows what it sounds like in the large echoing hall—as if he's driving a spike into hard ground with one hammer blow after another. Exactly the effect he intends.

"'And the rich man cried and said, Father Abraham, have mercy on me, and send Lazarus, that he may dip the tip of his finger in water, and cool my tongue; for I am tormented in this flame.

"'But Abraham said, Son, remember that thou in thy lifetime receivedst thy good things, and likewise Lazarus evil things: but now he is comforted, and thou art tormented.

"'And beside all this, between us and you there is a great gulf fixed: so that they which would pass from hence to you cannot; neither can they pass to us, that would come from thence.'

"The word of the Lord: Luke 16, verses 19 to 26. 'There is a great gulf fixed.'" He pauses for effect yet again. "'There is a great gulf fixed.'" Again, and then this time much louder. "'There is a great gulf fixed' between the rich man in this parable and the stinking hobo Lazarus, who dies in the ditch beside his driveway, with the dogs licking the sores on his filthy body."

This night, as on the night before, someone in the audience challenges him. "Who are you to condemn us?" But on this night his antagonist stands up to be recognized. He's a young man dressed in formal evening wear, and he jabs his forefinger at the Preacher as he calls out. "My father and every other man of consequence in this room have worked like *dogs* to accumulate what you see here." The young man's words are slurred, and at least one person is trying to pull him back into his seat. "They have earned it, and now you want to take it away from us with a few Bible verses. Go out and earn your own money, Preacher. My guess is that you've never worked a day in your life."

The Preacher raises both hands to shoulder height, one of them wrapped by Dr. McGuire the night before. At first you might think he is surrendering to the young fool's logic. "In my life, boy, I've farmed and I've laid brick. I've worked the railroad. I've mixed mortar for ten hours a day in the flatland sun, and I've driven nails for ten hours a day in the mountain winter. With these two hands. But this isn't about me, just as it isn't about you and your soft white hands.

"Yesterday, we fed over three hundred people down by the roundhouse in the river flats. Men, women, and children.

Among those we fed were out-of-work masons and carpenters and pipefitters and factory workers. We fed seamstresses and maids and women who take in laundry. Many of the children we fed—much younger than you—have worked in the bleachery or the tannery or the thread mill. They stink of the mill and they don't even know it because they're grown so used to the smell at such a young age. And every single person we fed would go to work tomorrow in your father's house or in his bank or in his factory if offered a job there."

He raises up his good left hand and slams it into the pulpit, careful to hit the wooden top with his open palm this time. "So you see, boy, this isn't about you or your father. Because I asked, and we didn't feed a single banker or lawyer or doctor or politician. We would have, if any had shown up with top hat in hand, but none materialized. If you and your friends had come to the river at noon yesterday, we would have fed you too. Why? Because we'll feed anybody." He is shouting loud enough to be heard in the street, and Bridget is blinking back tears at the raw cut of emotion in her father's voice. Boss Strong crushes out his cigar against one of the brass columns and edges toward the front of the crowd, where he can crouch directly beneath the pulpit.

"But it's not about you and me, is it? It's about the great gulf that exists between your father's house and my Father's house. Luke, chapter 16, verse 26: 'And beside all this, between us and you there is a great gulf fixed: so that they which would pass from hence to you cannot; neither can they pass to us, that would come from thence.'"

He is still shouting, though even his voice is beginning to crack. He thrusts his bruised and battered right arm into the air. "For I tell you now, boy, my Father's house is *above*, where there are many mansions, but none for the rich and famous. And your father's house is here." He thrusts his arm toward the south, in the general direction of Biltmore and the swanky side of town. "And until we find a way to erase the great gulf fixed between those two houses, between you and the leper Lazarus, then you too may suffer that rich man's fate. And you, and you, and you!"

He is growling now. "Help the poor! Give to the poor! Or someday you too may be thirsting for a single drop of water from a beggar's dirty fingertip!"

He turns and all but staggers toward the back of the small stage. Again, he has caught both Bridget and Cassandra unawares, and it is a long moment before the first plinking notes from the piano are heard, followed by Cassandra's plaintive voice.

But he hasn't caught Boss unawares. Boss stands tall and makes eye contact with the young man in tails who first challenged the Preacher. The young man and his friends—men and women also in evening attire—have edged out into the center aisle and are moving restlessly toward the front of the room. Boss shakes his hard, square head at them and holds up one scarred, battered hand, palm out to emphasize the message. Don't come any closer. The others in the party are sober enough to understand the gesture. They drag their drunken companion toward the exit.

The chief of police and his two cronies stand immediately when the Preacher turns away and the music begins. They head straight for a side door, Fingers following almost invisibly in their wake.

155

This Saturday night, they take in over seven thousand dollars in cash, along with a bucket half full of jewelry. Gabe and Bridget have to count the money, because Fingers doesn't show back up at the *Sword of the Lord* till dawn.

CHAPTER TWENTY-TWO

DEEP IN THE MIDDLE WATCH THAT NIGHT, he dreams that the French Broad River beside the railroad siding rises out of its banks and floods the fields where they are camped. Acres of muddy water on the move—verily a river of earth. As if in slow motion, he and the roustabouts raise the sides of the crusade tent so the waist-deep water can flow through, washing away benches and hymnals.

Bridget and Cassie and the boy Micah ride to safety on the backs of huge horses that materialize to carry them away, plodding sure-footed over the surface of the nightmare water.

When he wakes, first to escape the nightmare and then to walk outside to piss on the iron rails, he finds that the world is quiet and still, except for the distant whisper of the river, flowing safely within its normal course. He sees that the Swede, Cederberg, is sitting guard beside the *Sword of the Lord*, and he speaks to him before returning to the club car.

He dips cold water from the bucket on the platform stairs and then climbs up the steps to the club car. He sits for a moment on the side of the bed he shares with Cassie and watches her sleep in the dim, gray light. She has flung back the covers on this May night and is wonderfully corporeal, sprawled there in the pale sheets. She always sleeps naked, even in the winter, and her solid form is vastly reassuring to him: her shoulders, thick for a woman; one large, work-worn hand flung above her head; her modest but perfectly formed breasts, with nipples like small, overripe strawberries. Her belly not soft but sculpted by muscle.

She groans in her sleep, as if she too is inhabited by dreams, perhaps the same nightmare of the fluid earth in motion. The ancient flood that only Noah and his sons survived.

He is wearing a ragged undershirt and loose flannel pants, his accustomed pajamas for years, and suddenly it is the nightclothes that make him feel old and soft. They invite a chill into his blood rather than protecting him.

She sleeps as if nestled in Eden—abandoned, wild, unshorn.

He stands and strips the undershirt off over his head, yanks down the flannels, and kicks them under the bed. He can feel the slight breeze now through the open windows against his skin, fresh in a way that he'd lost for years.

Sleeping with Eve, he thinks as he slips back into bed. She turns toward him without waking, her form almost heavy against him. He flings one leg across her hip and pulls the sheet over both of them. She seems to be whispering something he can't quite hear, her mouth against his throat.

So simple, he thinks, sleepily.

Could we take off our skins too? he wonders, drifting deeper. Strip away layer after layer till the light shines?

Soul woven into soul—such proof against the streaming flood of the world.

CHAPTER TWENTY-THREE

Fingers materializes at dawn, sweaty and bedraggled, tired and full of news. "I followed them cops right down into the station house itself. Pretended at one point to be a rat-tailed informer talking to some beat cops who wandered in and out. Listening, always listening. And here's what I got to tell you."

He is talking to the Preacher over coffee. Cassie slipped into the saints' car when Fingers came knocking at the rear platform of the *Sword of the Lord*.

"What is it, Fingers? Spit it out."

"They're coming at noon today to arrest all them poor souls we're feeding. Arrest them as vagrants. They're going to use us as a goddamn means to their goddamn end. They mean to throw a cordon of officers around the big top and cut us off against the river. They plan to let the women and children go, but they'll throw every living man over the age of twelve into a wagon and haul them to the hoosegow."

"Why in hell would they do that?" The Preacher is fuming.

"You know perfectly well why. They mean to round up all the hobos who've been hiding out along the tracks and all the sorry folks who've been sleeping in the alleys and on the back porches in the dark side of town. Hell, and at the same time they get to show us up for fools. In their world, we're not feeding the poor: we're aiding and abetting the criminal class."

"Sons of bitches!"

"Pretty much that, what you said. But if you aim to feed the masses today, you better make up your mind what you're going to do when the cops show up, because they're sure enough coming."

"And we've got one more service to preach tonight."

"And one more chance to fill the coffers," Fingers adds. "It's your show. What are we going to do?"

"Let me think on it," the Preacher says. "There has to be a way."

"I'm going to get some sleep while you do that. I'm beat. You just be sure to let me and the Boss know your plan. Because if not, there's liable to be trouble. The ax-handle kind of trouble."

Later that morning, he tells Boss and Fingers to "send the boys out with food to the hobo camps and tell them to stay away from the big top till after dark. Unless they want to spend a warm night in jail. Send somebody else uptown and spread the word—you know where, Boss—and tell the men to lay low. We'll feed the women and children down by the river."

He can see they're skeptical, but he insists that they go ahead. He claims the Lord will protect those who can't protect themselves. Even so, as Boss and Fingers walk back toward *Saint John the Baptist,* they agree that they should tell the boys to be back by noon. "Just in case them coppers get restless," Fingers says.

By twelve, a crowd has gathered at the big top, but unlike the day before it is made up almost exclusively of women of all ages and children under the age of ten or so. There are three old hobos who've come in together, and when Fingers tries to run them off, they explain that they're tired and hungry. "The camps done wore us out, and the railroad bulls done beat us silly," one says. "We want to try jail for a while."

All the roustabouts return by noon or shortly thereafter, except for two who were sent up the hill to the far side of town. When the two horse-drawn paddy wagons pull up beside the railroad roundhouse and let out their squadrons of police, the ranks are about even. Six roustabouts, Gabe, and Fingers wait inside the tent while Boss, Sonny Smith, and Bridget walk out with the Preacher to meet the dozen armed cops who spread out in either direction as if to surround the big top. The cops are brandishing nightsticks, and most have revolvers strapped to their hips.

Boss recognizes one of the police chief's lieutenants from the night before, a young tough better than six feet tall with a prizefighter's scarred face, including a cleft lip. This, Boss thinks, is the man in charge. And sure enough, the lieutenant steps forward to meet them.

"You the man they call Solomon?" He pauses to unfold and refer to an official-looking document from his breast pocket. "Real name of Jedidiah Robbins?" The lieutenant's voice is hoarse, as if he's had his larynx crushed a time or two.

The Preacher nods and smiles his ironic smile. "Yes, sir, I am. How may I help you?"

"This here is a search-and-seizure warrant from Judge Samuel Garrett." He hands the Preacher the paper. "Me and these boys are here to arrest every man over the age of fourteen that we find in or around your tent or them two trains of yours."

The Preacher is studying the warrant. "Correction," he says after a moment.

"Correction of what?"

"Correction: you aren't here to arrest just any man you find. You're here to arrest as vagrant any *unemployed* man you find on the premises. That excuses any man who works for the crusade."

For the first time, the lieutenant's twisted lips writhe into a grin. "I figure to take every damn one and let the lawyers and judges sort em out. You know—the sheep from the goats."

"You don't have to do that," Boss steps forward, and suddenly the springtime air between the two groups seems to hum with electricity as the two bulls in the herd face off. "We can prove who works for Jedidiah and who don't." Boss' gravelly voice is deeper even than usual, edged with menace. "It ain't legal writ but it's evidence you'll understand."

The lieutenant steps forward, and it's suddenly apparent that he's taller than Boss, if not so thickly made. "What kind of evidence you got in mind, old man?"

Boss' hands fly up as if of their own accord. The lieutenant jerks, reaching automatically for his holstered revolver, but all Boss does is unbutton the top few buttons of his work shirt. He pulls back one lapel of his shirt and points to his chest.

The Preacher and Bridget both lean forward on either side of Boss to see what he is pointing to. Through the thicket of wiry gray hair on Boss' chest, they can see an Irish cross tattooed over his heart.

"Sign of the crusade," Boss says. "Every man of ours has one except the Preacher. He lives up in the clouds; he don't need one."

At this, Sonny Smith steps forward from where he has stood patiently, three steps behind the others. He carefully unbuttons the ancient worn dress shirt he has donned for the occasion and, without speaking, points to the same place on the left side of his wrinkled, scrawny chest. Against his agate skin, the cross is almost invisible, but the blue tinge of the ink is there nonetheless.

"Do you vouch for this shit?" the lieutenant points to the cross on Sonny's chest with his nightstick.

"Absolutely," the Preacher says. "Sign of the cross and the man is ours."

The lieutenant sighs, obviously disappointed. Shaking his head, he retreats to the paddy wagons and summons his men for a palaver. From where the crusade members stand, they can see the lieutenant pointing to his chest in explanation.

The Preacher reaches out and traces the cross on Boss' chest with his finger. "Did these just appear?" he asks, grinning. "The miraculous act of a loving God?"

"More like the miraculous act of a drunk tattoo artist in Jacksonville. Traded liquor for enough ink for all the boys."

"What about Hack Ramsey? He just joined in Hot Springs."

"I did his myself," Boss says proudly. "While the boys held him down. Son here held the ink bottle and sopped up the blood."

CHAPTER TWENTY-FOUR

To avoid any further bust-ups with the police, and to gain time, the roustabouts disassemble the big top after lunch on Sunday afternoon. They load it and the horses onto *Saint John the Baptist* and head out for points east. Specifically, they plan to pull into Morganton that night and begin to prepare the way for the crusade later in the week.

Everybody in the troupe will ride out on *Saint John the Baptist* except for the Preacher, Fingers, Bridget, and Cassandra, plus two trustworthy men to pass the collection pails. They will take a hired car away from the Masons' Temple as soon as the service is over, down the steep and winding road to the train station, where the *Sword of the Lord* will be waiting, boilers fired and ready to roll. It is one last night of a frighteningly successful three-night stand, and no one wants to hang around Asheville, North Carolina, to press their luck—with either the police or the rich folks whom they protect.

After the midday face-off with the police, who arrested the three hobo volunteers and a half dozen of the older boys from town, the Preacher knows what he intends to take as a text that evening. Since Thursday, when they arrived in Asheville, he's been staring at the Jackson Building down on Pack Square at the center of town. Three years old, it is the first skyscraper any of them have seen, and it towers over even the new town hall and courthouse, also monuments to human vanity.

And so he means to use as his text the story of the Tower of Babel from Genesis, chapter 11: "Therefore is the name of it called Babel; because the Lord did there confound the language of all the earth: and from thence did the Lord scatter them abroad upon the face of all the earth." He had dreamed the night before of towers reaching into the clouds; and in his dream, the towers had caught fire and burned, collapsing to the ground. And so, he thought, the language of all mankind has been confounded, till even plain English speakers can't understand one another. The rich man refuses to hear the poor man; the poor man only hears orders from the lips of the rich man. Man, he thinks, cannot understand woman, and woman has only disdain for man. Babel is the name of our language, he thought, for we are divided by money and by sex and by law. We cannot decipher each other's speech, no matter how hard we try. Even love cannot untangle the knot of our loneliness.

But when they arrive that night at the temple, they are surprised yet again by the nature of the crowd that awaits them. Rather than the Vanderbilt rich, Asheville's elite, this crowd is for the first time the working-class men and women they are used to. The Baptists and Methodists who make up the vast majority of the people they see, the people they serve. There are shopkeepers and repairmen, hotel maids and seamstresses, delivery men and draymen, farmers come in from the countryside smelling of wood smoke and the barn. Even a few of the beat cops who helped arrest the hobos down by the river are there, dressed in their off-duty clothes and blending into the crowd. There are no top hats and no furs, no silks and no satins except for the occasional necktie. The doctor, McGuire, who had wrapped the Preacher's arm, is there with a few of his midnight cronies, sharing a flask between them. These are mostly working men and women—people who sweat out their living with calloused hands and bent backs. For the first time, there is no privilege in the great hall and little sense of power. And Bibles; these people come carrying their Bibles, the covers worn and pages bent from midnight searching.

So he switches, suddenly, his plans for the sermon. He goes back to where he had intended to begin two nights before—to the fifth chapter of Matthew, the Sermon on the Mount. "'Blessed are the poor in spirit: for theirs is the kingdom of Heaven. Blessed are they that mourn…the meek…they which do hunger and thirst…the merciful…the pure in heart…the peacemakers…. Blessed are ye, when men shall revile you, and persecute you….'"

The evening has the sweet sense of a homecoming for him, a return to who they are in their essence. To whom they were meant to serve. Serving up to the people both alcohol and God, the fiery spirits from a bottle and that fiery Spirit from a book.

They leave the temple with only a few hundred dollars in cash, much of it in carefully hoarded nickels, dimes, and quarters. Any number of warm dollar bills, folded small to fit into watch pockets and the leather change purses that country women like to carry their money in. No furs, no jewelry, no finery of any kind—just the jangling coins that keep the great majority of humanity alive.

The *Sword of the Lord* pulls out of the Asheville train yards just after ten o'clock. It will take three hours for the slow, winding trip down the Old Fort grade, past Marion, where Cassandra's husband is still a Baptist minister and her father the county sheriff, and into Morganton—where *Saint John the Baptist* is already cooling on a siding in the rail yard.

At eleven o'clock, only Bridget and Cassandra are left to sit up with the Preacher. With Papa, for that is what Bridget has always called him, or Jed, for that is what Cassie calls him now, Jedidiah having too many syllables for pillow talk.

They break out the brandy, and the only light in the club car is from two oil lamps, filled and wicks trimmed to steady the yellow light. He unwraps his arm while he listens to the two women talk. There is an easy glow within the three—fed by the brandy—as the twisting black snake of the train winds its way down and around the sharp curves on the mountain grade.

At one point, when the brandy has taken the edge off their thoughts, Cassie asks Bridget if she's going to see the boy, Gabriel's son. The Preacher glances up at this, having lost track of where they are on the map relative to Bridget and her Gabe.

Bridget nods at Cassie. "Oh, yes. I mean to see him. Gabe's terrified, of course. That I'll slap the woman or hate the child, I don't know. But I've told him straightaway that if we're to have a chance at all, I need to see what's his. Maybe even love what's his." And then, after a long moment and a glance at her Papa, "Will it be strange to ride through Marion? Knowing that your father is less than a mile away, sleeping in his bed, and you passing through like a ghost?"

Cassie shakes her head. "Not so strange. It would be much stranger if we were to stop. Much stranger, scarier, to see him. Him or my husband." She stares at Jed as she says this, even though she is answering Bridget's question. "You forgot to mention the husband that I have hanging around my neck."

"Would you like to get a divorce?" he asks her quietly. Almost as if the thought is coming to him, to either of them, for the first time on this slow nighttime journey down the steep, silent mountainside.

"Can you divorce a minister of God?" she asks, her lips twitching as if she would smile. "Can you divorce someone named Agape?"

"With the right lawyer, you can do most anything," he says, smiling at her. "Mayhap we can find one in Morganton."

"Do it, Papa," Bridget says with some force. "Please. For Cassie's sake. Surely, if he beat her…"

He shrugs, letting his shoulders relax more deeply into the overstuffed chair where he sits, considering. "If that's what Cassie wants."

"You don't have to do that strange thing you do where you ask Mama," Bridget says. "Praying and dreaming, all such as that."

"Bridget!" Cassie says. "Let him be." And then, after a moment, "None of this is easy."

"Papa's time moves like a glacier sometimes," Bridget says to her. "Like one epoch sliding into another." She takes a sip of brandy. "Sometimes he might need just a little nudge."

Now it is he trying not to smile. "I already asked your mother," he says to Bridget. "If you must know, I asked her way back. In Hot Springs."

This is too much for Bridget, and she has to ask. "Well, then, what did she say?"

"She came to me in a dream. Right here in this car, and she told me that some things the woman must lead. That I must trust Cassie and that *she* trusts Cassie." He nods and smiles, with all the softness of the brandy and the lamplight. Nods to Cassie, who is blushing. "That she blesses Cassie each night while she sleeps."

Bridget starts to interrupt, but he goes on.

"That when Cassie is ready to go forward—against her husband, against her father—that I'm to help her." He shrugs again. "Not for my sake, but for her sake."

Cassie is smiling at Bridget now, radiant with the words and the brandy. "I'd like to get a lawyer," she whispers—speaking to him while staring at Bridget. "A good lawyer who isn't afraid."

He nods at Cassie. "Probably not in Morganton, then. Maybe Asheville. We might have to go back up there for such as that—a lawyer with rocks in his pocket."

"Will you do that?" Bridget asks her Papa. "Find a lawyer for Cassie who can deal with her father? Settle with her husband?"

He grins at his daughter. "Oh, we'll find him," he tells her. "If we have to go clear to the coast, Boss and I'll find him." And then, after a moment, "You worry about that boy in Morganton. Gabriel's son. Jackson, I believe is his name. You concern yourself with Gabe and that boy Jack, and let us," he nods at Cassie, "let us worry about Brother Bailey and the sheriff."

CHAPTER TWENTY-FIVE

T HE SEVERAL DAYS IN MORGANTON leading up to the Friday and Saturday tent meetings feel like a return, a return to normal country people coming into the county seat from farms and smaller towns flung out across the foothills.

The only unusual thing about the first night's service is that both Fingers and the Preacher notice a strange character in the audience. He is dressed in a wrinkled brown suit with a tie loose at his collar. Medium height, thin, intense. His hat, a battered Stetson, is pushed back on his hard, round head. He is smoking a thick cigar as he writes in a small notebook on his knee. When Gabe walks over to ask him to put it out because of the dry hay on the ground and the painted canvas all around, he carefully rubs the fire out of the tip against the edge of the bench and thrusts the unlit stub straight back into his mouth.

Journalist, the Preacher thinks to himself, although there is something about the man that doesn't fit with the local newspaper, or even some rag slightly farther afield, such as in Charlotte or Raleigh. Too intense, too self-obsessed, too focused on the words that he's scribbling furiously into his book.

Whoever he is, the Preacher thinks, here tonight in this place, we'll give him something to write about. And in a strange way he is stirred by the sight of someone so intent in the congregation. Someone who is—perhaps—so taken with the power of words. The power of *the* Word.

And so he dives deep into a text he hadn't really anticipated, the third chapter of Ecclesiastes: the words of the Preacher, the son of David, the King of Jerusalem. "'To every thing there is a season, and a time to every purpose under the Heaven. A time to be born, and a time to die; a time to plant, and a time to pluck up that which is planted. A time to kill, and a time to heal; a time to break down, and a time to build up.' And so on down through the end of time and seasons to the great Ecclesiastical admonishment: enjoy what you are given. Don't ask too many questions. Finally verse 13, something reassuring for tired and hungry humankind: 'that every man should eat and drink, and enjoy the good of all his labor, it is the gift of God.'"

That night, in the comfort of this broad tent they have made their own, in the way of the life he and his large traveling family have created, he means to go easy, to deliver a message of comfort and reassurance to the people who've come here. But something about the reporter in the back of the tent, about the sense of immediacy that seems to swim in the warm, spring air, pushes him deeper into the words of the biblical Preacher.

He finds that there are tears on his cheeks as he reads, and with them a sudden deep swimming of emotion. Although he means to focus on the back-and-forth of the seasons, his eye drifts forward to the final verse of this passage: "that every man should eat and drink, and enjoy the good of all his labor, it is the gift of God." Somehow he feels that this night is about gifts. And how they might be enjoyed for the brief period we are allowed. And for a flickering brief moment, he is aware of Cassie sitting with Bridget behind him.

And so, for the first time in many years, he preaches on the treasures of this earth: the warmth of a midwinter fire, the gentle breeze on the face that cools us as we work, the first light of day brushing the treetops, the long Southern evening that eases us toward rest.

At first, the congregation seems restless. They have come here expecting the harsh dealings of an Old Testament Jehovah. And they are receiving something entirely different in tone and meaning; they are being told to rest easy in their own beds and enjoy the fruits of their long labor.

"This earth is God's gift to you, and all the fruits of this earth are meant to be enjoyed as one season rolls over into another." He pauses for emphasis. "*All* the fruits of this earth."

And so on this one night, there is no altar call in the traditional sense, no fire-breathing, come-to-Jesus shout, but rather an invitation to enjoy what life we are given, and to come forward at the end of the service if, and only if, you plan to relish the morrow-day more than you did the yester-day.

Bridget and Cassie catch the mood of his sermon early on, and when he stops suddenly, almost in midsentence, they join in immediately—not with the tear-stained "Just as I Am" but with a slow, gentle version of "Shall We Gather at the River." The beautiful, the beautiful river that flows by the throne of God.

CHAPTER TWENTY-SIX

AFTER THE SERVICE, Bridget goes off with her Gabe to *Saint John the Baptist*. Cassie is settling into her usual chair with a book, having poured both herself and the Preacher a tot of brandy. Jezebel is curled beside her, burrowing against her hip, but when the knocking starts at the rear of the car, she leaps up to bark at the door.

It's the reporter from the service, demanding to see Solomon, the Preacher. Cassie lets him in just far enough to close the door behind him. She scoops Jezebel up. "Jedidiah's in the saints' car," she explains. "He'll be back in just a minute." She returns to reading, leaving the man standing.

When the Preacher comes back into the car a moment later, he smells the cigar smoke and immediately glances at the back door. "Who are you?" he asks.

"My name is Henry Mencken," the reporter growls, "and I'm here to—"

"Good God. 'Henry' as in H. L. Mencken? *The Baltimore Sun*, the *American Mercury* Henry Mencken?

"One and the same," the man says, grinning. He takes the cigar out of his mouth, though it doesn't seem to deter his talking. "Can I come in?"

"Of course you can. I'm one of your biggest fans. Cassie, pour the famous man a glass of brandy. He deserves it, after having to sit through the last couple of hours. Here is a chair, Mr. Mencken!"

"I'm not sure he's a friend, Jedidiah," Cassie replies.

"Of course he is. Pour Mr. Mencken his brandy."

"Henry. Please call me Henry. And yes to the brandy. Did I tell you why I'm here?"

"I assume you're here to expose me as a fraud. Isn't that what you do?"

Cassie looks up from pouring the brandy, watching Mencken closely to see how he responds.

"Well, yes. That is what I do. At least when it's called for."

"How in the world did you ever find us? Surely to God we're not any kind of news in Baltimore or any other place where you're celebrated."

"The courthouse sermon," Mencken says. "That's what caught my attention. Preaching against the saloon from inside a courtroom? That's a new one, even for me. Didn't even see that in Tennessee a few years back."

The Preacher raises his glass in salute. "Thank you," he says.

"It's not a compliment," Mencken replies, and raises his own glass in return. "I think you're some kind of hoax. Especially since we're sitting here drinking the very thing you were railing against."

"He was forced to preach that courthouse sermon," Cassie interrupts. "To get a friend of ours out of jail."

"A friend that was arrested for bootlegging, is what I hear."

The Preacher grins. "You do your homework, Henry. I'll give you credit. That's exactly what it was for, and that's exactly why that sermon was what it was."

"So you're not against liquor?"

"Careful," Cassie warns. "He's interviewing you."

"I'm against bad liquor. I'm against alcohol that's been poisoned by the government such that it gives a poor man the jake leg. I'm against bootleg rye so bad that it stinks of gasoline. I'm against some judge who drinks bonded whiskey in his parlor and condemns the Negro man who cooks a potful of liquor on his stove. Oh, I'm against a lot of things, but I'm not against what's in that glass you hold in your hand."

"Then why did you preach that sermon?"

"Did you read it, at least what was in the papers? It was ridiculous. Hopped-up Billy Sunday bunk that nobody in their right mind would take seriously."

"I read it, and here's what you don't grasp. Half the redneck people in that courtroom weren't in their right minds, and you know it. Hell, way more than half. Those poor crackers believed everything you said."

The Preacher shrugs. "I did what I had to do, and I even enjoyed it at the time. Surely to God someone like you, who writes such outrageous balderdash from time to time, can appreciate that."

At this, Cassie stands. "I'm going to bed," she says. "And let you two fight it out. You," she looks pointedly at the Preacher, "try to remember that he," she nods to Mencken, "can't be trusted."

"Can you be trusted?" he asks Mencken after she has gone and taken Jezebel with her.

"I can be trusted to tell the truth."

"As you see it?"

"As I see it."

"I'm not who you think I am," the Preacher says after a moment. "At least not who you thought I was when you came down here."

"So you're not an Anti-Saloon League moron? Do you even believe in the Bible?"

"I can answer both of those questions at once," he says. "Do you happen to recall that according to the Bible, Mary is the mother of Christ?"

"I've heard something about that."

"Did you know that she only speaks three times?"

"In her life, or in that book of yours?"

The Preacher gets up to pour Mencken some more brandy. "The real woman could have been downright chatty, but the Bible only records her speaking three times, and one of the three is at the marriage in Cana, when she suggests that her son—what's his name—turn the water into wine."

"If the marriage had been in Baltimore, it would have been beer," Mencken says.

The Preacher grins. "Then it would have been beer. But it would have been the best beer that anyone in Baltimore ever tasted."

"So all of this prohibition ranting and raving that goes on all over the benighted South from preachers like you is—"

"Politics. Pure and simple. Oh, some of my more narrow-minded brethren have been bitten by the same mania as Billy Sunday and his ilk, and they actually believe that liquor is poison. But mostly this is all about politics and money. How many rich people get arrested in Baltimore for serving up a hot toddy in the basement of the mansion? Not a single damn one, and you know it! Better yet, how many times has your house been raided?"

Mencken shakes his head roughly, as if to ward off the brandy fumes as well as the words. "But you're a preacher, damn it. And you sit here drinking. And that woman? I assume she's your wife."

The Preacher shrugs. "She's a friend who sings in the crusade. And none of your goddamn business, Henry...Louis... Mencken."

"I try not to throw stones."

He laughs. "You do little else but throw stones, but here's the truth in this. I think you and I are alike. Oh, you're famous and I'm not. You're a well-educated Northerner, and I'm by definition an ignorant Southerner. But the truth is that we're both word-cursed, you and I. You have trouble sleeping, don't you?"

Mencken shrugs and nods.

"Your dreams are haunted by reams, by rolls, by pages of words. You carry on conversations in your sleep. Every day, you read and write letters to dozens of people you've never even met. You work like a dray horse, and you drag around behind you a torrent of words. I know you because I'm like you. You write and I preach just to ease the pressure in the head, just to release the flood. Deny it if you can."

"Why would I deny it? But don't you think it's a blessing rather than a curse? That river of words you're describing?"

"Oh, I'll admit it's a blessing as well as a curse. Both together. But you ask why I take a drink. Or even why I admire a woman. You know the answer. It's to take the edge off. To slow the mind down enough just to sleep. To ease the constant flow of words, words, words."

"Like Hamlet?"

"Yes," the Preacher smiles. "People like you and me. We have the Hamlet disease."

They drink on into the night, and after a while Mencken gives the Preacher one of his prize cigars. Lights it for him with a kitchen match from his vest pocket.

Toward dawn, when it's obvious that they're both nearly exhausted, Mencken rises to go, intending to walk back to his room in the town's one hotel. At the door, he tells the Preacher, "You're a kind of cornfield Aristotle, aren't you—profiteer and prophet?"

"I accept the cornfield," he says. "I even take it as a compliment. But not Aristotle. His mind was far larger than mine… or yours. His mind was captivated by the myriad details of this world. I just keep trying to find ways to escape it all."

CHAPTER TWENTY-SEVEN

THE NEXT MORNING, he takes his coffee outside to sit on the iron steps on the rear platform of the *Sword of the Lord*. The air is young and fresh with late spring, the fluid syllables of birdsong woven throughout. He has slept only a few hours after his long discourse with Mencken. His head aches, and his throat is still dry from cigar smoke. But the early light soothes, and he has to smile at the memory of Henry Mencken's face when he realized that Solomon's Crusade sold liquor out of the same boxcar as Bibles.

His easy morning thoughts are disturbed, however, when he sees Bridget walking down the tracks toward him.

He can see from fifty feet away that his daughter is fighting back tears, and he motions her away from the tracks. "Let's go for a walk," he says, ever so gently, "and see some of this pretty morning."

She nods but doesn't speak, and again he has the intense sensation in his stomach that she's barely in control of herself. He sets his coffee mug down on the platform behind him and steps forward to meet her. Taking her by the hand, he leads her down the gravel embankment to a path that runs away from town and through the trees toward a creek.

"What in the world?" he says gently after a moment.

"Yesterday afternoon before the...before the service...we went...went...."

"You went to see Gabriel's son?"

She nods, furious with the effort not to cry. "To their house. She's married to some old man and they...they all of them together have a house."

He squeezes her hand reassuringly. "The boy's mother is married to the old man?"

A furious nod.

"And so she and her husband and the boy, Jackson, they all live together."

Again the nod.

"Well, that's good, isn't it? The boy has a home, a roof over his head. The mother has a husband so she's not trying to raise him up alone."

"I hate her."

He tries to hide his smile. "That's natural, given the circumstances."

"She is a short, skinny thing with freckles. Barely twenty if that, and as ugly as homemade sin."

"Oh, I doubt that, Bridget. At least the ugly part. What's the boy like?"

At this, she finally begins to cry. "Oh, Papa! He's the sweetest thing. He's just a baby, but he looks like Gabe, or at least I think so, and when Gabe was carrying Jackson around the yard, you could imagine Gabe at that age. Just a babe and laughing free as the breeze."

"Where was the mother? Her and her old husband?"

"Her husband was off at the mill, working his day job. She and I sat on the porch and drank the worst excuse for lemonade that I've ever put in my mouth. Tasted like horse piss."

"No, it didn't. And you know better. I take it you and she didn't get along."

"You take it correctly. After we sat and stared for a bit, drinking the horse piss, she suddenly up and asks me out of the blue, 'So, who are you, *Mrs.* Overbite?'"

This time he doesn't even try to stop himself from laughing. And though Bridget is crying still, she also begins to snicker through the tears. "Mrs. *Overbite!* She can't even get the father of her son's name right!"

"What did you say?"

"I said that no, I wasn't Mrs. *Overbay*, not yet. But that I had every intention."

"And how did she take that bit of news?"

They reach the edge of the creek, and he sits back against a large boulder, hoping the whisper sound of the water might soothe her nerves. After a moment, she sits beside him.

"She laughed and told me good luck. Said, 'I couldn't catch him, even with that.' And she nodded toward Jack, who is laughing out loud at the silly faces Gabe is making. 'We'll see if you can do any better,' says she."

"Well, it's as obvious as the day that he's yours if you want him. She could see that you've already reeled him in. Besides, their relationship is nothing to be jealous of. It couldn't have lasted more than a week if he was in town with the circus."

She suddenly sobs aloud and thrusts her head against his shoulder so hard she almost knocks him off the rock. Pushes against him till he puts his arm around her. "It lasted long enough for her to make a baby!" she wails.

"Bridget, darling, that doesn't take—"

"I keep trying and trying! Goddamn her, anyway."

"Oh," he says after a moment, his tired mind spinning in circles. "So *that's* what this is about."

"You say that like it's not the most important...important thing in the world, Papa."

"It may not be the *most* important thing," he whispers to her, meaning to comfort.

"It is if she can do it and I can't. Besides, what do you know about being a mother?" She is still sniffing, but the gasping and sobbing at least have subsided.

He shrugs. "Not much, I grant you. I had one—a mother, I mean—one that was awfully good to me in her quiet way, so I've seen it done from the start at least once." And then, after a moment, "I do know something about being a father. And I think that when it really matters to you, to you and Gabe both, when you're ready, then you'll have a child, or a child will come to you."

"What the hell does that even mean—a child will come to us? One will fall out of the sky?"

"Means that there are a lot of children in the world need raising. These days, it seems like I see them everywhere. And you, sweet thing, you will make a splendid mother when some of those children find you."

CHAPTER TWENTY-EIGHT

THAT NIGHT, AFTER THE SERVICE, the roustabouts break down the big top and pack it onto the *Saint John the Baptist* flatcar. They load the horses and prepare for an early-morning departure for the next stop—Hickory, North Carolina.

Once most everyone has turned in for the night, the Preacher walks out with Cassandra for some fresh air before sleep. They stroll hand in hand down the tracks to the first paved street they come to and then turn right onto a bridge over the Catawba River. As they walk along, he tells her about Bridget and her passion for a baby. They pause in the moonlight—relaxed, happy, used to each other. Any country couple.

That is, until they hear the voice. At first, it seems easy, smooth, almost oily. Somehow, he's slipped up on them from the town side of the bridge, and the first thing he says is this: "Take your hands off her, you pathetic old man."

At that instant, she knows who's speaking, and she is terrified. It takes him longer, not having grown up with the voice. He doesn't even recognize the thin, perfectly tailored figure until it takes another step forward, into the light cast by the two working street lamps in the center of the bridge. The man is holding a pistol that he has drawn from the holster on his belt, and he is pointing it with steady intent at the Preacher's chest.

"Father, no!" she says clearly. "Please, no." And in her own voice, she hears the echo of her childhood pleading.

"Stay there," the Preacher—Jedidiah—says to her. "Just stand still, and it will be all right." He gently untangles himself from her grip on his arm and slides sideways along the railing of the bridge, separating himself from her even as he edges slightly closer to William James, the High Sheriff of McDowell County.

"Don't get too close," James says.

"I mean no harm to you," the Preacher says very quietly, as if trying to soothe a dog or a drunk. "I just don't want you to shoot her by mistake." He thinks for a moment of the straight razor he carries in his pocket and how quickly he might have it open in his hand.

"I ain't here to shoot her," James says evenly, although the Preacher thinks he can detect a note of hysteria in the undertow of the man's voice. More sadness, perhaps, than anger. "I'm here to take her home." And then, almost as an afterthought. "And to take her away from you and your circus clowns."

"Don't you think that's her husband's job?" the Preacher asks almost conversationally, as if they'd just met at the post office and were discussing the weather.

"Her husband ain't worth the cloth and clay it took to make him," James says. "Beside which, he died."

"He *what?*" Cassie cries. "Died how?"

James, her father, pivots toward her almost as if her voice reminds him of her presence, his pistol turning with him till it points absentmindedly at her.

"Easy," the Preacher says to her. "Speak quietly. Let him talk to me, not you."

"That fool Bailey choked on a fish bone at one those covered dishes you people are always having. Sunday noon in the church-yard. Choked on a fish bone and then, while he was staggering around, managed to have a heart attack and pitched over a picnic table. Turned purple, I understand, though I wasn't there to see it."

"How long ago?" Jedidiah asks. And then again, louder, as James seems not to have heard. "How long ago, Sheriff?"

James pivots back to him, tightening his grip on the pistol. "Week before last, give or take a few days. The ladies of that church of his went crazy with grief. I would have telegraphed Cassie, but I didn't know where the high and mighty Solomon's Crusade might be hiding out."

"I'm sorry that happened," the Preacher says quietly. "I would never have wished it for him."

"Shit," James says. "You sure as hell wished it when you stole his wife away from him."

The Preacher can sense that Cassandra is about to speak, and he holds out his hand to silence her. "I didn't so much steal her as her husband ran her off. Don't you think?"

"Ain't what that Bible of yours says." James seems almost interested in the debate. "Says that if a woman is a whore and an adulterer, then her husband should cast her off."

"She's none of that, Sheriff," he says quietly. "You best not say that."

"I'll say what I damn well please to you." James steps toward him and raises the pistol to shoulder height, pointing it straight at the Preacher's face from perhaps three feet away. "Since you was the one that made a whore of her in the first place."

James' hand is shaking now, like his voice.

The Preacher can feel the muscles in his face and neck contract, painfully, expecting any second the impact of a bullet. He reaches into his pocket and grasps the handle of the straight razor.

"Slow down, Sheriff," a voice says. "Easy does it." This voice also comes from the town side of the bridge. Cassie and the Preacher know it immediately. It's the sound of gravel being shaken in a coal bucket—harsh, strong, and ever so dear. "Look at me, Sheriff," the voice says. "Before you let yourself get fancy with that trigger, look here to me."

Boss Strong has walked up on their little conclave while returning late from town, where he's dropped off a case of corn liquor in a backstreet speakeasy.

All three of their gazes shift toward his voice, both James and the Preacher turning their heads toward the sound. James' arm is still extended from his shoulder, his pistol pointing directly at the Preacher's head, but his face is turned to Boss.

Boss steps into the light and casually, almost as an afterthought, draws a snub-nosed .38 revolver from his coat pocket and raises it also to shoulder level, pointing it directly at the Sheriff's face, intending to hold his gaze with the barrel. The only difference is that his hand, despite years of hard drinking, is rock-solid still. That, and he is smiling at the sheriff, as if glad to see him.

"That man over there," Boss says conversationally. "My friend Jedidiah. He's like a brother to me. In fact, he's treated me far better than any old sorry-ass brother I could have had. And you've somehow gone astray such that you're pointing that police special of yours at him. I imagine it's loaded, ain't it?"

James nods. "Of course it's loaded, you con-*vict*."

"Fair enough. Mine's loaded too. So we're equal, wouldn't you say? And if you was so careless as to accidentally shoot that man, that man who is like a brother to me, even so much as to nick his earlobe or shoot off a hank of that pretty hair of his, then I would have to kill you. And just so you know, I can do it so fast that you'll be dead before it occurs to you to fall down."

"You can't scare me," James says. "You're nothing but a fucking criminal."

Boss nods. "That and worse. But here now, I don't want you scared. Scared men make mistakes. I want you smart. So smart that I want you to lower your arm nice and easy. Down to your side. And then I want you to bend over and lay that pistol of yours on the bridge. Everything so slow that nobody goes from here to the graveyard."

James doesn't move, although his right hand, holding the pistol, is shaking worse now. Uncontrollably, as if palsied.

"If you don't lower your arm, I'm going to kill you anyway," Boss shrugs and says after a moment. Boss glances at Cassandra to read her mind. Her face is in shadow, so he speaks. "Cassie, he's your father. Tell him I mean it."

After a slight pause, she does speak, as if measuring her words out with a spoon. "Boss is a tough man, Father. And he loves Jedidiah. He would like to shoot you."

Boss nods at her across the ten feet of lamp-lit air between them. "That's right," he says to the sheriff. "I actually would enjoy it." And then his voice deepens suddenly, into a harsh baritone whisper. "Lay the damn gun down, Sheriff, or I'll kill you where you stand before you have time to piss your pants."

"I ain't afraid," James says, his head starting to shake now like his hand. "I come here to punish him." He nods spastically at Jedidiah.

Boss sighs and look straight at Cassandra, his gun hand never wavering. "What do you want, Cassie? You get to choose: Jedidiah or this shit-ass excuse for a father. Which is it going to be?"

"Oh God," she whispers. "Don't make me choose." She can feel Boss' eyes drilling into her. "Don't let him hurt Jedidiah," she whispers finally to Boss. "Do what you have to do."

"Good girl," Boss says. "You heard her, Dad. Lay down the gun or die." He takes a step forward and cocks the .38.

James doesn't bend, but his grasp on the pistol grip relaxes, and the gun drops straight to the bridge deck, clattering harmlessly across the pavement toward Jedidiah.

Boss steps up to James and, with a broad roundhouse swing, whips him across his ear with the .38, knocking him to his knees. And again, backhanded, across the face, knocking him sideways to the ground.

The Preacher sighs, steps forward decisively, lifts the curled form of the sheriff as if picking up a bundle of dirty clothes, and tosses him over the bridge railing into the river below. "Son of a bitch," he says hoarsely. They hear the splash of body striking water.

"Sorry, Cassie," Boss says almost as an afterthought. "I hope he can swim."

She walks forward, ignoring Jedidiah for this moment, and puts her arms around Boss' shoulders. "Thank you," she whispers into his broad back. "Just…thank you."

Interlude

I F THE SOUTHERN CLERGYMAN IS THE EPITOME of dim-witted bullying, then it must be said that the redneck evangel-ical, the tent preacher, carries loud-mouthed ignorance to new and dizzying heights. Ranting and raving against anything that smells of culture or education or refinement, he thunders away like a poor man's Billy Sunday, reviling everything he doesn't understand and waving his hymn book like a club, ready to smite sin in the face—blissfully unaware that his own blindness and callowness are the crudest sort of sin. It is not enough that these men—and a surprising number of women—are besotted by their Bible; they are bred out of the poorest human stock imaginable and must stamp and howl like animals once they mount the pul-pit. They are not washed in the blood of the lamb; their champ-ing jaws are dripping with it. If ignorance were truly bliss, the Southern preacher would never shed a tear.

What do they hate, these apostles of buncombe? It would be easier to say what they don't hate, but a short list of their sworn enemies must include the arts, the letters, and any music not shaped and noted in the hymnal. They hate the North; they hate the city; they hate education of any sort that might lead their children to Darwin or to Dickens. They hate dancing, except when possessed by the Holy Spirit; and they hate any type of language not cornfield English unless it involves speaking in tongues. It goes without saying that they hate sex, for they fear and hate the human body. But most of all, they hate liquor. The spirit they worship does not allow those lesser spirits distilled in keg or barrel. And while they might imbibe in private, they are often found staging full frontal assaults on the local saloon.

Thus it was that I went down into the benighted South recently, my own fiery sword of journalistic purity raised high and ready to smite. I had read of one such brush-arbor pugilist who had preached a famous sermon against liquor not in the evangelical tent, not in the sanctuary of the local Baptist den, not even on the street corner; but in the courtroom of the county courthouse, mounting not the pulpit but a judge's bench. If this were any place on earth other than America—where we hold with separating church and state—I would not have been surprised to read about this infamous sermon. But as imprudent as American jurisprudence can sometimes be, this is surely a low point for the halls of justice—even in the South.

Thus I went down to North Carolina to find and impale this impostor of God, this Solomon—for that is his nom de preach—on the point of my pen. But when I arrived there, in a small red-clay town not far from where the infamous sermon itself is alleged to have taken place, I found something unexpected. I found a man, not a shaman.

Jedidiah Robbins, for that is his real name, is descended not from the postwar carpetbaggers who invaded his home state, but from the local white trash who were too poor to leave after the Confederacy threw away the war. Somehow, this son of starving, scratch-a-furrow-in-the-earth farmers got himself an education. And when I confronted him with his sins, he had the nerve to wave this august publication (*The American Mercury*) in my face and quote my own distinguished prose against me. Along with that of Montaigne and Marcus Aurelius. Strong words, indeed, from the mouth of an evangelical bred out of the teeming loins of pine-tree peasantry. But Montaigne, dear reader, is a Frenchman, and so may be dismissed for a prancing fool. And Marcus Aurelius, though he comes from strong Roman stock, has been dead for lo these many years.

Long, long into the night, we strove—this Solomon Robbins and I—with the result that we found ourselves more allies than enemies, and even I had to admit a strange kinship. For what this man hates is not education but ignorance, not music but discord, not language but babel. When he preaches, the lightning bolts he flings into the dark corners of his circus tent come so thick and so fast that I'm certain his audience—made up of the ignorant proletariat, both white and black—misses three-fourths of what he is trying to say.

What *is* he trying to say? *Feed the poor. Teach the children. Turn no one away.* Do I agree with him? Of course not, or at least not most of it, for it is soft-headed balderdash. What astounds me is that he actually believes these things, and that his beliefs are founded seemingly on knowledge, not ignorance. Where did this man come from? And for God's sake, rescue him out of the Southern desert before his inbred, cross-eyed cousins rise up and nail him to a tree!

—H. L. Mencken
The American Mercury

PART THREE

MAY 1927

CHAPTER TWENTY-NINE

HAVING SLEPT ALONE THE NIGHT after the confrontation on the bridge, the Preacher is up early, when it's still dark. By the light of a single candle, he pours water into the battered tin coffeepot, shakes ground coffee into the pot's metal basket, and sets it on the woodstove. He feeds the hot ashes in the stove just enough pine splinters to start a flame and then just enough kindling to boil his coffee.

He has dreamed in the night that he is a ghost rather than a man. In the dream, he first assumed he was alive but discovered that his hand passed through solid objects—and that when he drank or ate, he tasted nothing. It came to him that he was merely a spirit, precisely one-eighth alive and seven-eighths gone. *One-eighth* seemed to be important in the dream, for it left him with the curse of consciousness.

He wasn't frightened in the dream but rather resigned to his role, and as he wakes that morning, he wonders how ghosts—like his long-lost Rachel or like himself—manage to communicate. Could they, if they concentrated, move objects for the living? Could he speak in the dreams of others as Rachel talks to him in his? He doesn't know, but he will ask Rachel next time she visits him.

Still, though, he is glad that his hands, his arms, his shoulders at least seem to be real, returned to solid flesh even as it is still dark outside. When he pours out his first cup of coffee, he can feel the steam on his lips and eyelids as he blows on the surface to cool it. And he can, thank God, taste it hot and strong after the first few sips.

He knows now that he has been away during the night; but, for some reason, he has returned. He doesn't mind, he decides, having to come back. Doesn't mind the rough touch of the world—at least for now.

He decides to take his second cup and walk down the tracks to the bridge where they'd baptized Sheriff James the night before. He assumes the sheriff is long gone, returned to McDowell County to lick his wounds and plan his next assault. As he walks carefully along the tracks in the dark, the sky in the east features lighter shades of blue at horizon's edge, and the few high clouds are tinged with pink by the time he reaches the pavement and walks out onto the bridge.

What he sees there in the lamplight startles him. A man is standing just where the sheriff went over the railing. He is tall and thin, dressed all in khaki, as if in uniform. For a moment, the Preacher thinks that he is some sort of law enforcement, a deputy already on the case. But then the figure straightens from the railing and turns.

The Preacher begins to recognize him. His rough brogans and his battered fedora. In his surprise, the Preacher tries to recall where they've met, where he's seen this scarecrow before. Then the scarecrow speaks, and his fractured memories coalesce. There's a bluebird feather in his hatband now rather than red cardinal, but the voice is the same.

"Hidy!" The figure flings up one bony arm happily. "Hidy there, Preacher. What do you reckon the fishin is like here on this bridge? The water movin kinda slow down there, but I'm bettin on a trout or two."

"Festus?"

"Oh, yes sir, yes sir, that's right." The man is bobbing up and down like a cork on the water. "That's me. I'm proud and honored that you remember. And your name is Solo-mon the Wise, just like it says on the side of your train."

"What the hell are you doing here? This isn't your territory."

"I'm fishin, I tell you. Always a-fishin. And Preacher, I'll let you in on a little secret." The eyes grow big in the skeletal face. "I ain't got no locomotive like you, but I get around anyhow I can. Sometimes I even hop a freight when the yard bulls ain't lookin."

"How do you live? What do you eat?"

"Well, now." The bony old man stretches up to his full height and rubs at his raspy chin. "That's the question, ain't it? Truth is, I eat anything and everything. Anything livin—animal or vegetable—I'll eat it when the time comes. I'm always hungry, but I just can't seem to put on no weight."

"You aren't following us, are you? Following the crusade, I mean."

"Oh, no, I'm way too busy a man for that. I got appointments all up and down. I just happened to crisscross your path, Preacher. That's all. Don't you worry none about me. I'll see you when I see you." And this time the jaunty figure actually sweeps the hat off his bald head and bows to the Preacher before turning and walking away, his gait a strange kind of gimp and hitch as he disappears.

Later that morning, when he and Boss meet to compare notes on what next, the topic of the sheriff, Cassie's father, comes up. "Should we send Fingers up to Marion to look around?" Boss asks. "See if the bastard is all right?"

"I don't think so," the Preacher replies after a moment. "I think he's dead."

Boss looks up sharply from his coffee.

"I don't know," the Preacher says. "It's just a feeling."

CHAPTER THIRTY

Wᴵᴸᴸᴵᴬᴹ Jᴬᴹᴱˢ' ꜰᵁᴺᴱᴿᴬᴸ ᴵˢ ᴮᴵᴳ ᴺᴱᵂˢ in the foothills of western North Carolina. It isn't often that a sheriff dies while in office, and especially under suspicious circumstances. He apparently visited a neighboring town by himself at night and fell into the Catawba River, where two feet of rushing water smashed him into a bridge abutment and drowned him. The undertaker recommended that his casket be closed for the services.

The sheriff's daughter, Cassandra James Bailey, is the only next of kin other than his ancient sister, who came in from the country to identify the body. Interestingly enough, it is not the sheriff's deputies who suspect foul play, but the women of Marion. They are the ones who figure out that Solomon's Crusade was in Morganton the night the sheriff died, and that meant Cassie Bailey along with all the roughnecks who attend the trains. It is the women, of course, who begin to talk as soon as news of the sheriff's death reaches the streets of Marion. If men follow the trail of money, women follow the trail of blood or sex. Crying and sniffing the ground.

To dispel the rumors, the Preacher and Cassie decide to attend the sheriff's funeral, along with Gabe and Bridget. Together they represent the crusade, with three of the four there to support Cassie, the deceased's only child. The fact that she ran from her father's fists and hid from a husband who once or twice suffered those same fists is not lost on the assembled multitude. It only adds to the drama that is any funeral.

The First Baptist Church of Marion is located at 99 North Main, one of two paved streets in the whole town. It is deemed an appropriate site for the memorial observance because the sheriff had once attended a service there. That, and it is big enough to hold over three hundred people in its pews. Cassie sits in the family section, with Bridget to support her. The Preacher and Gabe sit a few rows back, where they can offer mute emotional reinforcement during the service.

When the Presbyterian minister comes in, he recognizes the Preacher. He leans over and, as he shakes the Preacher's hand, whispers to him. "Come on up, brother. You're a minister of Christ just like the rest of us. Come on up and say a few words." And though he resists briefly, the Preacher is led up to the platform behind the pulpit, where he takes a chair in the choir section along with several ministers of the town.

For as it turns out, Sheriff James hadn't belonged to any one church or denomination. He is reckoned the property of all these preachers equally, and since neither Cassie nor her aunt has chosen a lead, the town's ministers decided to take turns memorializing a man who was a known stranger to God.

So each in turn takes a shot—Presbyterian, Methodist, Baptist, Church of Christ—all before the Preacher rises to finish up, having been given the last spot on the roster as something like a visiting celebrity.

During the preliminary hymn and the somewhat mangled efforts of the first half dozen speakers, the Preacher has been staring at his daughter Bridget and at Cassandra beside her. He knows that Cassie's mother died when she was seventeen, and that the dead man in the coffin represents the last link to her history. As brutal as William James had been, he was her father. And somehow, he realizes, he must respond to that deep mystery. He himself is the only father that Bridget will ever have; William James is the only father that Cassie will ever have.

"'Verily, verily, I say unto you, Except a corn of wheat fall into the ground and die, it abideth alone: but if it die, it bringeth forth much fruit.'"

When it is his turn, he begins with this one verse, spoken from memory. He pauses. Then: "We are all, each of us, but a kernel. What John calls a *corn of wheat*—that is all we are in this world. We are none of us whole, none of us complete. We are here on this earth separated from God, so that we might learn and grow, and then someday return to Him through death—and, in returning, bear the fruit of our learning from this shadowy earth.

"The man or woman who can seem the most cold and distant is wrapped up in a cocoon. The man or woman who struggles to reach out, whom we struggle to reach, is like that corn of wheat, that hard kernel of feeling and thought, trying desperately to know and be known.

"We may condemn them out of hand because they are not open and fresh and available to us. But the truth is that all are available to God. All will blossom under the fierce light of His sun. For some of us, the summertime of the soul comes here and now; for some, it comes only when we fall."

It is just then that he notices the strange old man, Festus, seated in the very first row of the congregation. Somewhere, the old geezer has found a suit of black cloth and a blood-red tie. He is happily grinning, obviously enjoying the Preacher's remarks. And at the pause in the funeral sermon, he nods enthusiastically, urging the Preacher on into the champing maw of death.

"For some of us," the Preacher continues, "the fruit and the flower come only at the very last call, when we drop into the ground and die. For some of us, that last test is required to render us whole. And that, I believe, is the case with our brother

William James, whose body lies before us here. He seemed a careful, close man in life, but now, just now, he is made all of flaming color as he approaches the throne of God. He is all flowing gold and vermilion, magenta and royal purple. He is catching fire in response to the pure light that is God. I tell you now, he burns with joy."

Strangely, the old man Festus seems to almost float above the bench he sits on, so taken is he with the Preacher's words. His eyes are closed as he shakes in a kind of funereal ecstasy.

The four of them—Cassie plus the Preacher, Bridget, and Gabe—follow along with the line of mourners who walk solemnly to the town cemetery and see the plain wooden casket lowered into the ground by deputy sheriffs. It is here, finally, standing beside the open grave, that Cassie breaks down in tears and collapses—not into Bridget's arms but into his arms, those of her Jedidiah.

CHAPTER THIRTY-ONE

THE FUNERAL WAS ON A MONDAY AFTERNOON. The visitor comes to the *Sword of the Lord* the next night, a Tuesday. The *Saint John the Baptist* rig has already pulled out for the next town, with Gabe aboard, leaving Bridget behind to be with Cassie during the days immediately following her father's burial.

They are all in the club car—the Preacher, Cassie, and Bridget—when he comes knocking. And though the women are tempted to leave, the Preacher asks them to stay even after the portly, distinguished man in the fine suit introduces himself. The Preacher hopes the women's presence will discourage the visitor, send him sooner on his way.

"My name is Mark Dixon," he explains. "Perhaps you've heard of me. I'm a former lawman myself, like our dearly departed sheriff." With this he nods at Cassandra. "But now I ply my trade as a banker. And I greet you in the name of the Sacred, Unfailing Being."

Jezebel streaks forward and nips at the banker's legs, who swats at the dog with a bundle of papers he clutches in his hand. The Preacher picks Jezebel up as she continues to snarl at Dixon and tosses her out the backdoor of the club car.

The Preacher almost offers Mark Dixon a drink to make up for Jezebel but stops himself, imagining that a glass in Dixon's hand can only detain him, when neither the Preacher nor the women want any of the outside world on this sad evening, unfailing being or no.

After the briefest pleasantries, including extending an invitation to sit down in the most uncomfortable chair in the car, he asks Dixon to state his business. "I know I'm being short with you, sir, but as you can see, we're in mourning."

"Not at all. Not at all. Let us not stand on ceremony. I'm here as the representative of a social organization with which you, yourself, share many important values." And then after a pause. "May I speak freely, sir? Before you and the ladies."

He nods. "Of course you may. The ladies are my family. And we have no secrets between us."

Dixon clears his throat. "I am come to you as the Kleagle of western North Carolina, the whole western half of our great state."

"What did you say?" he asks. "Beagle?"

"Oh, no," Dixon chuckles as if he's never heard the joke before. "Kleagle. It's a term we use for a certain rank of leadership. I am one of founders of the Klavern of western North Carolina. A young and vibrant part of the new-style Ku Klux Klan—which, I might add, is growing daily across our great state and nation."

"But isn't the Klan against Negroes? We none of us here are against the colored man." He thinks of Gabe with his Melungeon blood as he says this, and glances at Bridget. He thinks of Jesus the Son-of-God Smith and smiles.

"Oh no, no," Dixon says. "Those were the old days. The days after the war. We aren't against the good, solid, Protestant colored man at all. We're against liquor. That's what I meant. We're against liquor, and you, sir, of all people, are famously against it as well. In fact, since your courthouse sermon, you are like a hero to us.

"And yesterday, when I saw you again, standing tall in the pulpit, preaching over the body of one of our fallen comrades, I was suddenly inspired—as if God had flung a lightning bolt down out of the sky and hit me in the head."

"You're saying that my father belonged to the Klan?" Cassie asked.

"Belonged! Why, he was one of our first and one of our best. He saw before anyone else that the forces of law and justice alone couldn't stop the flow of whiskey into our communities. He knew that he and his deputies would need help to confound the evil influence of the saloon and the speakeasy.

"He knew that a happy marriage between the sheriff's office and the Secret Brotherhood could create an army for good. An undeniable force for God, the Protestant church, and the Anglo-Saxon race."

Bridget moves over to sit beside Cassie on the divan. Puts her arm around Cassie's shoulders and pulls her close.

"We believe you," the Preacher says. "So the good sheriff was a soldier in your cause."

"More than that," Dixon exclaims. "Sheriff James was a veritable dragon in our cause." Then he leans forward, as if to speak in confidence. "And that, Brother Solomon, is what I've come to talk to you about. We need you. We need you to become a recruiter to the Secret Brotherhood, a shining example of purity and commitment. I assume you know that we have taken pithy excerpts from your courthouse sermon and captured them in a series of pamphlets that are designed to draw every true Christian into our ranks." Dixon carefully places three colorful brochures on the desk in front of the Preacher. Each of the brochures is adorned with a white cross displayed against a blood-red background. Dixon taps the image with his forefinger. "I have a vision, Preacher Solomon, that I believe is divinely inspired. I have a vision of that blood-drop cross painted on every car on this train, taking our image and our message into every city and town you come to."

"Did it ever occur to you to ask for permission to quote that sermon in your…pamphlets?"

Dixon draws back with a dramatic flourish. "How can anyone ask permission to quote the direct and inspired word of God? For you, sir, are the mouthpiece of the divine. You are the source of our inspiration!"

"I'm just a man, Mr. Dixon, with very little of the divine to speak of."

"I beg to disagree. And because of that, I want to ask you to become a leader in our movement. We are organizing in this, your home state, to fight those who make and sell the liquor—especially the Jews, the niggers, and the Catholics."

"Come again?"

"You know full well that the liquor problem is not really an issue for the Anglo-Saxon race. We don't imbibe so that we can subvert the social order, run amok, and break the law. If and when people like us take a small nip, it's so that we can lay down the heavy burdens of maintaining our culture and supporting our intellectual heritage. We, sir, are not the problem."

"If we aren't, who is?"

"Why, the dissatisfied among us. The nigger who don't know his natural place. The Jew who cares only for money and nothing else. The Catholic who worships Christ's mother rather than Christ himself. These are the cancers in our body politic, sir, and I have a feeling you know exactly what I'm talking about. One of our favorite sayings in the Klavern is that we will wipe out the homebrew *and* the Hebrew." Dixon rocked back in his straight chair, emitting a squeal like a rusty spring. They realize after a moment that he is laughing, chortling at his own humor.

"Is there a place for us women in your new religion, Mr. Dixon?" Bridget asks innocently.

"Oh, I'm so glad you asked that," the man exclaims. "Have you heard of the WKKK?"

Bridget shakes her head no.

"It's the Women of the Klan. There are thousands of members already in Indiana. Thousands more in Oregon and Washington state. We have long hoped to launch a branch here in North Carolina, and you and Miss Cassandra would be the perfect starting point. And like Preacher Solomon here," he pauses to nod deferentially, "you would be in a perfect position to recruit new members as you travel across the country."

"I believe you mentioned the Negro, the Jew, and the Catholic as our enemies," Bridget says, smiling brightly. "Is there anybody else out there that we should steer clear of while we're... recruiting?"

Dixon leans forward and lowers his voice. "I can tell you-all this, even though we don't go around saying it in public just yet. My colleagues in Indiana, with whom I'm in almost daily contact through the mails—they worry about the Irish. You have to imagine the pubs of our great Northern cities, run by an old toper named Mick O'Conner or some such. My colleagues in the North call them green niggers." He pauses expectantly for effect, and indeed there is a smile growing on the Preacher's face. "And you have to remember that every Paddy who ever lived takes his orders straight from the pope."

The Preacher can contain himself no longer and laughs outright. "The pope? In Rome?"

Dixon, encouraged, winks at him and says, "Ladies, you may want to cover your ears. Preacher, do you know what happens when a nigger gal marries an Irish?"

Cassie has begun quietly to cry, and Bridget, realizing this, shakes her head ever so slightly at her father. Who starts to interrupt Dixon but is too late.

"Up North they call em leprecoons!" crows Dixon. And begins again to rock and squeak. So pleased with himself that he doesn't notice that he's the only one laughing. From the rear platform, Jezebel begins to bark.

"That's enough," the Preacher says with his pulpit voice. "That's enough from you."

"What?" Dixon is slowly recovering himself. Too slowly.

"We will not help you," the Preacher says slowly. "The New Testament forbids it. And we couldn't join you even if we would. In our troupe, we employ a man named Scully. Cassie, help me."

"Irish," she whispers, "with a tattoo of the Virgin on his thigh."

"A man named Klein, who is our veterinarian and doctor."

"Jewish." Cassie has stopped crying but is still sniffing.

"A man named Blaesius."

"German, although he is learning to speak English."

"A man named Jesus the-Son-of-God Smith."

"A very black man."

"A man named Overbay."

Cassie glances at Bridget, who shrugs and answers for her. "Only God knows what Gabe is. Brown skin, blue eyes...."

"And a man named Robbins along with his daughter."

"Who are undisputedly Irish bogtrotters." Bridget again. "With just enough Scots, blood stirred in to make us mongrels."

CHAPTER THIRTY-TWO

THE FOLLOWING FRIDAY NIGHT. Hickory, North Carolina. The crusade tent set up on an elementary school playground near the train station. The evening is as sweet as stick candy. A hint of tree-shaded wildflowers and birdsong in the sultry air.

The children from the school spent recess that day watching as the roustabouts with the Percherons set up the big top, astonished by the size of the men and even more so of the horses, especially when the boy Micah led the beasts about as if they were enormous, very tame dogs. Dogs that like to play with the boy as if he were a ball or a wisp of straw. Several of the horses love to nudge him from behind with their giant heads to see if they can push him over, and one likes best of all to munch on Micah's hair whenever he is within reach. It is obvious to the children that the horses love the boy, and they are as jealous of him and his life as it is possible for any one human being to be of another.

It occurs to the Preacher that the children from the school will bring their parents back to the service that night, if only so that they might have another chance to see the horses.

"What we need," he says to Cassie as they sit in the sun that afternoon, down by tracks where the *Sword of the Lord* is parked. "What we need is a children's crusade. Singing and storytelling. No adults allowed."

"And horseback rides." She shades her eyes against the sun as she smiles at him.

"And horseback rides," he says. And then after a pause, "That, most of all."

"And some goats. I've always wanted to have some goats."

211

He opens his eyes to study her face. "What in the world would we do with goats?"

She shrugs. "I just like them. They're curious. They're funny. Children love them, especially the baby goats."

"Goats have devil eyes."

"Well, so do you sometimes."

He laughs out loud. "I suppose so. I suppose we all do."

"How do you feel about children, Jedidiah? Really feel about them? You and your children's crusade."

"I wish Bridget could have one."

Cassie pauses for a moment, considering. "She's trying very hard."

"I'm sure she is. She seems to want a baby more than anything."

Now Cassie has shut her eyes, resting them from the hot sunlight as she leans back on both hands. "She thinks that will tie Gabe to her."

"That's silly. Can't she tell she has him wrapped around her finger and tied in a knot?"

"She knows that in her head, but deeper down in her body, she's afraid that somehow she'll lose him."

"Afraid because of that other child? That boy in Morganton?"

Cassie nods and says, "Jackson. His name is Jackson. And yes, she's afraid because of that."

That evening, as Bridget and Cassandra walk up the path from the train station toward the school where the tent is pitched, Cassie suddenly grabs her friend's arm. Bridget turns to study her face, but Cassie doesn't speak, only shakes her head. She darts into the trees beside the path, bends from the waist, and vomits into the dusty weeds. Once, twice, and then a dry retching.

After a long moment, Cassie steps back onto the path, and Bridget hands her a handkerchief to wipe her mouth.

"Have you told him yet?" she asks.

Cassie shakes her head. "I tried this afternoon," she gasps, still catching her breath. "Don't look at me like that. Sometimes he can be as dense as…"

"I know how he is. Do you want me to tell him?"

"No. Not yet. He's not ready yet."

That night, lightning bugs circulate in the trees that line the elementary school playground. The smell of red clay mixes with the fragrance of pine woods in the late spring evening.

The place and time feel slow to the Preacher, slow with an almost palpable sweetness in the air. For some indefinable reason, he is sad tonight. Melancholy with the Kingdom Come beauty of it all. He feels transparent, as he often does these days. Almost as if he is permeable to the rays of light that drift through the honeysuckle evening.

So he preaches more softly tonight, with a more measured tone. And he takes his text from Matthew, the sixth chapter. "'Consider the lilies of the field, how they grow; they toil not, neither do they spin.'"

He swings his arms wide with this verse, letting in all of ambient nature with its thronging, throbbing life. The katydids chirp in the honey-thick night beyond the tent. "'And yet I say unto you, that even Solomon in all his glory was not arrayed like one of these.'" He brings his hands together before his chest and bows his head, while the people laugh at his little scriptural joke on himself. "'Take therefore no thought for the morrow: for the morrow shall take thought for the things of itself.'"

After a moment of prayer, with the afternoon's thoughts about children ghosting through his mind, he begins. "The truth," he says evenly, conversationally, "the truth is that we don't trust God. The truth is that we think we must manufacture our own happiness, build our own lives out of brick and mortar. The truth is that we trust our own judgment sometimes more than we trust God's. We care for our own thoughts more than the Creator's thoughts, our own tears more than those of Jesus weeping at the tomb of Lazarus.

"And perhaps our ceaseless striving, our unremitting effort, our constant worrying and fretting and scheming—perhaps that is what stands between us and God. Like a wall made out of our own sweat. Perhaps that is what Matthew is warning us against in his gospel. Could we not be as simple as, as beautiful as, the lilies in the field? Could we not care for—"

He is interrupted by a scream from the back of the tent.

Later, they will find out that it began with a child, a young boy sent outside by his mother to answer the call of nature, where he sees the hooded figures actually dousing the giant cross with kerosene. When he runs back in and grabs his mother's arm, she turns and sees the flames close to the tent and screams for help. And then, sobbing, calling out, "Oh, my dear Jesus. Fire!"

It is a hot night for almost summer, and the sides of the tent are rolled halfway up, so the crowd flees in all directions. Men dragging women, women screaming for their children.

The roustabouts filter through the crowd and gather around Boss Strong, who stands in the open doorway of the big top facing the half dozen cloaked and hooded figures guarding the burning cross.

Gabe recruits a few of the men to help him soak the canvas closest to the flames with buckets of water from the nearby hose spigot. But the hard cases—Cederberg, Klein, Scully, Fingers Spivey, and Jesus the-Son-of-God—line up beside Boss, whose face takes on a dark, harsh light in the reflected flames. The six Klansmen stand in formation with folded arms around the flaming cross. The one to Boss' right holds a shotgun across his chest and seems to be breathing especially hard.

Boss ignores the shotgun and walks forward until his face is inches away from the hooded head of the leader, who stands front and center before the cross. It is sizzling hot this close to the flames, and Boss' voice is even more hoarse than usual in the furnace. It growls from deep in his throat.

"You boys done shit the bed," Boss whispers. "You done thought all you had to deal with was women and children and sorry sons of God who would run like scalded dogs when you lit up your fireworks. You didn't count on us, and now we're going to rip them sheets off you and beat you till you piss blood."

"You and your ilk have no rights here," the leader proclaims loudly, as if declaiming to an imaginary crowd. "You are trespassers in a God-fearing community, and we are representatives of the Sacred, Unfailing Being."

As Boss is discoursing with the lead Klansman, Fingers edges around to the sheet holding the shotgun. He smiles and nods, and then, without even glancing down, he slips the double barrel out of the man's hands, breaks it open, and ejects the two shells onto the ground. Casually, he tosses the shotgun to the side as if discarding a broken tool. "Don't mind me," he says out of the side of his mouth to Boss. "Go on about your business."

The lead Klansman is apparently a short, fat man, but he does have the blood-drop cross embroidered on the front of his robe and so must be some sort of sergeant or lieutenant in the secret society. After Fingers speaks, Boss hawks loudly from his throat, spits into his hand, and smears the tobacco-stained spittle over the cross.

"You goddamned cur, you—"

This before Boss hits him so hard between his eye slits that he falls back against the cross and his hood catches fire.

Two of the Klansmen run fast and away, so there are only four left to deal with. They are overrun almost immediately by the roughnecks, for whom this sort of melee was an every-Saturday-night occurrence in the circus world. After they have laid out the Klansmen and cut their robes off of them, they tip back each pale, white face before it passes out, holding the straining jaws wide so that Jesus the-Son-of-God can hawk and spit into their gaping mouths.

CHAPTER THIRTY-THREE

FOR THE FIRST TIME since her father's funeral, Cassandra Bailey stays through the night with the Preacher, safely inside his arms. Once they are mostly asleep, Jezebel joins them, curling up on the Preacher's side of the bed, down at his feet. All this—the woman and the dog, a quiet night—this is paradise, he decides before he drifts off. This peace, this passion…a prelude to what is to come. On earth as it is in Heaven, and he smiles in his sleep. With her arms around him, he is not afraid of his dreams—even dreams haunted by hooded figures.

It is in the dark middle watch that Heaven is invaded by the metallic stench and lurid light of Hell.

When he gently separates himself from her arms and rises to go outside to the privy, he sees down the tracks what looks like a bonfire, except it is located directly underneath *Saint John the Baptist*.

He yells to alert Cassie and the dog.

Jezebel is down the iron steps and with him in a flash, even as he starts to run. He goes in his boxer shorts and an old torn shirt, barefoot in the harsh gravel, yelling out warnings. The dog races ahead, barking her own alarm.

Someone has thrown bales of hay under the two central cars on the rig and set them ablaze. As yet, the fire is only licking up around the edges of the cars, probing for air and fuel. Jezebel's frantic barking and the Preacher's hoarse shouts bring men pouring out of the passenger car, where Bridget, Gabe, and the roustabouts sleep. They are in all stages of undress, these men. Men, yes, but no Bridget.

So he half limps, half runs into the middle of the fire, up the platform steps, the hot iron burning his feet. The interior of the car is full of acrid gray smoke, billowing inside the constricted space. He is shouting her name as he all but crashes into her in the dark, dragging Gabe behind her, already a victim of the smoke. Together they drag the boy out the door, wrenching his unconscious body free of the opening and down the iron stairs.

There is shouting and yelling all around as the German, Blaesius, picks Gabe up and carries him farther from the flames. Bridget follows in just her slip, the once-white fabric blackened like her skin by the smoke. Even as she follows her unconscious lover, she screams at the men to get the horses.

For inside the second car are the Percherons—and young Micah. Hack Ramsey, Micah's father, ignores the searing heat and leads the men charging into the stable car. He emerges a moment later carrying Micah over his shoulder as the boy fights him to go back to the horses.

He hands Micah to Boss, who has just come running up, naked except for a fedora jammed onto his head. Boss takes the thrashing, squirming boy into a bear hug, and Hack dashes back up the ramp. Straw is burning now on the floor of the stable car, and the heat is bubbling the paint off the steel walls. The horses are screaming and crashing against the sides of the car in pain and fear. With a nod at Jedidiah, Boss turns and walks steadily away from the fire, carrying the boy over his shoulder, away from the horror.

Cassie has brought Jedidiah's shoes and makes him put them on his burned and blistered feet before running on to help Bridget with Gabe.

Jedidiah grabs Fingers as he rushes by with a bucket. "Get Cederberg, unhook on both sides," he pants. "Unhook the cars on…sides of the fire." Fingers grasps his meaning at once and starts yelling for the Swede and Jesus, the Swede to fire the engine while he and Jesus unhook the rest of the train fore and aft.

One by one, the roughnecks manage to get soaking-wet tow sacks over the heads of the horses and lead them screaming and kicking down the ramp and away from the fire. One, then two side by side, then one more leaping over the ramp and galloping away toward town. Hack Ramsey climbs the ramp a final time, willing himself into the black square of the door surrounded now by leaping flame, coughing up smoke as he goes into Hell for the last horse.

The rear cars of the train, the storage car and Bible car, are rolling safely away now, down a slight incline toward the *Sword of the Lord,* Jesus trotting along beside them. The front is unhooked behind the flatcar. Fingers and Cederberg are working heroically to fire the boilers for steam enough to pull it to safety.

The burning stable car finally collapses into a snarling, writhing pandemonium of flame, engulfing the last Percheron and killing Hack Ramsey instantly. The horse screams horribly in pain, the man not at all.

CHAPTER THIRTY-FOUR

THE PREACHER IS EXHAUSTED from the long night. His feet are fire-blistered. The boy Micah is with Cassandra in the saints' car on the *Sword of the Lord*. After the fire, she gives him milk laced with brandy and holds him till he falls finally into a restless, tear-stained sleep. Gabe is in the local clinic, suffering from smoke inhalation and watched over by Bridget, who only leaves his side during the night to find temporary stabling for the four horses that survived the fire.

And so they are three—the Preacher, Boss, and Fingers—sharing a full pot of coffee in the club car at first light.

"We should've posted a watchman," the Preacher begins.

"I never thought they'd come back," Boss admits, "after what we done to them earlier. And now we got two large-ass problems. We got a smoking wreck instead of housing for the boys and stabling for the horses. That's one. And two, we got the goddamned Klan painted a target on us." Boss waves restlessly at a fly buzzing over his coffee before sipping from his mug.

"Two more," the Preacher says, blowing on his coffee to cool it. "Although maybe they go together."

"What am I missing?"

"We got a dead body in the wreckage," Fingers says. He pauses and plucks the fly that is aggravating Boss cleanly out of the air. "Gotta be a funeral."

"That's one problem," the Preacher nods. "Plus we've got an orphan on our hands."

Boss shakes his head. "That's no problem. Micah belongs with us. We're his family now."

221

"He's awful young. What is he? Ten?"

"Twelve," Fingers says. "Small for his age."

"He goes with us," Boss says stubbornly.

"What about school? Boy has to have schooling."

Boss shrugs. "I never had no schooling to matter, but I do see your point." He tastes his coffee and then adds another spoonful of cane sugar to it. "He'll live in a different world than the one we make do in."

Fingers shakes his head. "We got our own school," he says. "Miss Bridget teaches Gabe to read and write. She teaches Jerry to speak English, and she's started teaching Jesus his letters. Micah can go to school with her for a teacher." He looks up at the Preacher. "I vote with Boss. His mama's dead, and we can't let him go off by hisself into them dark hills."

"All right. He stays with us. What about the train cars and the Klan?"

"Leave the two cars to me," Fingers says. We got four gen-u-wine train men on the payroll, including yours truly, by the by. The way I figure it, this sorry-ass town owes us two or three boxcars at least, and if we can't scrounge them up, then I've lost my touch."

"Soon as you locate them and get them hooked on, paint them," the Preacher says. "So their previous owner won't try to reclaim."

Boss nods in agreement. "Hidden in plain sight."

"What about the Klan?"

"That's me," Boss says. "You take care of getting Hack Ramsey's bones in some sort of box. You and Cassie deliver him back up home and into the ground. Take Micah with you so he can see it done honorable. I'll take care of this Klan business."

"You sure? In case you haven't noticed, you're only one man."

Boss grins. "Yeah, but it's a hell of a man, ain't it, Fingers?"

Fingers nods and smiles grimly. "Plus, if it comes to it, the boys'll go along for the fun. They expect payout for Hack."

"What was the name of that banker that come to see you?" Boss asks the Preacher. "The dragon, or whatever the hell he styles himself."

The Preacher sifts back through his memory before answering. "His name is Mark Dixon, and he claims to be the lord high Kleagle. You figure to start with him?"

"They done brought us fire twice now since you told him to take a hike. Twice in one night. Plus they killed one of ours. Before I'm done, he'll give us the blessing or I'll roast him till his goddamn fat crackles."

CHAPTER THIRTY-FIVE

Hᴀᴄᴋ Rᴀᴍsᴇʏ's ꜰᴜɴᴇʀᴀʟ is held at the Dorland Memorial Presbyterian Church in the tiny hamlet of Hot Springs. Everyone in town says that Mrs. Ramsey, Micah's grandmother, was a pillar of that congregation till the day she died. The service itself is sparsely attended. There is the elderly Reverend McBride, who doubles as the chaplain at the Dorland-Bell School across the road, and perhaps a dozen Hot Springs women who make it their business to ornament any occasion at the church.

McBride leads a scrawny hymn, with only Cassandra's voice rising over the empty pews and up to the rafters. The Preacher himself recites from the book of John, the fourteenth chapter, the verses that have haunted so many of his dreams: "'In my Father's house are many mansions: if it were not so, I would have told you. I go to prepare a place for you.'" He looks down at Micah as he intones this last, meaning the boy to hear that his father is safe in Heaven—warm, with plenty of beans and bacon to eat.

Afterward, one of the churchwomen thinks she can recall the funeral of Hack's mother, Naomi, and that she must be buried in the Odd Fellows Cemetery on the shoulder of the ridge above Spring Creek. Based on that rumor, the Preacher hires two town men named Gehagan with a wagon and a span of mules to haul the pine box containing Hack's bones up to the cemetery and, while there, to dig a grave. Micah chooses to ride in the wagon with his father, sitting on a folded horse blanket beside the box and sniffing quietly to himself. The Preacher walks along behind with Cassandra, the two of them holding hands from time to time in the dusty sunshine.

After a long climb up from Spring Creek, they reach the cemetery, a loose collection of graves strewn across a meadow and into the trees along its edge. They let Micah choose a spot for his father, and he selects a plot in the shade of an ancient hemlock. The Gehagan boys shrug off their shirts and begin to dig with pick and shovel. The box containing Hack Ramsey's bones is perhaps half the size of a normal coffin, for which they are grateful.

The boy runs off into the woods to look for his grandmother's grave, but really to escape the adults and explore among the trees. The Preacher and Cassie sit quietly together, leaning back against a log at the edge of the woods. Enjoying the sun even as its radiant heat causes him to loosen his collar and her to pull her dress up over her knees.

"What will happen to Micah now?" Cassie asks her Jedidiah. Easy and warm in the lemon light.

"Boss and Fingers have decided that he will stay with us and that Bridget will school him."

She shades her eyes to study his profile. "What do you mean *they have decided*? Don't you have a say?"

He shrugs. "I always wanted the boy to stay. Anybody can have a home with us who needs such."

"And you let them think they talked you into it?"

He grins. "Something like that."

"Don't you think he might get lonely for other children?"

"Why, as far as that goes, Gabe is near about a child. As are several of the others."

She shakes her head. "Not what I mean. I mean he might miss real children to play with. A younger brother or sister."

It's his turn now to turn and study her face. "What did you have in mind? That we should borrow a child or two to keep him company? Steal babies from cradles like the fairies of old?"

She reaches out and takes his near hand, pulls it to her, and rests it comfortably on the slight bulge of her stomach. Covers his hand warmly with both of hers. "I hate to always be a shock to you, but it seems we can make our own."

During the long moment of blooming understanding, his face grows numb, and his mind—always so nimble—trips over itself. "What are you...doing? Saying?"

"I'm saying that I have assumed for years that I was barren, but apparently I was wrong. I'm saying that we brought Micah's little brother up here with us."

His hand on her stomach involuntarily closes into a fist, taking in a hank of her dress. The fist trembles for a moment as if his whole body were under a gripping strain. But then slowly, as slowly as the deepest breath, it relaxes into a human hand again. Something that might touch or even comfort her.

"Are you upset?" she asks, her voice atremble. "At being a father, I mean."

He turns his face to her, a sly smile playing on his lips. "So now you're claiming I'm the father?"

She thrusts his hand roughly away and shoves to her feet. "Jedidiah Robbins! You...you...you know full well that you're the father! Who the hell else?"

"Well, there's men all around. There's Fingers, there's the roustabouts, there's Jesus himself. And then there's this whole business of immaculate conception."

"This conception was not very immaculate, goddamn you. What about Boss? You left out Boss. He might be the father of your child."

He pauses to consider. "Nobody better. I'd be proud if Boss were the father of my child. Or rather your child."

She sits back down on the log, her first flush of anger and disappointment giving in to his teasing. "I wish Boss *were* the father. He, at least, would take it seriously," she says.

He nods. "He would at that. Very seriously. And he will take your child seriously, even if it happened to be me who was present at conception."

"Present at conception, my ass. You were an enthusiastic participant, as I recall."

"Yes, I was." He is grinning at her now, so looks years younger. Younger and more foolish. "Every single time, I was a volunteer."

"And just so you know, I don't spread my favors around. My mother taught me to eat one dish at a time." She is grinning back at him, meeting his challenge.

"Taught you to chew every bite, did she?"

After a glance at the Gehagan boys, who are waist-deep in the earth, she reaches down to place her hand directly on the sun-warmed fabric over his crotch. "Taught me to chew every bite nice and slow."

CHAPTER THIRTY-SIX

MICAH IS RUNNING AND PLAYING IN THE WOODS, ignoring the adults with all their talking. At the edge of the woods, he finds—of all things—a brindled white-and-black dog. Smaller than their Jezebel, and mostly white with pink around the eyes and muzzle.

The boy crouches and holds out his hand to the little dog. It comes to him creeping on its belly with its ears back. He pets it ever so gently, rubbing first the top of its head and neck, and then working his way slowly down to its ears and then its face around the eyes. After a bit, it begins to lick his hands in gratitude.

He straightens up just long enough to pull a tangle of string out of his pocket. As he works to unknot his string, he talks quietly to the dog, who lies still on its belly, watching him intently. "This here can make a leash," he tells the dog. "It is exactly five feet and three inches long. I know because I measured it with daddy's folding rule. And when I'm grown entirely, I expect to be as tall as this cord is long."

The dog—he already thinks of it as his—stares at him with limpid brown eyes. It is so thin that you can count most every rib.

"I'm going to tie the end of this around your neck," he says. "Don't be afraid, but you ain't got no collar, and I don't know how to keep you. I'm lonely for a friend just now, and maybe you are too." He is careful to tie a square knot when he loops the end of the string around the pup's neck so that the makeshift collar won't slip and choke it. "I want to take you along with me to meet Jedidiah and Cassie. They're my other friends, but they're older'n hell, and we'll have to convince them to like you."

Once he stands, the small dog—a mongrel of some indeterminate sort, who limps badly on one hind leg—is quite happy to go along with him as he walks back toward the sound of voices. He finds the Preacher and Cassie standing together beside the open grave. The Gehagan boys have finished digging and, using ropes, have lowered the box containing his father's bones down into the opening.

The Preacher prays, holding Micah's hand, while the boy keeps a tight grip with the other on the dog's improvised leash. The prayer is short. Later, Micah will remember the soothing sound of the Preacher's voice more than the words themselves.

After the prayer, all three stand for a moment in the warm sunshine before the open grave, still holding hands, with eyes closed. There is an early summer peace in the air, woven with the flowing warble of birdsong from the trees and the hasty clicking of cicadas. Cassandra doesn't want Micah to see and hear the dirt being shoveled in upon his father, so she asks if the boy would like to bring his dog and walk with her down to the creek.

Micah is happy to go with Cassandra, and the dog—who is afraid of the men—is happy to go along as well.

CHAPTER THIRTY-SEVEN

THE PREACHER NOTICES that Cassie has one hand gathered at her lower back as she walks away, a new gesture for her. And so he thinks again of the unborn child. It is a new thought still, a warm notion but a frightening one. "Can I stay?" he wonders to himself. "Can I stay long enough to see the child grown and happy?"

He takes off his suit coat, folds it carefully inside out to protect it, and lays it over a tombstone. Is equally careful to put his tie in the pocket of the coat. And then, in order to hide his own thoughts from himself, he takes turn and turn about with the Gehagan boys, using their shovels to throw first the lumps of clay and then the dark, loose topsoil into the grave.

He sweats freely in the afternoon glare of the sun, and soon his shirt sticks to him, so he unbuttons it down almost to his waist. He and the older brother finish up by placing the few sparse tufts of grass back in place on the mound. The younger Gehagan finds a chunk of white quartz among the trees, so that they can mark the grave with something fine against the addition of a future stone.

When they are done, he pays the men twenty cash dollars each, and the two brothers start back down the mountain in the wagon. He sits for a while in the shade, letting the breeze cool his flesh. When he stands finally and retrieves his jacket, he notices that there is a stranger laboring up the hill from the Spring Creek road, apparently late for the burial.

He starts down to where their paths might cross. Seen closer, the figure turns out to be a startlingly thin man with his sleeves rolled up in the heat and his suit coat draped over one arm. There is a strange stutter and stumble in his walk, as if his back pains him, or his hips. Even so, there is a sense of familiarity about him, something about his loose-jointed, scarecrow walk. Then the figure looks up to orient himself, and the Preacher sees his bony face for the first time.

"Well met, well met, Preacher Solo-mon," Festus says by way of greeting. "I hoped beyond measure to see you here."

"What the hell are you about?"

"Why, you know I never miss a funeral." Festus pauses to catch his breath. "That fire at your train the other night caught me by surprise, I confess, and I was late to the service down at the chapel. So I made my way up here to pay my respects. It's a beautiful spot, ain't it?"

"No. I mean, yes, it is beautiful. What I mean to say is why do you carry on so about funerals and such?" The Preacher is close on Festus now, staring downhill at him from a few feet away. "Why are you so obsessed with the dead?" He means to threaten the old man, but his words have the opposite effect. Festus looks up from under his hat brim and starts to laugh, cackle almost.

"Why, don't you know? For a preacher, you ought to be ashamed. I am the most important figure in the play. Life is just the prelude to the banquet Old Death serves up at the end. Lord help me, for such a wise old Solo-mon, you are downright simple at times."

"I grant you that death matters. It means something. But why are *you* so drawn to it?"

Festus removes his hat and draws one arm across his bald head to fling the sweat away. He glances side to side as if to check for someone spying on them. "Oh, I have a role to play," he says quietly after a moment. And as if entertained by his own words, he chuckles again. "A role to play…that's rich as sin."

"Who are you, the devil himself?" The Preacher begins this question as a joke, but realizes halfway through that there are chill bumps on his arms, even in the sweaty heat of the day.

"Lord, no. Though he and I are on a first-name basis." Festus chortles again and steps uphill to stand beside the Preacher. "Trust me, you'll know old Scratch when you see him…or her."

"What do you mean?"

"I mean that the devil can appear as man or woman according to the circumstance, makes no difference."

"You say this like you've seen it."

"Have seen it. Both. The devil works with fire. That's the sign. Surely after the other night, you know that. A fire burning up a cross outside your tent. Who do you think puts the match to such as that? Who do you think burned your man down to a pile of greasy bones, some shit-ass local boy? That's strong work, even for white trash." Festus turns and spits over his shoulder. "Do you know what dry charcoal crumbled up in your hand smells like?"

The Preacher nods. "Bout like those two train cars smelled the next day. Or that goddamned cross they left smoking in the pasture in front of our tent."

"Just so, Solo-mon. That's how you'll know the Old One. He or she is as pretty as dawn over the ocean, but the stench is always there. The fetor of burning flesh sticks despite any spice or perfume." Festus pauses for a moment, as if to consider. "The devil can fly, too, though you rarely see it."

"What the hell, fly?"

"Why, the beast can do most anything. Anything except wrestle with God one to one. Takes a human to do that."

"Anything he can't do? Or *she* can't do?"

"Hates water. Won't cross water or abide its touch."

"How come you to know all this?"

Festus smiles, a death's-head grin wearing a country-store fedora. "I can see a little further in and out than most folks," he says. "Since I am present at the end."

"By the end, you mean *death*?"

"Yes, sir. That's me. However you choose to call me."

It is a breathless, cold moment, but then Festus grins again, and the Preacher can see his long, yellow horse teeth. "But don't you worry. I have no business with you today. It seems that you and me are getting to be best pals, and I won't take advantage of a friend on such a nice afternoon."

The Preacher swallows painfully, his mouth suddenly dry in the dusty heat. "If we're such good friends, Festus, I need you to do something for me."

"What's that, brother mine?"

"Stay away from that boy down there by the creek. His name is Micah Ramsey."

Festus nods, his head jerking up and down as if on a string. "What about the woman?" he asks. "Can I have her?"

"Her too. Leave her be."

"What's her name? I have to know their names if there's to be a con-tract."

"Her name is Cassandra Bailey. But it'll soon be Robbins. Cassandra Robbins."

"I'll make note of it. Micah and Cassandra. For how long? How many weeks or months you trading for?"

"Fifty years…each. At least that."

Festus snorts. "Half a century? That's a long damn time, especially for the woman and her bearing. What will you give me for half a century? What coin you got in your pocket?"

"You know what I'll give you."

Festus regards him solemnly for a long moment. The eyes in that bony face are ancient, fever-bright but blurred with a centuries-old weariness. Perhaps there is even sorrow. "Yes, I know what you'll give in trade. I know exactly what. For that sort of deal, what you're asking and offering, you have to shake my hand. You have to touch me of your own determination."

He reaches out with his stick-thin right arm and extends the forefinger. In the brazen glare from the sun, it appears unnaturally long and made all of bone with barely a parchment of ash-colored skin. The nail on the end of the finger is long and sharp, hard as horn.

The Preacher masters the sudden urge to recoil from such a thing, a finger like a spear. After swallowing his own sour bile, he reaches out and grasps the long frigid finger. It is exactly like holding an icicle with joints—hard, slick, and burning cold. "Fifty years for each of them," he says into the grinning face, "and you can do what you will with me."

"Done," Festus agrees. "A contract knotted up between two old friends."

The Preacher releases the icy finger and stifles a gasp at what he's done.

Festus himself seems relieved. He drops his jacket on the grass and stretches luxuriously in the sun, his joints groaning and popping. There is warmth again pooling in the air around them, where before was clammy mist. He nods to the Preacher and whispers. "I believe I'll go stretch out on one of these here graves. I can't afford to sleep, you know, but I so like to rest myself on a lonesome, sun-varnished grave."

CHAPTER THIRTY-EIGHT

WHEN THE PREACHER, CASSANDRA, AND MICAH return from Hot Springs to Hickory, they find that Fingers and the roustabouts have been busy in their absence. Both locomotives—*Saint John the Baptist* and *Sword of the Lord*—are parked on a long siding below the train station. There are three—not two—new cars hooked onto *Saint John the Baptist,* two passenger cars and a boxcar. The whole rig is being painted carefully in the bright sun. The train is already the color of new stove blacking, plus every car is having its lettering renewed:

SOLOMON'S CRUSADE

SAINT JOHN the BAPTIST TRAIN

And on the coal tender car behind the engine appears an added verse from the book of Matthew, carefully drawn out and painted in full:

> I INDEED BAPTIZE YOU WITH WATER UNTO
> REPENTANCE. BUT HE THAT COMETH AFTER ME
> IS MIGHTIER THAN I: HE SHALL BAPTIZE YOU
> WITH THE HOLY GHOST, AND WITH FIRE.

Fingers and Bridget are especially happy with the paint job and with the comfortable stable that several of the boys have knocked together in the new boxcar. She immediately takes Micah by the hand and leads him with his puppy away to show him how they—boy and dog—will sleep in the car with the horses, where the workers have carved out a bedroom just for him, with a bunk and with shelves for his clothes and schoolbooks.

When the Preacher is through exclaiming over the quick work Fingers and his crew have made of the destroyed equipment, he asks about Boss. Fingers shrugs and admits that they've neither seen nor heard from him for several days.

"He left the same day you did," Fingers explains. "Took Zeke Scully and Lost John Stoddard with him for moral support. It's been three days and no sign. But my guess is that unless they run foul of the law, we'll see them in a day or so. I figure there's nothing that walks the earth will stay Boss from his man."

Boss and the two others return to camp that evening. They are laughing as they walk up to the *Sword of the Lord,* although Scully has a black eye and Stoddard a split lip. They've been fist-fighting sometime in the previous day or night, and they're alive with it. They stink of male sweat and a trickle of blood.

Boss is wearing a suit of clothes like nothing the Preacher has ever seen on him before. Gray gabardine trousers and dark blue jacket coming apart at the shoulders from the pressure of muscle and bone. Plus he has a necktie hanging loose around his neck—of all the things in the known world, a necktie.

"You taking up preaching?" he asks Boss as they walk up, and all three of the men burst into laughter.

"Look closely," Boss says, "and you will see that I am a well-heeled, goddamn businessman."

And so they let it rest till later that night, when once again the three conspirators can sit together—the Preacher, Boss, and Fingers. Only this time there is pure white liquor rather than coffee. Each takes his dram as he prefers. The Preacher with honey, Fingers with water to cut, and Boss straight in a tin cup.

"Can we sleep safe in our beds?" the Preacher asks Boss after a bit. "Without the damn Klan burning us up alive in the middle of the night?"

"You and me are as safe as God ever intended," Boss says, sipping at the whiskey. "The boys and I guaranteed our passage. Anywhere in the western half of the state."

"You track the Klansman down to his lair?"

"We found him in Marion. First at his bank, and then we followed him home after work."

"I'm surprised you didn't take him up right there on his front porch."

"We considered it. But his wife and his little girl was there. Plus there showed up each evening a McDowell County deputy. Something rich and strange about that. Whoever took James' place when he went swimming must be in direct cahoots with the Klan, cause every evening about dusk, an off-duty deputy would show up to sit on the porch till the break of day. Napping often as not, but there nonetheless."

"You didn't bury him in the flower garden, this deputy?"

"The boys wanted to. But you'd have been proud. I counseled patience and consideration. And so after two nights of seeing the daughter through the window and the wife throwing her dishwater out into the yard, we decided to have our conference at the bank, where Dixon spends his days."

"Big bank, downtown street corner?"

"As big as they got in Marion, which is not so big as you might imagine. We scouted around a bit, and I bought this suit secondhand from a fellow I know runs a little juice joint up above a feed store. Then yesterday afternoon, we walked in during the heat of the afternoon. Wearing my new suit, I asked all peaches-and-cream to see Mr. Dixon about a business deal while these two commenced to flirting with the lady teller, playing the fool with the customers, and generally smelling up the front of the bank.

"Directly, a big old slick head sticks out from behind an office door—the door where this Dixon is supposed to see me—and the fat head starts to come out to brace up the boys. Assuming he's our man, I grab his arm and steer him straight back in. Shut the door and lock it behind me. And so it was there in his office we had a chance to palaver a bit."

"Surprised they didn't have a guard," the Preacher says.

"He was down the street at the drugstore, having a piss," Boss explains. "But directly he come strolling back and tries to throw Zeke and Lost John out of the bank, but they began first to scuffle and then to scrap—in the lobby of the bank and then on the porch. Nothing too serious, cause I'd told em not to end up in jail, but serious enough so that Dixon and I had ten minutes of uninterrupted time to reason together. Ain't that the biblical? To sit and reason together?"

"'Come now, and let us reason together.' Book of Isaiah. How did you reason with him?"

"Told him who I was. Told him that we knew perfectly damn well who he was, great beagle of the local bedsheet boys. Told him that we knew some of his crowd had fired the train, and that they'd killed Hack Ramsey in the process. He started to bluster and blather, so I leaned over the desk and slapped him so hard his dentures went sideways in his mouth.

"He got all teary-eyed about that, and while he was rubbing his ear and rearranging his teeth, I stepped around the desk and grabbed him up by his shirtfront and stuck my handsome mug in his." Boss grins. "I had ate an onion on the street right before we went in, thinking I might have to breathe on him just a bit. Safe to say that he didn't care for the smell of me up close.

"While my nose was stuck in his eye, I whispered nice and familiar that Hack had left an orphaned son, just about the same age as his own girl, Hortense, who we'd been admiring through the kitchen window. And then I explained that if trouble of any kind—any kind at all—should come our way, from his Klan boys or from the High Sheriff his own self, that we would burn his house to the ground with him in it, and it would be his baby girl facing life without a daddy. I added that part where we believe in an eye for an eye and a tooth for a jaw because we are godly men."

"What did he say to that?"

"Well, he was crying so hard by that point, whether from the slapping or the onion I don't know, that he could barely say anything. But he did finally blubber out a promise that he'd keep all his crowd away from us. Free rein to go and come, such as that. I also told him that he was lucky it was me paying him a visit cause I wa'nt a patch on you. You wanted to hang him up by the neck in his own bank and cut his balls off. More or less as an example to sinners everywhere."

The Preacher guffaws. "You ruined the effect. No way in hell he believed that."

Boss shrugs. "Don't bet on it. He'd have believed pretty much anything at that point."

CHAPTER THIRTY-NINE

AFTER SOME DELICIOUS DISCUSSION, Bridget and Cassandra decide they want to hold a double wedding, and that they want to get married in a place where beauty reigns—not some dusty crossroads that has nothing to recommend it. Some place high, wide, and steep with beauty.

Brides will have their way.

And so the entire company travels back up to Hot Springs in mid-summer, when there is a week-long break in the crusade schedule. Fingers and Cederberg hitch the club car to the rear of *Saint John the Baptist* so everyone can travel in comfort on their own rig. Even the horses are part of the wedding party, as Bridget and Micah will not leave them, and they grow restless if neither the woman nor the boy is underfoot.

Lester Caldwell, the good old man who baptized most all of them in April, agrees to come down to the springs to meet them. He will, if he is satisfied, perform the ceremony. The negotiation, when they meet on the Hot Springs train platform, is mock-solemn and playful.

"Who's it to be?" Lester asks. "I ain't fixed to marry no heathens." This with a perfectly straight face.

They all turn to the Preacher. "Well, Lester, three of the four I can vouch for. That Gabriel there, he's one of the grooms. And in the past year or so, he's learned to read just so he can devour the King James. And one of the brides is my daughter, Bridget, who is the picture postcard of her mother, a sainted lady. The other bride is Mrs. Cassandra Bailey, a preacher's widow who can quote the Bible, chapter and verse." He nods to each of the three in turn: Gabe nervous and unsure, the two women grinning back at Lester Caldwell.

"Fair enough," Lester admits, the first signs of a smile teasing the edge of his mouth. "That's three out of four. What about the other groom? Does he know Jesus?"

"I am he, and he is me," the Preacher says with a wink. "It is up to you to judge the sanctity."

Lester Caldwell reaches out and, with only a forefinger, touches the Preacher on the chest, directly over his heart, as if to take the measure of him. Again, the Preacher is struck by the electrical force of the man, as if Lester is conduit to an unseen current that surges through his hands.

"I believe you just might do as well," Lester says after a moment. "You do have an old soul but, all in all, one that is fresh enough and green enough for your young bride."

"Are you sure of that?" he asks suddenly, painfully aware even as he says it that both Bridget and Cassie are listening closely.

Lester pulls his hand back far enough to fold it into a fist and then punches the Preacher hard—just over his heart. "You're young if I say you are young," he intones, his voice as clear as a bell. "Young enough to father, I'd say."

In his dreams of that night, the night before the wedding, he walks again by the river where they—he and Micah Ramsey—had discovered the drowned body of the little girl from Highlands. He is wading in the shallows of the river and then along its edge, stepping on the water-woven sand among the rocks. In the dream, it is night but with a dawning hint of day just breaking through.

It is as if he is awake, and then asleep, in the water and without, waking as it were along the edge of a dark river of sleep, where he might swim deeper if he chose.

Just where Micah found the body of the girl, he comes upon the statue of a woman. She, the statue, is sitting on a rounded boulder at the water's edge, her marble feet buried in the current. The statue's hands are behind her on the rock, her elbows locked, so that she leans back languorously. Her head is turned to the river, her eyes open as she stares out into the rushing current. The water silent and silver in midnight passage.

She is completely naked, thin and muscular—beautifully frozen in silent wonder, including the ivory bounty of her breasts, small but rich enough to nourish all the known world. She is, he thinks, perfected.

As he comes closer to her, he realizes that what had appeared first as stone—silent, still marble, the handiwork of some long-dead Greek—is in fact skin; her hair, human hair. Her stone nipples suddenly alive in the chill night, hard from the cold wash of the mountain streaming over her feet.

Everything about her is real—somehow alive but utterly and completely still. More still and more silent than anyone or anything he has ever yet seen in this shadowy world.

"Rachel?" he says to her tentatively. And ever so slightly, her eyebrows gather in consternation. He glances out at the river, following the line of her sight. When he looks back again, her quiet, marble mouth is open, as if in speech.

From far away, he hears a high, musical vibration, and from it gleans a few tingling words that quiver the skin on the back of his neck. "I am that girl who drowned." So say the words. "I do not now recall her name, but know that I am she."

He approaches her then, and in her stone face, her marble eyes, her still lips and tongue, he can perceive the faintest resemblance to Lillie Goforth.

"What would you have of me, spirit?" he whispers. "What will you tell me?"

He realizes that he is too much alive, too much of this world, to understand her marble voice; but still he leans forward, aching for her message.

The music, high and skyborne, has not abated, only woven itself into the whisper of the river. "Three," it says, "fifteen." And then: "Three…eleven and fifteen."

He feels a faint flush of anger that he can't know, can't unlock this riddle. It is a language too far, too distant from the present moment. And he is too weak, too human, to understand.

He thinks that if he steps farther out, deeper into the rushing river, he can turn to face her. He will see her more clearly, beyond the dark and wavering glass that hovers between them. But when he turns toward the deeper water, her head tremors from side to side. "No," she is saying, the movement either so incredibly fast or so monstrously slow that he can only just perceive it. "No deeper," he believes she is saying to him. "Not now deeper."

She is fading now; he is beginning to see beyond her, through her. "Why *three?*" he blurts out. Reaching out to clasp her arm, seeking to keep her hard, cold presence. "Why *eleven*, why *fifteen?*"

But she is fading now and then gone, her beauty an alabaster memory.

It is only as he rises from the swirling depths of sleep, swimming slowly up through the layers of his waking mind, that he realizes what he has seen, is seeing still in the afterimage of his burning eye.

It is an angel who spoke, who speaks, to him. Warning him....

When he wakes fully, twisted in his sheet, he finds the Bible beside him on the bed. His own tattered copy of the King James. It lies open to Ecclesiastes, where in the early evening he had been blindly reading. He turns with shaking hands to the third chapter, searching for the eleventh and fifteenth verses.

CHAPTER FORTY

The spot that Bridget and Cassie choose is a quarter mile from the river, in a sweeping oxbow bend of Spring Creek. It lies on a gentle, grassy slope, broken here and there by large flat rocks, one of which serves as a platform for Lester Caldwell to stand on, slightly above the two couples. Earlier that year, they are told, the entire bend was underwater, washed through by spring floods.

From left to right in front of Lester stand first Gabriel Overbay, then his bride, Bridget; her father, Jedidiah, and the second bride, Cassandra. What Gabe will remember in later years is the sound of singing: Bridget and Cassie in harmony, both before and after the short ceremony. What Bridget will recall is her father's pale, serious face throughout, only opening into a flush of pleasure at the conclusion. What Cassie will hold on to is the sense of impending change—that the river from that day forward is forever different—explosively, even dangerously so, in rocks and rapids.

Jedidiah Robbins, the Preacher, will remember little of the ceremony itself, because he is mesmerized by the whisper of the creek and the sound of the breeze rattling in the summer leaves. Lester's quiet, sure words on the endurance of love, lifted from First Corinthians, drift through his questing mind and roam freely inside the sound of wind and water, mingling with the passages from Ecclesiastes the angel had riddled him with the night before.

"He hath made every thing beautiful in his time. Love suffereth long, and is kind. *He hath set the world in their heart.* Love

envieth not, is not puffed up. *No man can find out the work that God maketh from the beginning to the end.* Love doth not behave itself unseemly. *That which hath been is now.* Love is not easily provoked, thinketh no evil. *And that which is to be hath already been.* Love rejoiceth not in iniquity, but rejoiceth in the truth. *God requireth that which is past.* Love beareth all things, believeth all things...*now and then*...hopeth all things...*in the truth...* endureth all things. *The truth.*"

Somehow the angel's skyborne music and Lester Caldwell's slight, laconic drawl merge into one stitched quilt that becomes his own internal voice, speechless and speaking, flowing freely on and on—until the pressure of Cassie's large, warm hand in his own and her steady presence beside him bring him back to the present. Slowly his wits gather into the moment, and he can feel a smile growing on his face, his skin relaxing and blushing. When he turns to look at Cassie, the only voice that he hears is Lester's sweet, tobacco-stained syllables: "Love beareth all things, believeth all things, hopeth all things, endureth all things."

For that brief, bright moment, he is fully happy in the fresh and sun-bright air. Forgiven and forgiving.

CHAPTER FORTY-ONE

He has arranged rooms for the two couples at Sunnybank, a boardinghouse on Bridge Street where the four of them might have a few nights away from the trains—away from the smell of coal dust and horses, the constant aroma of sweaty roughnecks wreathed in cigar smoke.

But first there is the celebration of their nuptials, hosted by Boss and Fingers down by the railroad siding where the *Saint John the Baptist* Bible car provides a constant stream of whiskey and brandy, and where the entire company gathers to eat and laugh and sing.

The men tend two bonfires: one blazing high for warmth against the evening air and for light as the evening advances. The other has already burned down to coals so that Scully and Cederberg can braise the smoking-hot meat, enough beef and pork to feed the entire town, as the entire town has been invited.

Bridget and Cassie stand by to greet each and all, Bridget sipping a glass of brandy refilled from time to time by Gabe, who is constantly being pulled away by the men for a slap on the back and a nip from a jar.

As the party gains heat and momentum, Boss leads Jedidiah off to one side and hands him a glass tumbler half full of a dark brown liquor.

He smells it suspiciously. "What's in it?" he asks. "Be like you to knock me out and steal the bride."

"Yes, it would," Boss admits. "Wish I'd thought of that myself, as you don't half deserve her. What's in it is a little brandy

251

and a double dose of that 'sang tea that Bridget and Cassie are always brewing up. Guaranteed to raise up your Ebenezer."

"What Ebenezer?"

"That sorry little piece you got in your pants. I don't want you to embarrass us on your wedding night."

"How you know what I got in my pants? Besides, this stuff smells like the black draught my grandma used to dose me with. It had coal oil in it."

"It is a little rank," Boss admits. "But I had my eye on you lately, and it seems to me you're going through one of your thinking spells. Working over something inside that head of yours till you've worn it out, warp and woof. Time to come on back to reality, and that little Cassie is about as real as it gets."

He smells of the tonic again and shakes his head. "I don't know, Boss. You sure there's no kerosene?"

Boss sticks a dirty forefinger into the glass and sucks a little of the liquid off his fingertip. Blows in and out like a horse and mutters, "It's fine, Jedidiah." Clears his throat. "Goes down easy. Besides, who's that dead fellah Jesus come along and raised up?"

"Lazarus?"

"Yeah, him. I figure that even if your dick is as dead as Lazarus, this here'll raise it on up and make it dance."

The Preacher sticks a finger of his own into the glass and, without breathing, licks the brazen mixture off. "Oh God, Boss."

"Well, hell, Jedidiah. Be a man for once and take your medicine!" Boss returns to the fire, shaking his head as he goes.

After a moment, the Preacher sighs, holds his nose, and tosses back the contents of the glass. His eyes go dark and his stomach roils inside him for a long moment before the spasm passes. He tosses the tumbler into the weeds and staggers toward the line of people who have come in congratulation and celebration.

"Are you all right?" Cassie asks him, when he steps up beside her. "You're as pale as a ghost."

"I'm the ghost...of Lazarus," he mutters, shaking his head to clear the fog from his eyes. "Raised up a new man."

Later, after much meat and more drink, after a hymn or two and long storytelling, first Bridget with her Gabriel and then he with his Cassandra ease out of the flickering circle of firelight and start down the street toward Sunnybank. They can hear behind them snatches of song, here and there a fiddle, much laughter.

He and Cassie follow the younger couple up the steep sidewalk in front of the house, pausing at one point to stand with their arms around each other while gazing at the stars strewn across the liquid sky. The lamplight from within the house washes over them for a moment when Gabe and Bridget open the door to enter. Then darkness again, and they kiss.

It is new, this kiss, not unlike the sudden rendezvous in the bathhouse months before, but now with no hesitation. Here, they are both more hungry for it, more insistent, more desperate since they know now what they might have. Biting and licking each other in their hurry to taste and be tasted. The salt of life.

Once inside the house, they climb the stairs while simultaneously trying to bite each other and hold each other and walk, tripping over one step at a time. His hand is inside the back of her dress, her hand tearing off one of his buttons and inside his shirt, running up and down over him, counting the ribs beneath his skin.

Inside the first room at the top of the stairs—no notion if it is their room or not—they slam the door by thrusting each other against it. Her insistence of hip and thigh pulsing against something in him she's never felt before. She tears the remaining buttons off his shirt while he pushes her dress, the dress she was married in, down over her shoulders, her breasts, to her hips. He kneels to push it further, and while there, thrusts his face between her thighs, his tongue into the secret, dappled dainty of her.

She makes inarticulate groans to a god unknown, sounds he's never heard a woman make before, as they find ways to strip away the rags of clothing that are left. Abandoning any thought, he bounces her on the bed and falls over her, trying to touch all of her all at once, belly and breast, elbow, knee, and ankle.

He on her, and the bed rocks like a ship at sea. His stone rooster crowing inside her pulsing, thrusting passage. She wrestles hard, louder and stronger against him, growling into his ear to urge him on.

Somewhere deep within the sea beneath them, there is a bell tolling, a deep, resonant tide of clanging. The bed groans and squeals beneath the collision of hip and thigh, the smoldering, blistering of what they are together making, rolling on, coming in tides.

The bed gives way beneath them just as the typhoon finally, achingly breaks through and explodes all thought, any name, all words. Collapses onto the floor with a rending crash that silences the bell and sucks all sound out of the air except the gasping weeping.

One breath between them that barely survives. One breath conspired between two stripped and straining bodies.

Somewhere from the open sky above their roof, beyond her, beyond him, they can hear the jubilee. The music of planets grinding together.

Barely surviving the shipwreck of their bed, their soul, their mind. One body alone is left—limbs strewn carelessly in intricate pattern—to tell the tale.

CHAPTER FORTY-TWO

"WHAT IN RED HELL WERE YOU THINKING?" Boss' gravelly voice the next morning as he and the Preacher sit over coffee on the Sunnybank porch. "Bouncing that poor girl all over the room like that, and her with child!"

"My back hurts."

"Shit on your back. You owe me for that bed. I had to pay Mrs. Gentry for it, as she was game to throw the two of you out in the street this morning. You and Cassie woke her up out of a sound sleep. Said she thought a tree had fell on the house."

"I'll pay for the damn bed. Did I tell you my back hurts? And oh God, my head."

"Your *ass* ought to hurt. Besides, your back hurts because you are an old man. Most as old as me. And you owe Fingers for that bell you two crushed under the bedstead."

"*What* bell?"

"We hung cowbells in the springs of both your beds, just for shivaree and to see who might have the power and the glory to ring em."

"So there *was* a bell. I thought I'd dreamed it."

"Hell no, you didn't dream it. And I'll give you this. You and Cassie rang it like a champion right up till you tore down the bed and destroyed the bell. I won ten dollars off of Fingers because of you and Cassie."

"What about Gabe and Bridget?"

"I lost the ten dollars back on those two. I bet on them and they didn't make a damn sound." He shakes his head in sad disappointment. "Don't know what the hell the younger generation is coming to."

"What were you and Fingers doing? Lurking in the hallway with your ears to the door?"

"More or less. We was sitting on the steps having a toddy. Keeping score on the bedstead wars."

"Pour me some more coffee. My head's in a vise."

"Shouldn't ought to have drunk so much. Like I said."

"It was that damn tonic you poured down my throat. Poisoned me."

"Yeah, well. It worked, didn't it? Confess, you old sinner. You'd drink it off again, wouldn't you?"

He grins. "Maybe."

"Maybe, my ass. Do you think we should bottle it?"

"Bottle what?"

"The sex draught. We could sell it out of the advance rig when we first hit town. Call it Lazarus Arise or some such as that."

"You're serious, aren't you?"

"Hell, yes. It'd have people rutting in every back room and barn loft within twenty miles. They'd have to come to the crusade then, to get saved from all that sin. We'd get em going and coming…so to speak."

"Yeah, well, it might also blow their damn brains straight out of their ears. Then we'd just get rode out of town on a rail."

"Maybe. Maybe we paste directions on the bottle—take only one tablespoon a day on account of your liver—you know, like medicine."

Bridget walks out onto the porch with her own coffee cup. "Did you two hear that crash last night, not long after we went to bed?" she asks. "Gabe thought somebody'd drove a jalopy into the side of the house."

"Didn't hear a thing," the Preacher says.

CHAPTER FORTY-THREE

MYSTERIOUSLY, AFTER BREAKFAST, first Bridget with her Gabriel and then Boss all disappear. It being Sunday morning, the Preacher and Cassie are left to walk to church alone, down to the Dorland Memorial Presbyterian Church where once before they had attended the funeral for Hack Ramsey. As they are leaving out the front door of Sunnybank, they pass the stern and watchful eye of the proprietor, Mrs. Gentry, who sits and fans herself in one of the porch rockers.

"We believe we may go down to church, Mrs. Gentry. Atone for our sins," says Cassie, conscious of the slight swell of her own belly.

The woman's broad face breaks into a grin. "Well, honey, after last night, I spect you better." She guffaws. "And maybe pray forward for a bit too. Cover the next few nights just in case grandpa there gets his engine cranked up again."

The sanctuary of the church is cool and, with the windows thrown open, breezy and flush with birdsong. Outside, clouds are gathering and a patter of rain is pocketing the dust. There are perhaps two dozen folks in the church that morning, including half a dozen sleepy children. The local chaplain has invited Lester Caldwell to pinch-hit in the pulpit, and in honor of the previous spring's flood, Lester chooses to visit in the book of Genesis, chapters 6 through 9. The first and greatest flood of them all.

"Neighbors, friends," Lester begins, "I don't know that I'm up to the task. These late days, my eyes are too cloudy, my grip on things too shaky, to visit with old Noah all by myself. So I'm going to invite Brother Godwin over there on the left—the local man—and Brother Robbins over here on the right. . . . I'm going to invite them to talk along of me. I'm going to throw out some verses and perhaps a word or two, and then I'd favor for one of them to take up the thread and weave in his own thoughts about how this incredible story gets told. Between the three of us, we'll swim through to the end. To the re-creation of man and beast." The rain on the roof is steady now, and a deacon rises to pull the open windows halfway closed against the wet.

Lester walks down from the pulpit and sits with his open Bible on the short stage in the front of the chapel. "This here story comes not long after the Garden of Eden and our great fall from grace. Men and women have taken a liking to each other and set about multiplying."

Outside, there is a rumble of thunder in the air. Like a loaded wagon pulled over stones.

Lester continues. "Verse 4 even tells us that 'there were giants in the earth in those days; and also after that, when the sons of God came in unto the daughters of men, and they bore children to them, the same became mighty men which were of old, men of renown.' Giants and men of renown. Sounds pretty fine, don't it? But there was a problem. 'God saw that the wickedness of man was great in the earth, and that every imagination of the thoughts of his heart was only evil continually.' And the Lord was sorry He made man. The earth, His creation, grieved Him." And then after a pause. "What say, Brother Godwin?"

"God wepth." Godwin has a high, reedy voice and a definite lisp.

What in the world made him become a minister, Cassie thinks to herself.

"God wepth to see what He hath wroth," Godwin continues.

Out of pity, he, Solomon, takes the reins. "'But Noah found grace in the eyes of the Lord.'" This from memory. "Noah was a just man and perfect in his generations, and Noah walked with God."

"He hath some sons too," Godwin interrupts him. "Shemth, Hamth, and Japheth." The children now are awake, listening intently to their Preacher Godwin, knowing full well that if he gets revved up and spitting, it will be more fun than the radio.

"That's right," the Preacher agrees. "Shem, Ham, and Japheth, along with their wives. But the rest of the earth was corrupt and full of violence, and God decides to destroy it all excepting Noah and his generations." He, the Preacher, nods at Lester Caldwell, who is obviously enjoying himself.

"'Make thee an ark of gopher wood,'" Lester intones, his voice pushed as deep as it will go to signify God talking. "'Rooms shalt thou make in the ark, and shalt pitch it within and without with pitch.'"

"What's gopher wood?" A child's sleepy voice.

"Hush!" The mother's whispered reply. "It's like dogwood, only gopher."

"'The length is three hundred cubiths.'" Godwin again. "'The breadth of it fifty cubiths, the heighth of it thirty cubiths.'" There is a giggle from the third pew, cut off by a mother's pinch.

"And so there is a covenant," the Preacher says, "between God and Noah, like an agreement or a contract. The storm is coming. Death and destruction are coming. But God will save Noah and his family—Noah's wife, his sons, and his sons' wives." He squeezes Cassie's hand where he holds it warm against his thigh. "But Noah has a big job to do in return. He must take up every living thing of the flesh—two of every sort, male and female. And then there are the sevens. This good old story is full of sevens." He pauses to wink at the little girl who is kneeling backward on the pew in front of him and Cassie, staring wide-eyed at him, hanging on his every word. "He is to take seven pair of the clean beasts and also seven pair of all the fowls of the air."

"The birds?" the little girl asks.

He nods. "The birds. Seven pair of each. Which shows us how much God loves the birds. And then there is another seven. Do you know what it is? He and his sons had only seven days to gather all the animals, just seven days before they had to shut up the ark and prepare for the storm."

"Did they find em all?" the little girl whispers. "The animals, I mean. And the birds?"

"Find them? Yes, they did. And gathered them together. And just as God promised in His covenant with Noah, it began to rain. For forty days and forty nights it rained, and the waters covered even the highest mountains."

"Even our mountains?"

"Yes, child. Even our mountains. The earth was one huge ocean, and the ark was tossed on the waves."

"Did everything that was evil die?" Lester's voice again, assisting him with a question.

"The waters remained high for a hundred and fifty days, and everything that was left on the ground—men, cattle, creeping and crawling things—all were destroyed. The only life left on earth was in the ark with Noah."

"Even the little children?" the girl asks. "Did they drown?"

How do you answer such a question? Can little children be evil? Cassie is squeezing his hand now. Hard. Telling him to be careful.

"No," he says to the girl. "No, the children of the earth became as fowls of the air. They took on the form of birds and flew above the waters."

The little girl—brunette pigtails and chocolate-brown eyes—nods vigorously. *Birds of the air* is satisfactory to her.

"God sent a strong wind," he says now, "to dry up the waters. He has given the entire earth a bath. He has cleansed the world, and then He sent a wind to dry it off, prepare it for a new day."

"Did the sun come out?"

"Yes, child, the sun came out. And the waters receded. Do you know what *receded* means?"

She nods, again vigorously.

"The waters receded and the ark came to rest on the high mountains. Somewhere around here, I expect. And Noah sent out first a raven and then a dove to discover if it was safe to open up the door and come down out of the ark. The raven never returned. That's why the raven lives in the highest mountains to this day. And when the dove came back, she was soaking wet. She had found no safe place to land. Noah waited seven days—"

"Seven again," the little girl says.

"Seven again. Seven days, and then he sent out the dove again, and this time she didn't come back. So he knew she had found safety. So Noah opened up the door of the ark and looked out and saw dry land. He was still afraid, though. Noah was six hundred years old and even so, he was afraid. So he waited on God to give him the high sign, and after a bit, God spake unto him and told him to go forth with all his family and all the living things of the world. And he built up an altar out of stones and made a sacrifice to God, and God liked it pretty well. So well, in fact, that He made a promise to Noah and the animals. 'I will not again curse the ground,' He said. 'Neither will I again smite anymore everything living.' And He sent a bow to seal the deal. God called it a bow, but we call it a rain-bow."

"Is a rainbow good?"

"A rainbow is among the very best things, child. For it means that God will never again destroy us. It means that the earth is safe from His wrath."

"Say what you mean by *wrath*, brother." Lester's whisper, reminding him to explain God to the children.

"Do you know what *God's wrath* means?" he says to the little brown-eyed girl.

She nods enthusiastically yes, but then hesitates, and after a second's pause shakes her whole head no, her pigtails flying into her face.

"It means God is angry."

"God was mad at the children," she whispers.

"God was mad," he admits, "at the children and at their mothers and fathers."

"Why did He kill the animals then?" Tears are welling up in those brown eyes. "They didn't do nothing."

"No, they didn't," he admits before he has time to think. "You're right."

"Then, why did He do it? He didn't have to kill them. He could have turned them into birds, like the children."

He is in deep water, he knows. Debating with this child. And all the children who are within earshot.

"In the old days," he says. Now he himself is whispering, and people are leaning in to hear. "In the old days, long ago, God was an angry being. Like an angry father who comes home and finds things wrong with the house. Finds fault with his wife and his children."

"Did He throw things and yell?"

"He did. He threw the very first family out of the house altogether. And then one day, the time we're talking about, He flooded the whole earth."

"He is a bad pap," the little girl says. "I bet He run off after that." The tears are slipping out of her eyes now, though she blinks to hold them back. He can feel his own eyes swelling, and Cassie gripping his right hand hard in both of hers, gripping till it hurts.

"He was an angry father, in the old days, but then He was sorry for it. When He saw what He'd done, He was sorry for it."

"Sorry for His wrath?" Again Lester's whisper, urgent now.

"He was sorry for His wrath, and He sent a rainbow as His sign that there would never be another flood. He would never again smite every living thing."

"Never?" The little girl.

He nods. "Never again."

After the service, he stands with Lester Caldwell in the first flirtation of sun following the morning's rain. The clouds are breaking, and they take pleasure in the clean rays of light striking down on the mountains.

"Preacher," Lester asks after a moment, "do you know what old Noah did after the ark finally landed and he had a chance to gather his intellects?"

His mind is still in the sanctuary with the little girl, tangled in her fear for the children and her love for the animals. Wondering at the lies he had told her. He shakes his head to clear the thoughts. "No, Lester, sad to say that I can't recall."

"He planted him a vineyard." Lester pronounces it as two distinct syllables. Vine yard.

"Made wine, did he?"

"Yes, he did, and I suspect after all he'd seen, he needed him a cup or two to even out the death and destruction."

The sunlight is warm now on their heads and shoulders. He can see Cassie standing across the narrow street, talking and laughing with the little girl and her family. "I suspect he needed more than a cup or two. And I seem to recall something about nakedness."

Lester nods and grins. "Yes, that too. Old Noah drank of the wine, and was drunken; and he was uncovered in his tent. His youngest son saw him laid out naked and made fun of him. But his oldest two, they shut their eyes and covered him up."

"They were embarrassed by the old man?"

"Oh, no. Them oldest two, they covered him up out of respect and said no more about it."

They are both laughing now. At the thought of Noah drunk, sprawling naked in his tent.

"Listen, Preacher." Lester grips his arm now. Affectionately, easily, as a father or older brother might. "At first, I didn't care for the smell of alcohol around your traveling church. Liquor and booze and such. No need to look at me funny. I wasn't born yesterday. But here lately, I begin to understand you better, and I think you might just be all right. Might provide God's people more salvation than sin. Even if it's some of that vine-yard salvation."

He nods. "Maybe. I hope so, anyway."

"But I will say this," Lester continues with a wink. "I'm glad that girl of yours," he nods across the street at Cassie, "is bearing. I believe you need you some sons to cover up your nakedness."

CHAPTER FORTY-FOUR

"WHERE IN THE WORLD DID THEY GO?" he asks.

It is evening now, and they linger over a supper of broiled mutton, alone together—Jedidiah and Cassandra, mister and missus—in Mrs. Gentry's dining room at Sunnybank.

"Where did *who* go?"

He glances up at her suspiciously. "You know perfectly well who. Bridget and Gabriel and Boss. And, come to think of it, Fingers. He seems to have disappeared as well."

A faint smile tugs at the corners of her mouth. "Maybe they took a vacation," she says.

He lays down his fork and leans forward, seeking her eyes. "Took a vacation from their vacation, did they? All four of them? Simultaneously?"

She nods, still looking down at her plate. "Maybe."

He clears his throat, trying not to laugh out loud at her face.

"And where might they go on vacation, if they was to take one? India or China?"

"Maybe India or China. Maybe Morganton."

"Morganton? Definitely a garden spot of the Western Hemisphere. And what in the hell? I mean, just what might the four of them be planning to do while they're in...?"

"Well, you know they went to see Gabe's little boy." She is looking up at him now, full in the face, and he is startled to see tears glistening in the corners of her eyes. They were playing, and now there are tears.

"Well," he says, "I can imagine Bridget dragging Gabe to see little Jack, but what in... What do they need Boss and Fingers for?"

She is smiling at him helplessly now, a tear tracking down over the alabaster of her cheek. It strikes him that she is afraid to answer.

"Good God Almighty. They've gone to steal that child, haven't they? Cassie, answer me."

"I don't think *steal* is exactly the right word."

"Well, what the hell *is* the right word? *Borrow*? You don't borrow a child from its mother."

She shrugs. "I wish you wouldn't curse at me. And I don't think they mean to borrow *or* steal. Beg, maybe. Barter."

"I'm not cursing at you. I'm cursing at them. Kidnapping is a felony, so far as I know."

"So is transporting and selling liquor, Jed. And you've been doing that ever since I first met you, and you took advantage of me while we were praying."

"No, *you* took advantage of *me,* as I recall. We were in the middle of forgiving each other's trespasses when you stuck your hand in my.... Don't try to distract me, Cassie. So they took Boss along to—"

"Negotiate. To discuss with all concerned what's best for the child, given this complex, modern age in which we live."

"*Negotiate*? That's a good one! Boss Strong, Peacemaker. And they took Fingers along in case the negotiations break down?"

"Something like that."

He pauses, considers. "When were you all going to tell me about this?"

She smiles. "Oh, we weren't going to tell you at all if it didn't work."

"But what if it does work?"

"Boss said you'd look up one day about a year from now and ask who the new boy playing with Micah might be."

"I'm not *that* dense. And when Boss gets back, I'm going to kick his ass down the tracks for agreeing to this."

"He'd do anything for Bridget, and…"

"And what?"

"So would you, and you know it."

"Kidnapping?"

"Don't pretend for one sacred second that you haven't thought of it yourself."

He looks down at his plate now, hiding his own grin. "Thinking ain't doing."

"Sometimes, doing is what's called for. I've only heard you say that about a thousand times. Besides," she says, "I think it's time we went upstairs and did some Bible study. I'm lonesome for my Bible."

He looks up. "What did you have in mind? Some more of that praying you were talking about?"

She nods. "That too, but first I think we need to study the Song of Solomon. Your very own book, named after you, which for some reason you've never read to me. Chapter 2 says…"

He looks momentarily blank.

Her voice is husky now. "Don't tell me you don't remember chapter 2." Her voice little more than a whisper. "'I am the rose of Sharon, and the lily of the valleys. As the lily among thorns, so is my love among the daughters.'" She spreads her hands wide on the tabletop and leans toward him. He is mesmerized, lost in the depths of her face as she pauses to lick her lips with the glistening tip of her pink tongue. "'As the apple tree among the trees of the wood,'" she whispers, "'so is my beloved among the sons. I sat down under his shadow with great delight, and his fruit was sweet to my taste.'"

Interlude

"SO YOU SAID I WOULDN'T TAKE NOTICE for a year." It wasn't a question, more of a statement. He, the Preacher, is talking to Boss. They're both sitting on the iron steps of the club car with cigars in hand, breathing out the end of a long day.

They are watching bath time, done Hot Springs style. Micah is helping Bridget give Jackson a bath in the large tin washtub that Gabe has faithfully filled with buckets of hot mineral water from the springs. The little boy is walking and talking—or at least the beginning of walking and talking. Gabe is *Papa* and Bridget is *Bidget*. *Micah* is not in the boy's mouth yet, though his eyes follow the older child everywhere.

"I did say that," Boss admits as he knocks the ash off his cigar against the iron railing. "I'm surprised you took account of the child this soon. Only a few days since—"

"Since you four carried him off and brought him here. Care to tell me how you came into possession of him?"

Jackson is obviously enjoying the splashing water, hypnotized by Micah, who talks endless baby talk to him, and in love with Bidget, who has barely let him out of her sight since his arrival.

Boss considers for a moment, drawing in a long, even puff of smoke. "Didn't steal him," he says eventually. "Nor did we borrow him. More like we *traded* for him."

"Was the mother really ready to let him go?"

When they get the child out to dry him off, he evades both Micah and Bridget and begins to toddle madly across the grass toward the trees and the creek, laughing so hard that he can barely breathe. Micah chases after him while Bridget watches, enthralled.

"Have you noticed that the boy is about as brown-skinned as you can be, this side of the color line?" Boss is pointing with his cigar.

"I've noticed. Blue eyes and Cherokee-black hair."

"Where do you think it originates?"

"All Gabriel, I believe. Melungeon blood." He bends to knock the ash off his own cigar against his shoe heel.

"Portugee?" Boss asks.

He nods. "Tablespoon of black blood, I expect. Or more than a tablespoon."

Boss nods. "Jack's mama was done with that worn-out husband of hers. Said she needed to make a new chapter. New life somewhere hot. So all in all, she was happy to let Jack go. Less baggage for her to tote going forward."

"Just like that?"

"Well, I give her fifty dollars and two jars of brandy in trade. My guess is she was on the train south that very night, and her deacon husband is still looking out the window, wondering where in the hell everybody's at."

"So you bought the boy?"

Boss shrugs. "We done what needed to be done. Does the Negro blood bother you? For a grandson, I mean."

"Hell, no. We got our own Jesus riding with us, and he's as black a man as I've ever seen."

Boss nods and, after a moment, grins. "Yes, he is."

PART FOUR

DECEMBER 1927

CHAPTER FORTY-FIVE

BY THE FIRST WEEK IN DECEMBER, the crusade has made a sweep through middle and eastern Tennessee, filling the big top in towns like Murfreesboro and Johnson City. Now they are on the rails again from Knoxville, headed back to North Carolina for Christmas, through Hot Springs, Marshall, and into Asheville for at least three nights' work.

It sleeted hard on them in Chattanooga, and the roustabouts had to roll up the big canvas soaking wet, something Gabe had always warned against. The entire troupe is recovering from their labors when the two rigs roll through Knoxville one after the other, and though the horses are restless in the stock car, most of the human cargo is fast asleep.

The last newspaper the Preacher saw in Chattanooga described a winter storm thrusting inland from the Gulf of Mexico and another rolling up the Atlantic coast from Florida. The world is made up all of freezing rain, or so it seems. From Virginia to Florida, Nashville to the coast. And wind enough to shake the birds out of the trees and rock the trees from the earth.

Cassie sleeps exhausted in the club car while the rig sits for a time in the Knoxville yard, sidetracked by several long freights headed west. He—the Preacher—can't rest, for somehow the storm disturbs him, and he sits up with his book, though he's too uneasy to read.

At times the rain lashes the side of the club car so hard that he wonders how they can go on that night, but eventually Fingers climbs the iron steps and taps on the door. Warns him that they are about to push on, despite the weather. He nods dumbly, trusting the crew's experience more than his own nerves.

When they jerk into motion again, he goes and sits on the side of the bed to watch Cassie sleep. She is lying on her side, curled around the living ball of her belly. At one point she begins to groan, and he knows that she is dreaming, perhaps caught up in a nightmare. Lately, she has suffered from midnight visions of losing the baby, or losing him, or both. He lies down and wraps his arms around her struggling form, whispers in her ear that she is safe. He is there, beside her, and the baby is safe. All are secure.

The storm rages outside, bashing the side of the car as the rig struggles south and east, winding along the river. But here, inside, he murmurs into her ear, all are safe. And slowly, she calms, eases more deeply into some haven. He rubs her warm shoulder absently, not quite sure that he shares her ease. Can he believe his own words?

He wishes he'd insisted that Bridget and the child Jack transfer back into the *Sword of the Lord,* but when he'd suggested it in Murfreesboro, Bridget had laughed. Said she'd come back when Cassie was ready to deliver, but until then they were making up a family of their own, and she was needed more on *Saint John the Baptist.* Could that be right? Could she be needed more elsewhere than with him, her own father? In the howling of this wretched night?

Even Jezebel is no comfort to him. She has taken to sleeping underneath their bed, and she is dreaming there tonight. Quiet and undisturbed in what must feel to her like a warm nest.

When they cross into North Carolina at Paint Rock, the rain actually increases, and for half an hour the sky above *Saint John the Baptist* and the *Sword of the Lord* moans with long, bashing bouts of thunder. The windows of the club car are iridescent with flashes of lightning. This brings Jezebel out from under the bed, trembling against his legs, and he picks the little dog up and carries her back to the easy chair, where he can sit and cradle her against his chest. The old-time preachers would shout that God is punishing us for our sins, he thinks, and smiles at the thought. Maybe this is the ark and I am Noah.

The rigs slow at what must be Hot Springs, for he can hear first Cederberg's whistle bleating a warning to the town and then Fingers' closer, louder blast five minutes later, as they cross the Spring Creek trestle and then Bridge Street. The place where we were married is under water yet again, he thinks, imagining the Spring Creek lapping up that beautiful green lawn.

Though it is hard to tell in the dark, it seems to him that they're staying at the slower speed of the town crossing, Cederberg and Fingers playing it safe as they approach the Deep Water Trestle above the springs. He carries Jezebel to the closest window and opens the blinds to stare out into the shrieking black night, just as one last bolt of lightning strikes the superstructure of the trestle, sending a faint buzz of electricity through the whole car. Jezebel scratches free from his arms and scrambles under the bed again as he stares in horror out over the river. It is within five feet of the trestle and raging almost from one mountain wall to the other. "Please, God," he mutters involuntarily, as the whole train struggles on into the storm. "Let us find some higher ground."

CHAPTER FORTY-SIX

MORNING. ALTHOUGH THE RAIN HAS STOPPED, the sun has yet to burn through the angry, billowing clouds that stream away to the north and west, borne on the gusting wind. The world is steel-gray above the furious miles of pooling, swirling, racing water.

They have made it to the wide valley surrounding Asheville, though the tracks were covered in water for the last few miles, and at least one trestle collapsed behind them.

The river is a mile wide at the Southern Railway station below the city, but from the siding they are able to wade through the bone-cold water to higher ground, the men leading the Percherons, and with Micah and Jackson, Bridget and Cassie clinging to the horses' backs. The Preacher carries Jezebel under one arm, while Micah clutches his own dog to his chest.

They establish the entire troupe—including the horses—inside a giant abandoned tobacco warehouse that stinks of old burley. The roustabouts bust up tobacco baskets and oak pallets to build a bonfire just outside the doorway. They find only one chair in the whole establishment, which is given, by unanimous consent, to Cassie, who in her ninth month is treated like an invalid by every man present. Micah stands guard by her chair, though she shoos him away irritably from time to time. Bridget watches over everything while Gabe with young Jack search for more firewood.

Fingers and Doc Klein volunteer for the trek up the hill toward town to search for provisions, food for everyone, and milk for Cassie and the boys. Even more to the immediate point, Sheedy and Cederberg are dispatched with buckets in search of drinking water, since every well in the valley must be contaminated.

Once the duties are shared out and the women settled, the Preacher climbs with Boss up a steep street that curves back along the river, where a crowd has gathered beside a half-flooded house. The mob is restless, murmuring. The two push through to a policeman, who is pointing out over the water, beyond the train tracks, to where the old brick tannery squats in the flood waters a hundred yards from shore.

A half dozen people are standing on the roof of the tannery, waving and yelling, and after a moment it becomes apparent why. The upstream end of the building is crumbling under the constant hammering of water and flood debris. Even as they watch, a large, uprooted tree smashes into the nearest, upstream corner and wrenches a stout brick pillar from under part of the roof, which leans precariously and then shears off into the muddy stream.

Absurdly, ironically, wooden coffins float by in the current, and the cop blandly explains that the Acme Casket Company's warehouse is less than a hundred yards upstream.

The people in the crowd edge back from the bank, for it too is sloughing off into the water below. From behind them, farther up the hill, someone yells and points, and when the crowd pivots back to the river, they can see a rowboat with two Negro men at the oars attempting to reach the tannery. They sweep valiantly downstream, running with the current and rowing toward the upper end of the collapsing building.

What happens next occurs in the space of a few breaths. The rowboat is tossed among the debris against the back of the building. One of the occupants clutches a tree branch, while the other scrambles into the flooded building. He helps one slight figure—perhaps a child or a woman—into the boat just as the first man loses his grip and the boat spins precariously down the side of the building, to be swept past the lower end.

The crowd holds its collective breath until the man left in the boat seizes control of the oars and straightens course so that he and the girl—for it seems to be a girl—might survive to reach shore.

One of the men in the crowd, a young white man wearing a starched shirt and a bright red tie, steps forward beside the policeman and turns to face the crowd. He raises a closed Bible over his head and begins to harangue them.

"This is the ancient flood of God's anger," he screeches. "This is the biblical rout. This is the result of your liquor and your whoring. This is the payback on your adultery and your thievery. This is the—"

Between Boss and Jedidiah, a young woman with a horribly scarred face begins loudly, dreadfully to weep. Jedidiah puts his arm around the woman to steady her, and she whispers through her sobs that her father is among those on the roof of the tannery, her father and her brother stranded on the crumbling brick.

"All this," the young preacher cries out and waves his other arm at the mile of racing water, "all this is God's righteous anger at your dirty, filthy sin." He pauses to gasp for breath and then screams again. "God will not be mocked. God will cleanse the world of your nasty, putrid ways. God will—"

Jedidiah looks at Boss over the weeping girl's head. "For God's sake, shut him up," he mutters.

Boss nods and shoves forward through the mesmerized crowd.

"God hates a whore," the man yells, "and God hates the liquor sot. God hates the red-hot adulterer and the sneak thief. God hates the—"

They will never know who else God hates, for Boss hits the young preacher so hard in his open mouth that the blow flings him backward off the trembling bank and into waist-deep water.

"Ain't you never heard of the New Testament, you sorry shit?" Boss shouts after the flailing body. And when he turns back to the crowd, most of whom are laughing now, he continues, "That boy ain't studied half his Bible."

CHAPTER FORTY-SEVEN

It seems to the Preacher that all his life, he has been coming to this place—to this flooded riverbank and to this particular moment in the ancient, folded quilt of time.

He is almost running as he leads Boss by the arm back down the steep street to the warehouse. There, by the bonfire, they pause only long enough to yell for Gabe and Lost John Stoddard to join them in a search for rope—long rope of any kind. Inside the warehouse, they find and reject balls of twine and snarls of string.

Back out in the street again, they see Fingers returning with sacks of what must be food. "Give that to Bridget," he yells, "and come on." Gasping for breath, he explains to Fingers that they need both a light but stout line and also a heavier cable. Each long enough to reach from the *Sword of the Lord* to the tannery. "Fifty or sixty yards," Boss adds, and Fingers nods. Nods and then pauses.

"Hell, we got all we need on the flatcar with the tent," Fingers says. "Both the light line and the cable. We use them all—"

"What the hell do you have in mind?" Boss interrupts.

The Preacher, catching Fingers' meaning, ignores Boss and leads the ragtag crew on the run down into the water. When they are waist-deep and almost on the trains, he directs Fingers and John upstream to the flatcar for cordage, and leads Boss on to the *Sword of the Lord*.

The water is, if anything, colder than before, fed by the myriad and swollen mountain streams leaping down out of the hills. It is a relief to climb up out of the frigid current.

He thinks of Rachel, as he always does, when they cut through the club car to get to the back platform, the closest point in all that teeming waterscape to the crumbling tannery. Thinks of Rachel and, now, of Cassie as well.

Suspended between the two women in his mind, he feels all the more certain that this is what he is meant to do, why he has traveled so many thousands of miles chasing after death, longing for this chance at life. That he must dive far out and sink in, that he must reach the people on that building. "Swim into the darkest—"

"What the hell did you say?" Boss' voice like gravel, interrupting him.

"I didn't say anything."

"Yes, you did. Something about swimming far out. We can find a way to get the line to them, Jedidiah, without... Hell, I can throw it that far, shoot it out of a shotgun, lash it to a log upstream. We can—"

"You know better, Boss. You know I have to go."

"Goddamn it, Jedidiah." And his voice is not angry but resigned. Deep and sighing in his chest. "You about to be a father. Let me go."

"You can't swim ten feet, Boss, and you know it. Besides, we got to have the strong man here. To pull them back across. Fingers'll rig a sling for them to ride in, and you've got to—"

"And to pull you back across," Boss whispers. "Don't forget that part."

He strips to his shorts and sits cross-legged on his desk to sip at a glass of brandy while Fingers and Boss secure the long cord they have found to the iron railing of the club car porch. The water is in the car now, washing over their feet.

Lost John stands by with Boss while the Preacher and Fingers climb up and walk along the roofs of the various cars upstream toward the engine. When they've gone as far as they can, Fingers ties the end of the cord securely to a leather belt around the Preacher's waist. Then, just before he goes, Fingers does something he's never done before. He shakes the Preacher's hand. "You been good to me," Fingers shouts in order to be heard over the torrential sluicing of the water around the train. "So don't get lost out there. Come on back when you're done."

He waits for a drowned mule to float by, out of his way. And then, so that he doesn't have to think anymore about it, he leaps as far out and upstream as he can.

The sensation is that of being torn out of the air into the maelstrom of the flood.

He swims high in the water, aiming well above the tannery and fighting across the deep swell of the current. Within ten yards, he is deafened by the drumming and streaming of what sounds like ocean waves. Within twenty yards, he can barely feel his hands or his feet.

But something in his blood claims the torrent. Something in his heart thrills to finally swim against fate and death. Upon one strong stroke, he almost laughs for joy, and has to spit out the muddy water that splashes into his throat.

CHAPTER FORTY-EIGHT

H<small>E SWIMS SO HARD AND FAR UPSTREAM</small> that Boss and Lost John are forced to haul on the line, reeling him back so that he doesn't swim past the tannery and into the deep, fast water beyond.

Boss yells a warning till his throat almost splits, but he is out of earshot, so they maneuver the line to angle him gently in toward the debris piled at the head of the tannery—more a brick island now than anything resembling a building.

Jedidiah crawls over the logs and lumber, even a few half-submerged coffins, gasping and laughing, carefully pulling the line along behind him so that it doesn't get tangled. His arms and legs are so numb that he has to watch his hands struggle with the rope, for his fingers feel nothing.

Two men rush down from the roof to help him to his feet and onto the flooded tannery floor, where the water is pooled knee-deep and choked with floating tan bark. The rancid stench of raw cowhides is almost overbearing. He can't as yet speak, but he motions them to untie the rope from his belt and pass it from window to window until they have it free on the roof. "Use it," he gasps, bent at the waist, his hands on his knees. And then louder, to be heard. "Use it to haul over the stronger rope...the cable. Tie...it...tie the cable off as high as...you can." And then, after a moment, as they've grasped the idea and are rushing to pass the rope to others on the roof, "Tie it secure, for God's sake. Secure or we drown."

When he can finally feel his arms and legs again, when his breathing has slowed to something close to normal, he climbs up the makeshift ladder to the roof. There are the half-dozen figures they'd spotted from shore. The heroic Negro man from the rowboat, the three men who are busy with the rope—father and son, perhaps, plus another. A man who sits with his back against the great chimney, his leg strapped to a plank. A woman, in rags almost, who kneels to comfort him.

Everywhere there is water.

A moment more and his hands are tingling with new blood, and though he still shakes with cold, he joins the four men hauling on the line, and in a moment they fish up the end of a hempen rope three inches thick. Lashed to the rope is a canvas bundle and the end of another, smaller rope like that he'd pulled over the torrent ten minutes before.

The Negro man and one of the tannery workers immediately set to work cutting and unraveling the end of the cable, so that they can splice it into the iron stanchion that supports the chimney. It is obvious that they know what they are doing, so Jedidiah begins unfolding the canvas bundle, which turns out to be a sort of hammock into which a human being can be safely lashed.

In the next thirty minutes, Boss and the crusade roustabouts haul six human beings to safety. When they begin, the building is already trembling, and all of them work from breath to breath in anticipation of its collapse. First the man with the broken leg, barely conscious when they fold him roughly into the hammock. Then the woman, who obviously frets for the broken man. Then the three tannery workers, who will remain nameless until they become heroes of record in the local paper. Then finally the Negro man, who has refused passage until the last, splintered moment.

The roof shudders at first, then shakes, and finally, just when Jedidiah pulls the hammock back across for the last time, the chimney itself collapses and the cable is swept far and away.

With a long rending groan, the entirety of the world above the deluge tilts over and collapses beneath the rushing water, thousands of bricks swept downstream in the gushing waves.

Jedidiah dives far out toward shore as he feels the coarse asphalt shingles beneath his feet slide into the water. He senses no immediate danger. He doesn't need to reach the *Sword of the Lord;* he knows that. He has only to keep swimming across the current until he comes to something on shore—a tree, a house, a straining human hand.

He knows that Boss and the roustabouts are already on the move, wading through the shallows, tracking him downstream.

Even now, he feels most alive in the water. Most intensely afraid and at the same time thrilled with breath and reach and thought.

He keeps whispering Rachel's name deep in his mind, proud that somehow with her help he has succeeded where, before, he failed. Lives whereas before she died.

He pulls high on every fifth stroke to judge the shore, again almost laughing though barely able to breathe. He is close, almost within hailing distance to figures waving and calling out to him.

On the next full stroke, he swims head-on into a submerged stone pillar, and his awareness of the world implodes.

CHAPTER FORTY-NINE

A WORLD MADE ALL OF WATER in a dark dance of time.

Being borne away through a blind and twisted passage. Human voices calling out but far beyond some invisible surface above, some impenetrable boundary. Human hands touching someone, touching him perhaps, but too late and too far. His skin no longer within the scope of his knowing. Like the rest of his body, shed and forgotten.

Somewhere far away, he hears a train whistle...but where?

What he sees there—beyond—is an ancient barn. All nut-browns and glistening, pearly grays. The barn stands just at the edge of a pasture up against a vaulting ridgeline cloaked in brilliant green woods. Chestnuts and maples and oaks in all their clean spring purity. Higher on the ridge, a stand of hemlocks wave their soft branches in the breeze.

He is expected within the barn. He knows this even as he wades through the knee-high pasture grass. There is no hurry; time is not an element in this place. As he comes closer to the flank of the ridge, he can hear a wood thrush trilling just within the green canopy by the barn. And then he sees the bird, a long streak of brown brushed across the face of the lush and emerald leaves.

He pauses in the barn door for his eyes to adjust, but strangely there is no variance in the clarity and purity of the light within. He sees a man in stained work pants and a patched shirt seated at a long table made of planks laid over sawhorses. There is no noticeable chill in the still air, but even so, the man sits beside a cast-iron stove in which burns a small fire of wood shavings and pinecones. Jedidiah can smell smoke and old wood and the thin oil used to sharpen a knife.

The man is clean-shaven, and the skin on his round face is tanned the color of an old penny. He wears a faded green or brown cap pushed back on his balding head, and he leans over something on the table, something that absorbs him.

After a moment, the man looks up and smiles. And Jedidiah is struck dumb. For the man is familiar in the most puzzling and haunting way. It's as if he's looking at a photograph of his own father, but an image that is more shockingly intense than anything recorded by the eye.

The man speaks to Jedidiah, and when he does, Jedidiah realizes that he is ancient. Made up of time as well as flesh, sight as well as knowledge.

In one hand the man holds a small wooden animal half-formed out of dark wood. Walnut perhaps. In his other hand he holds loosely what might be a pocketknife, the blade of which is so worn and so sharp that it appears a sliver of light rather than steel.

Jedidiah notices that the top of the long table is littered with shavings of different kinds of wood—shavings that will end up in the stove, he is sure. At one end, close to the barn door, there are all sizes of blocks of wood, rough-hewn by saw and rasp in the general shapes of animals. Deer, bear, fox, bird perhaps. Yes: birds.

When Jedidiah doesn't speak, the man leans to his work again, and after a few moments, the piece of walnut curled in his hands takes on the shape of a bear standing on its hind legs. He sets the carving down on the table in front of him and says something under his breath. The carving seems to shiver, as if waking. The ancient one learns forward and blows ever so gently on the head of the wooden bear. After a moment, the bear drops to all fours and ambles toward the far end of the table, where it disappears into the shadows there.

"I know who you are," Jedidiah says.

The ancient one nods and grins. Picks up a pair of spectacles and hooks them carefully over his ears. He picks up another, smaller piece of wood, maple by the look of it. "This here will make a fox pup," he says, and taps the spectacles with the blade of his knife. "Some seasons, I need my glasses for such fine work."

"I don't believe in you," Jedidiah says. "Or at least I haven't believed in you for many years."

"What's a year?" the ancient one says, peering at the fox-to-be. And then looks up at Jedidiah. "I mean to say, what's a year except a tiny sliver of something else?"

"Must I believe in you?" Jedidiah says. "I don't like to think that you are real."

The ancient man looks up from his blade and stares kindly at Jedidiah over the lens of the spectacles. "My job is the making of things," he says, "my job...and my joy. But there's no need for you to believe in me or anything else. Especially if it is painful to you."

"But must I believe in order to stay here, with you?"

The old man shrugs and rolls his shoulders. Gives the fox a careful touch or two of the blade. "You cannot stay," he says.

"What do you mean? I've earned it, and I want to see—"

The man is shaking his head and smiling at the same time. Jedidiah realizes that the old man's hands are at work even though his eyes are focused on Jedidiah's face. The fox—though ever so tiny—is almost finished.

"You see that I have a lot to do here, do you not?" The man's voice is clear and calm, neither tired nor complaining. "Much life awaits."

Jedidiah nods. It's all he can do.

"You have much to do as well. Cassandra and Bridget and those boys. You are needed, especially now."

"Can I tell you something?" Jedidiah asks. He feels the dampness on his cheeks.

The ancient one smiles. Nods.

"Now that I know you to be a workingman—with your hands, I mean. Now that I see you working, your shirt stained with sweat, I like you very well."

"You will love me before you're done, Jedidiah, though it take you a thousand years." The ancient one laughs, and it is the sound of the wind in springtime, ruffling the trees beside a pasture spring.

Everything in the barn seems to be fading now, the colors running like paint, but still the voice. "Go on home, Jedidiah. You're wanted there. And Jedidiah?"

Yes, he is trying to say. Yes, God?

"Next time you visit, bring some of that good brandy."

CHAPTER FIFTY

T HEY DRAG HIS NAKED, UNCONSCIOUS BODY out of the
shallows and carry him limp and frozen into a flooded farmyard
behind an empty house. There, at Doc Klein's direction, they
lay him facedown over a large upended barrel. With two of them
holding his arms and two his legs, they begin to roll him back and
forth over the barrel to force the water out of his lungs.

He can hear them talking before he can see them or form any
coherent notion of where he is. "He ain't breathing." "Damn,
he swallowed half the river." "Puking his guts out." "He ain't
breathing, I tell you."

"Should we blow air in his lungs?" A distant voice that
sounds like the man named Fingers, desperate for some reason.

"I don't know!" Klein's voice. "I don't—"

"Roll him over. Try this here." Whose voice is this? "Hold
his jaw closed."

Now he is laid on his back over the barrel, his legs dangling
on one side, his head and arms on the other. It occurs to him
obscurely that this hurts—that his spine is stretched beyond its
capacity to bend.

Doc Klein holds his head up and his mouth closed while
Sonny Smith covers his nose with his own mouth and blows cigar
smoke straight into the depths of him. Once, and then, after a
second long pull on the cigar, again.

The coughing that results is so violent that he—the
Preacher—is flung sideways off the barrel and onto his hands
and knees in the mud. Those that aren't dancing around him
in celebration are whacking him on the back to help pound the

water out of him. The coughing is wretched, wrenching, tearing, but gasps of air are flowing inside him again.

"Jesus," he croaks after a moment, "stop it. I can...breathe."

"Well, *Jesus* is the one who done it to you," Cederberg says, and they all lapse into hoots of laughter. Even the-Son-of-God himself has to take the cigar out of his mouth to chuckle modestly.

Eventually, they help him to his feet and lead him carefully onto the porch of the old farmhouse, where one lonely rocking chair rests in the chill, humid air. They sit him tenderly down in the chair and cover him with an old quilt they find inside. He is shivering even in the warm air, but is giddy with having lived. The simple thrill of being alive. Here and now.

As his eyes clear and, more slowly, his mind, he looks around him. The sun is breaking out overhead; there are runs of ethereal sky, although fletches of steel-gray cloud still chase downwind.

The roustabouts are all around him, lounging on the porch, soaking wet, laughing and talking about the heroic rescue. They are all there except one.

"Where's Boss?" he whispers, easily, conversationally. Almost the first words out of his mouth after *I can breathe*.

A pall falls over the whole group. As if a thick cloud is passing before the sun.

The men turn and look at Fingers, their natural leader now, waiting on him. Fingers squats on his haunches in front of the Preacher and reaches out to grasp the arms of his rocking chair.

"He's gone, Jedidiah." This is the first time that Fingers has ever said his name.

"Gone where?"

"Gone. When the tannery collapsed and the cable went, he tried to swim out to you. When he hit deep water, he didn't last ten feet before he went under."

CHAPTER FIFTY-ONE

THE ROUSTABOUTS WANT TO RAISE THE BIG TOP for Boss' funeral, but even three days later, any suitable spot remains either half underwater or soaked from freezing rain.

And so Fingers engages the Masonic Temple for the occasion. At first the Masons are reluctant to surrender the temple for the funeral of a non-Mason, but when Jedidiah joins Fingers in the negotiations, they have to relent. For he is a hero. And they do, after all, portray themselves as community-minded men.

They even allow Boss' closed casket to be brought into the great room the evening before the funeral so that various members of the troupe can sit up that night with the body, as is the custom in the hills.

And so it comes to pass that four days after Solomon the Preacher rescued the poor souls stranded on the tannery roof—and somehow survived his own drowning—and two days after Boss' body was found wedged among the flood debris left when the waters receded below the Weaver Power Plant, they return, body and soul, to the Masonic Temple.

At first, it is a crowded and chaotic evening. The roughnecks stand watch for a few hours, along with Jedidiah and his small family. When Jedidiah tells them to go back to the trains to rest, Zeke Scully, their Irishman, steps forward to stand before Boss' open coffin. He begins with a long, low moan that seems to emerge from the pit of his stomach, and then he throws his head back and screeches.

"What in the world…?" Cassie whispers.

"Keening," Jedidiah answers. "He's mourning Boss in the old way."

Zeke pauses only long enough to catch his breath before again offering up a high, plaintive scream. Somewhere out on the street, a dog howls in reply, and as it does, a small man—a janitor at the temple—steps forward out of the shadows to join Zeke, adding his voice to the lament. Then two women—ancient crones dressed in the rags of those who live in the corners and back alleys—come in through the open door and creep forward to the casket. They shake out their hair and straighten up their crooked backs to join in the calling out—so that now there are four.

It is the groaning of the wind against a high mountain cliff at midnight. It is old Ireland. It is an ancient and terrifying sound that creeps in the blood.

Three mountain women, who have been sitting patiently outside waiting for some secret signal, enter the great room now and walk forward to join in with their voices. Two old and one young, with dark red hair, all dressed as they came from the farm. They pull deep breaths, throw their heads back, and begin to moan.

Zeke Scully begins to strike his chest, pounding out a slow, steady rhythm that gives the quilt of sound a new shape and meaning. Moved by brotherhood, Jedidiah and the other men in the room walk forward to stand beside and behind Zeke with their heads bowed. They have no notion of how to join the keening but, even so, their collective breath slows to match the pounding and wailing of this most ancient human sound.

And then, with a last, quavering cry from the oldest woman there, it is done. The waking is over and the long watch begun.

No one speaks while Zeke and the other roustabouts file out, followed by the women from the street. No one speaks for long moments after, as the air under the high, vaulted ceiling seems to tremble with the echo of primeval and pagan song.

By midnight, only four remain, seated together on two padded wooden benches facing the open casket. Jedidiah and his Cassandra, Bridget and her Gabriel. They have put the boys, Micah and Jackson, to rest on cots in a warm room just off the hall, and only these four sit up with Boss' remains.

At two o'clock, Cassandra and Gabe are each stretched out asleep on the benches, and now it is just Jedidiah and his daughter, Bridget, alpha and omega of these people and their traveling show. They are both deeply sad and yet glad to be there alone together. After all the others have taken a step back from Boss and his life, they remain—dedicated to the man before them. His terrible strengths and his astonishing frailties.

"What will you preach from tomorrow?" she asks quietly, not wishing to wake Gabe, whose head is nestled in her lap.

After a moment, he replies. "Why, I'll preach about the many mansions there are above."

"Is he there? Boss, I mean?"

"Yes, he is. It's funny to think that in his dying, as in almost everything, he's gone on before us. Scouting things out, preparing the way."

"Saint John the Baptist."

"That's right. He is John the Baptist."

"Papa?"

"Hmmm?"

"What was Boss' real name? Not Boss, surely."

"That's all I ever heard him called, in all these years. For obvious reasons. But that's not what his mother named him."

"What, then?"

"Robert. His name was Robert William Strong."

"So all this time, you could have been calling your best friend on earth Robbie or Bob or Bobby."

He chuckles quietly. "I tried it once. Called him Rob, and he made a face like he was eating a green persimmon. I don't think he favored it."

They are quiet for a bit, each trying to imagine the man before them as any name at all that wasn't Boss.

"Did you know he was an orphan?" Jedidiah to his daughter.

She sits up suddenly and almost spills Gabe onto the floor. "No! You never told me!"

"He didn't like it known," her father says quietly. "Thought it would make people feel sorry for him. Something he couldn't stand."

"Is that why he loved children so much, always bringing candy to Micah, and now to Jackson? Always bringing toys."

He nods. "I'm sure it is. He climbed over the fence and ran away from the Baptist Children's Home when he was thirteen. Never looked back."

"Where do you think he is now, Papa? Tell me true. What do you think happens when we die?"

"I know exactly where he is." The words sound new and unexpected in his mouth, and the saying of them brings tears to his eyes.

"What do you mean *exactly*?" She turns her head to stare suspiciously at him.

"He's helping out an old man I met…on a beautiful farm high in the mountains." He pauses. "Time doesn't seem to have much play on that farm."

"What do you mean, a man you met? Met where?"

"I was dead for a while when I was in the water, Bridget. I caught a long glimpse of the other side. But the old man who works that farm over there, he made me come back."

She stares at the side of his face for the longest time before answering. "I'm glad he did," she whispers finally.

When it is almost dawn, even Bridget falls into a doze, leaving him by himself with his thoughts. All his loved ones gathered within reach, and yet he is alone with time to think. He will miss Boss, he realizes, in the same way that for years he missed Rachel—talking out each thought, each feeling with him as the days spin forward into weeks and months.

After a bit, an old and very tired figure shuffles out of the street into the Masons' great hall. The man's clothes hang on him as if on a skeleton, and Jedidiah knows at once that it is Festus, come to pay his own sort of respects.

"I've been expecting you for some time now," he says evenly to Festus. "Hell, I expected you at the tannery. And then I expected to travel with you myself, see where you call home."

Festus takes off his hat as he approaches Boss' coffin. Reaches out one bony hand and rests it for a moment on the edge of the open box. "I been a horrible busy man these last few days, Solomon. Forty-three lives swallowed up by that river."

"Oh, my God. Forty-three."

Festus nods. "Men, women, children. Every sort of your kind that God ever made."

"Damn you, mister." He sighs. "You took the wrong man here. You were meant to take me and leave that better man be."

"Well, you know, I tried my best. I certainly did. I had you in my grip, Solo-mon, and I was just a-squeezin. But sometimes that Old Farmer takes matters into His own hands. That Rascal has the final say when He cares to take it."

CHAPTER FIFTY-TWO

PERHAPS THEY EXPECT SOMETHING like a quiet and private service. Attended by those closest to Boss, those in the troupe and those few who knew him one way or another in the backstreets and byways of Asheville.

How could any of them imagine the number of people whose lives Boss had touched? Touched with an open hand, touched with a dollar bill or a five or a ten. Touched by unscrewing the lid of a jar and sharing the contents. Touched with a ham sandwich or the coat off his back. Touched to the core with his body. Or his mind. Or his heart.

How could they have known, since none had followed him into the dark corners of his world?

The funeral is set for three o'clock in the afternoon, and at two the central hall of the Mason's grand temple is packed, with people lining the walls and a crowd milling in the street, threatening to close off traffic.

To start the service, Bridget and Cassandra stand up precisely on time and, after the massive crowd quiets, sing "Down in the Valley to Pray." It is an old, old tune, and is the beginning and ending of music. There is something plaintive and sad about their voices in tandem, never more lovely than on this day. Many in the audience are already in tears. And yet, in the end, there is also something that lifts them above that sadness, spreading wry smiles through the multitudes of people that have come.

He—Jedidiah—sends Micah Ramsey out to the pulpit first. To say his memories of Boss, to give the proceedings a flavor that Boss himself would have liked, for Boss always had more patience for children than adults. Micah is twelve years old now and after a year with the horses and after suffering the loss of his father, is afraid of neither the room nor the people.

Micah stands beside the makeshift pulpit and tells what happened when his own father, Hack Ramsey, died. "Everybody was sad, sure enough, and everybody was nice to me for a week or so. But there was only one who visited me each evening when we were shutting up shop for the night. Only one who would bring carrots for the horses and bring cookies or a piece of cake or some pie wrapped in a napkin…for me. Maybe a sandwich if I had missed my supper. There was only one man—or woman either—who would come night after night, every night he was with the train, to sit with me and talk. Or sometimes just sit with me and not say a word. That was Boss.

"He wasn't no showboat, Boss wasn't. He wasn't loud like some of the men. But everything he said had a thought behind it. Everything he said meant something there on the spot, though sometimes the meaning didn't come clear to me till later, when I needed it.

"And though I only heard him say it once, the last thing he told me when we reached Asheville in the middle of the flood was to take care of the horses, to watch after Miss Bridget and Miss Cassie, and that…" Here the boy pauses to wipe the tears from his eyes with his shirt sleeves. "He said he loved me. And since my daddy died in the fire, not a single other human being anywhere has ever told me that. Nobody else but Boss. And since I never heard him say it out loud to nobody else, I know he meant it."

And so Jedidiah is blinking back his own tears when he stands up to the pulpit. To think that in all the hurly-burly of their lives, nobody ever thought to see about Micah, nobody except Boss.

He prays silently for a bit before he trusts himself to speak out. Just stands there with his eyes closed, remembering the Old Farmer in the barn at the edge of the pasture. Seeking His memory—or, more to the point, His present spirit. And when, in his mind, the Ancient One looks up at him and nods, he begins.

"From his hat to his boots, Boss Strong was a beautiful man. If he was standing here today in the flesh, he would like as not hit me in the face for saying that."

A ripple of laughter runs through the crowd. "Amen," shouts a man's rough voice from the side of the crowd. More laughter.

"He was such because he was unaware of his beauty. He knew his own strength—which was legendary—but he never knew how fine was his spirit.

"I am fortunate to have known Boss for over thirty years, and I never saw him hurt anyone who didn't need hurting. He saved my life—and I mean *saved my life*—at least three times, once on a bridge. And was on his way to save it again when death finally got a grip on him."

He can sense the crowd growing reflective. Searching into themselves. "How many of you can say the same?" he calls out. "How many of you can say that Boss saved you?"

And for a few minutes, various ones in attendance stand and testify as though this were a simple country church rather than a great public hall. It is so quiet that they can actually be heard from wall to wall.

"He done broke me out of jail oncet. Down there in Anderson, South Carolina. I'd'a died in that jail else."

"He turned his pockets inside out on a street corner one time to buy me some supper. Made me promise him to buy food with the money and not that bad liquor."

"When I was a little flower girl before the war, back at the Mountain Park before it burned, Boss saw that I was beat up one day. Had a black eye and a bloody lip. Boss said, Who done that to you, gal. And I told him the man in room 212. He won't do it again, Boss said, come Hell or high water. And the next time I seen that fancy man from 212, he looked worse than me." Many nods and some appreciative laughter from the crowd. "And you know that man wouldn't even pause to speak to me after that, he was so afraid of Boss." She sits suddenly down but then pops back up. "And afterwards, Boss would always buy my flowers when he come to the Park."

"Boss and I were partners in a business venture over in Tennessee just after the war." This testimony from one of the best-dressed men in the room. "I won't say what kind of business, except that the sheriff would have taken an interest had he known. And the thing that stands out to me about those hard-and-fast years is how honest Boss was. He never stole from me, though he had numerous chances to do so. I wish now that I could say the same."

No one to say that Boss was rich. Or supported the church. Or graduated first in his class. Or led the dance at the ball. Or sat on the judge's bench. But many to say that he laughed and fought and…

When Jedidiah stands back up, he begins with those strange, eerie verses from the Gospel of John.

"'Let not your heart be troubled: ye believe in God, believe also in me. In my Father's house are many mansions: if it were not so, I would have told you. I go to prepare a place for you….

And whither I go ye know, and the way ye know.' I can't hear those words now except they sound like Boss is speaking them. In that voice that sounds like a sledgehammer breaking rock." Most everyone in the room relishing the memory of the voice.

"For many of my fifty-plus years, I didn't believe in God." He pauses to let that truth sink in. "I had seen too much suffering and felt too much death close by.

"But here of late, I've begun to see and hear and feel something behind this thin veil. Or more precisely, *beyond* it. Something more than just this sorry old world. And that reality just might contain a Godlike spirit. A spirit who toils to replace all this pain with love and all this death with life. I hope…I hope to God that I'm right, for just the thought of such ravishes me."

A man in the front row below him begins silently to weep. Many others as well.

"For how else can you explain a man like Boss? How can you explain a man who is strong enough to take anything he wants, to take anyone he wants? And yet, and yet, for all his strength, he was always giving himself away.

"There is no explanation for a man like Boss Strong unless you factor in the existence of a God—who breathes into Boss the meaning of his life. And into this world the meaning of our lives."

At Riverside Cemetery, Fingers has haggled with his own cash, set aside for him over the months, for a site just above the long rows of soldiers' graves, beneath an old oak with gnarled bark. The roughnecks have thrust the regular gravediggers aside, insisting that only they could carve out Boss' resting place.

So when the caravan of cars from the temple winds down the hill to the grave site, everything is ready and waiting.

And it is here that the last memorable event of this winter day occurs. The boys lift the heavy coffin out of the hearse and set it gently on the grass beside the grave. Jedidiah leads the crowd in a deep, resonant version of the Lord's Prayer in the King James style: "'Forgive us our trespasses as we forgive those who trespass against us.'"

Just as the crowd starts to disperse, first one and then a number of women come forward to place flowers on the coffin. Sensing their evident sisterhood, several in the crowd link arms and kneel in the grass, leaning over the casket as if kneeling beside a bed to pray. It is a restful event, only the sound of a mockingbird's trill woven into their quiet tears.

That is to say, it is quiet and restful until one of the women—surprisingly young—faints, topples slowly over, and falls into the open grave.

For years after, when the roustabouts tell the story, they will explain just how much they enjoyed lifting her supple body out of the ground and how grateful she was for their relief.

CHAPTER FIFTY-THREE

Two weeks after the funeral, the floodwaters have receded enough so that the crew can drive both the *Sword of the Lord* and *Saint John the Baptist* upriver past Biltmore to an old side track in an open, grassy field that was largely untouched by the storm.

The men erect the big top in the bright January sunshine to allow it to dry thoroughly inside and out, so the canvas won't rot and they can repaint it yet one more time.

During the second day there—near a little town called Swannanoa—they rest and play cards and repair equipment. They discover that a leak in the roof of the Bible car has ruined half their stock of sales Bibles but left the corn liquor and apple brandy untouched. For which there is a general thanksgiving.

On the morning of the third day there, Jedidiah convenes a general meeting of the whole company. They gather inside the tent and build a bonfire to warm them as they talk. He tells them that their run together may be finished. That he cannot imagine going forward without Boss to move the liquor stock and navigate the dark and lonesome side of their work. That he himself may have lost his desire to fool every rube, hick, and boob in the South.

There is a long silence in the tent, and he notices that to one side, a wood thrush is trilling its flute-like syllable. And on the other an equally stubborn blue jay is imitating a hawk, perhaps to hush up the sweet thrush.

"What about me?" Gabriel jumps to his feet. "You put me apprentice to Boss a long time ago, and surely to God I can take his place. Take the lead on that *Baptist* train."

Again silence, somewhat embarrassed. What Jedidiah wants to say is that no man in the troupe can take Boss' place. Fingers saves him the trouble. "Sit down, Gabe," he says from where he sits off to one side, chewing on a birch twig. "We done discussed this. Your job stops with the Bibles and the canvas. Nothing personal."

General nods of agreement, and Bridget leans over to pat Gabe's shoulder reassuringly. After a moment, one of the men—Son Smith, perhaps—speaks quietly. "Tell him, Fingers. Tell him what we decided."

Fingers stands up and steps forward, closer to the front of the group. "Well, Preacher, while we was holed up in that Asheville burg and while Mrs. Robbins was doing her blessed duty," he pauses to nod to Cassandra, sitting to one side of the fire, "we all, the boys and me, held a meeting, and we done reached a decision."

"Voted, did you?" Jedidiah is smiling.

"Well, yes, we did. After a manner of speaking. We decided that this crusade needs to be a joint stock company, share and share alike. You, being a founder of the company, get three votes in any set decision, and Miss Bridget gets two. Otherwise, one vote per man." Again he nods to Cassie. "Or woman."

"How about Micah and Jackson, do they get a vote?"

Fingers shakes his head. "Not till they come of age. Before that, they can speak but they can't vote."

"What is the accountable age?"

"We reckon fourteen."

Jedidiah nods. "How is the money to be divided?" he asks, assuming that he's driven Fingers to ground on this one.

"We done thought of that too. Equal shares for every man and every woman, except that you get three shares and Miss

Bridget gets two—as with the votes. In part because you each have children to feed and clothe. You two are responsible for the children."

"I don't need three shares."

"Yes, you do. Besides, I'm a communist, not a thief." Fingers says this with a grin, and a good deal of laughter follows, causing Jedidiah to smile and shake his head. To laugh himself, if truth be known, and it is the first time he has laughed out loud since Boss' funeral.

He looks over this rough group of men, along with the two women he loves most in the world, and he realizes that they are survivors all. Beaten, bruised, wounded by life, but alive none-theless. "I don't know that I have the will to preach," he says simply. Quietly.

"It's not up to you," Son Smith says. "We done elected you to preach. Besides, you'll get your voice back."

"I don't know that."

"I do," Son says. "Besides which, if you don't travel about, taking the dollars and cents out of the hands of the shiftless and ignorant, who will? It's your calling."

Again laughter. And he realizes he trusts Son's instincts now more than his own. His own are stripped naked by grief.

"All right," he says. "I'll try. But we still haven't solved who's to take Boss' place. Who is man enough—"

Fingers clears his throat. "You are correct. Ain't nobody man enough, and this knot troubled us for some time, but then Cederberg nominated and we voted."

"What the hell you mean, nominated?"

Fingers grins ironically. "Ain't nobody man enough, but Miss Bridget is woman enough. We elected her boss of the *Saint John the Baptist* rig and primary sales agent."

"Goddamn it, Fingers, I don't want her going alone into every backwoods booze parlor and gin joint south of Virginia."

"Oh, she won't go alone. She'll go armed, and one or two of the boys will always be with her. Bridget?"

"I am almost twenty-six years old, Papa. And I'm the toughest man—or woman—on the lead train."

He has to turn away to hide his smile.

"Besides, Jedidiah," Cassie speaks for the first time from where she sits off to one side, nursing little Robbie Robbins, born just ten days before. "Don't pretend for one minute that you didn't already think of it yourself."

IN THE END

February 1948

JEDIDIAH ROBBINS DOESN'T MUCH LIKE THE MORNINGS these February days, for it is a cold winter, and when he first climbs out of bed, he is too stiff to walk. And he hates stumping around and hawking the spit out of his throat like an old man.

For all that, he is an old man.

He eats his breakfast with the boarders so as to be less trouble to Cassie and Bridget. Now that Robbie is gone off to Berea College and Bridget's girls mind the livestock, there is little for him to do after breakfast. Most Saturdays, Micah will come in to sit with him. Since Micah took up preaching in the local churches around Hot Springs, the boy likes to try out his sermons on the old man first. Always wanting pointers about language or gesture. When to shout and when to whisper.

What can he even tell Micah when he is still so young in the world? Watch the crowd and adjust accordingly. Preach out of your heart and trust your instincts.

"Instincts?" Micah asks.

"Yes, damn it, instincts," he growls and then winks. "You got em in there somewhere."

But today is not a Saturday. He will not see Micah today, and it is just as well.

He is going for a walk today. Once his joints loosen up and the coffee primes what pump he has left, he will walk across Bridge Street, up the hill by Sunnybank, and on over toward

Spring Creek. Perhaps as far as the swale where they were all married in the summer of '28.

The night before, he dreamed of their marriage, drenched in warm sunshine and a flood of beautiful words. The dream so immediate, so present in his mind that his eyes were wet when he woke. Crying from the occasional happiness of his well-seasoned life.

He has been thinking of that spot lately, the rippling run of the creek around the bend against the rocks, and he wants to see how it flows this midwinter day. Time and water rushing away to the sea.

He doesn't pack any food for his walk, though either Cassie or Bridget would make him a sandwich. Rather he takes the jar of brandy from under the bed he shares with Cassie and wraps it in an old shirt so he can carry it along in a paper poke. Brandy to shield against the sharp air, he tells himself, and then too, he might meet someone who would like to share a sip or two.

By the time he reaches the top of the hill just beside Sunny-bank, he is out of breath, dizzy from the effort of even so slight a climb. Sparkles of light flash inside his eyes, as they often do of late, and the voices rise up.

They are friendly, even loving, these voices. Chatting to each other and to him. The voices of the living—Bridget and Cassie always, Micah and Robbie, even Thomas, Bridget's new husband—but also the voice of Rachel, who is friendly among the women, and the hoarse, gravelly tone that could only be Boss. Theirs are living voices as well. They make a kind of conversation inside his mind. A conversation that is most always there, so that when he is out for a walk, he can speak freely and easily with one and all, and they with him.

It is, he believes, a communion.

That which hath been is now…

It sounds to him like music, and he recalls a marble angel whose face, whose voice, whose stone breasts…

You just the kind of disciple we been needing…Jesus the-Son-of-God…Smith…and Jezebel…a time to be born and…the sweetest dog…die…beside the beautiful, beautiful river that flows…forth into the sea…all the fruits of this earth…if your dick is as dead as Lazarus…a time to plant…to pluck up…I sat down under his shadow with great delight…and his fruit was sweet to my taste… and honey on my tongue…

That which is to be hath already been…

It seems to him that their voices, old time and new, sing through him each to each like a choir of stone angels. His mother's seldom-heard contralto and his father's sweet tenor, harmonizing now with all his people, before and after, here and there inside his mind, as a kind of harmonious light sparkling in his eyes. A river of radiance.

The skeletal figure finds Jedidiah lying on the grass beside Spring Creek just below the wedding rock. The crazy old Preacher has taken his shoes off, oddly enough, and his bare feet are being bathed in the rushing stream itself, lifted first one and then the other by the flashing current. Festus, for that's who surveys the scene, leans over Jedidiah and touches his cheek with an impossibly long, sharp finger. There is no movement, neither twitch nor groan.

"Done gone," Festus complains under his breath. "Slipped away while nobody was looking." He straightens, joints cracking and groaning. "You always was a sly one, Solo-mon. Even to the last. Taking your own life and leaving naught for me." Festus removes his jaunty fedora and places it over the old man's face, for there is a smile there that unnerves him, a stubborn sweetness in the face of death.

A world made all of mist, struck through by slant rays of sunlight in the dark dance of time.

Somewhere far away he hears a train whistle, calling down the lonely track. But where? Where…?

What he sees there, beyond, is the ancient barn he remembers from before, the browns and grays fading into the stark white of mountain winter. There is snow in the pasture as he walks toward the barn, but no ice and no cold. It's as if snow is perfected, a windswept field of white to remind us of our lust for the sun.

As he walks forward, he feels a weight at the end of one arm. When he looks down, he is surprised to see a fruit jar wrapped in a tattered shirt. There is a thick, brown liquor in the jar, and it matters that he carries it safe. He can hear Boss whispering to him about the jar.

He hears a fluttering of wings and looks up to see a long streak of brown brushed across the quilt-work of winter trees. The trilling of a wood thrush.

As he nears the barn, someone steps forward from inside. A balding man in stained work pants and a patched shirt stands in the door. He reaches forth to Jedidiah in welcome. To steady his progress through the stiff pasture grass. The Ancient One smiles, his countenance radiant in the quiet air.

Jedidiah's voices now are one, a symphony of spun light, as if the planets themselves are caroling. "Please let me stay," he whispers to the old farmer, reaching out a tired hand in supplication.

"Come warm by the stove," God says. "There is much to be done."

About the Author

TERRY ROBERTS' DIRECT ANCESTORS have lived in the mountains of Western North Carolina since the time of the Revolutionary War. His family farmed in the Big Pine section of Madison County for generations and is also prominent in the Madison County town of Hot Springs, a consistent setting in his novels. Among his forebears are prominent bootleggers and preachers but no one who, like Jedidiah Robbins, combines both preoccupations.

His debut novel, *A Short Time to Stay Here*, won the Willie Morris Award for Southern Fiction, and his second novel, *That Bright Land*, won the Thomas Wolfe Memorial Literary Award as well as the James Still Award for Writing about the Appalachian South.

Born and raised near Weaverville, North Carolina, Roberts is the Director of the National Paideia Center and lives in Asheville, North Carolina.

Printed in the USA
CPSIA information can be obtained
at www.ICGtesting.com
JSHW022208140824
68134JS00018B/930